FOR THE LOVE OF YOU

Tarshima Washington

Washington

ISBN - Paperback: 979-8-218-69261-2

First Edition : April 2025

C O N T E N T S

1

Progress

"Why is there so much traffic?" Sheena thought to herself as she sat in bumper-to-bumper traffic at a red light on Hancock Street. "My goodness, hurry up. This baby is on my bladder," she yelled out her window as she rubbed her belly and tightened her thigh muscles while trying to will away the urge to relieve herself.

As traffic slowly began moving along, Sheena could not help but realize that after three years of coming to this same address on Beale Street, three days a week, today would be her last day. Before Sheena could even think to get emotional, again she felt that strong urge to urinate as the baby made a few strong movements before settling down.

"Ugh, thank God," Sheena sighed as she pulled into the driveway of the unassuming, well-maintained Colonial single-family home that bore a simple "Welcome" sign hanging from the porch. Sheena quickly put her car in park, hopped out of the vehicle, snatched her purse from the driver's seat, and quickly waddled up the front steps while holding onto her eight-month pregnant belly.

"Sorry, I'm late, Doc! Traffic was a beast!" Sheena yelled as she burst through the front door and ran directly to the bathroom. "Ahhhhh!" She sighed loudly as she felt the pressure in her bladder dissipate.

"No worries, Dear. Take your time. After our session, the only thing I have scheduled is to finish packing."

"Ohhh, don't remind me, Doc!" She yells through the door as she washes her hands in the sink. I can't believe this is it!" She says sullenly as she walks into the living room, which has been converted into a waiting room. There, she sees Dr. Angel removing her college degrees, psychology accolades, and certifications from the walls, gently wrapping them in bubble wrap, and placing them in a cardboard packing box.

"Oh, Dear, come now. You are going to be fine; you've made tremendous progress. No…no, you've made magnificent progress. You were committed to doing the work and you succeeded, Dear."

Dr. Angel looked up at Sheena, standing in the doorway, rubbing her protruding belly, smiling, and appearing to have a sense of accomplishment on her face. Dr. Angel walked toward Sheena, took both of her hands, and whispered, "You did it. You are strong, loving, amazing, and deserve all the happiness you have worked for."

Dr. Angel then placed both hands on Sheena's stomach and continued, "You are going to be an inspiration for this beautiful baby girl, and she is going to be one lucky girl because you decided to reclaim yourself. Remember that."

"Thanks, Doc. I couldn't have gotten here without you," she said, looking at Dr. Angel with genuine adoration and appreciation.

"Have I ever told you, you look like Jane Fonda?" She asked with a sheepish grin.

Dr. Angel laughed heartily, "Oh Dear, I haven't heard that in years. Jane is quite the looker. Oh dear, I think I'm blushing now," she said, her cheeks turning flush pink as she walked back over to the box and placed the last frame from the wall into it.

"Okay, Sheena. I would like us to try something different for our last session. Come, let's get comfortable in my office," Dr. Angel says while leading the way to a designated therapy room.

"I'll miss this room," Sheena stated as they walked into the mid-sized room that she guesses used to be a bedroom.

Sheena found the pastel yellow and blue walls calming, along with the oversized ivory colored chaise lounge chairs and tabletop serenity water fountain. Scrolled on the walls in the most elegant calligraphy was the quote, "The purpose of psychotherapy is to set people free." Sheena found this quote so simple yet profound. And, as she sat in this room at this moment, rubbing her stomach and feeling the movement of her baby girl, she couldn't help but relish in the feeling of freedom.

"What is it that you think you'll miss?" Dr. Angel asked while sitting in a recliner, looking around the room, tapping the top of her pen on the tip of her nose. "What is it about this room, Dear?" She asked again, now looking directly at Sheena.

"Honestly, it's this," she stated, pointing at the wall.

"It all makes sense now. I feel like I have a strength I never knew was possible. I feel like I have control, and I've never felt this way before. I feel free from my past and can love her and show her love I never had, but know that I deserve," she said while holding her belly.

"Excellent, Dear," Dr. Angel responded while smiling.

"Quite excellent. I'll tell you what, since you enjoy this Rollo May quote so much, I want you to have it," she said, getting up from her seat and walking towards the wall.

"It's a decal and will come off easily," she says while peeling the decals off the wall.

"When you get home, put these words up to remind you of how far you have come and how much wisdom you will have to share with your little one," she said while handing Sheena the decals.

"Thanks, Doc, thank you for everything. I know your daughter must be so excited to have you moving back home to help out."

"Oh, yes, Dear. It's all so very exciting. She and her wife have been trying to get pregnant for quite some time now. I can't wait to be a Grandma," she replied, smiling.

"Listen, Doc. You're way too glamorous to be called someone's Grandma," Sheena said, exaggerating her look of disagreement.

"You, Miss Thang, are what they now call a Glam-Ma. "

"Ha! Oh Dear!" Dr. Angel snickered; her head flung back while laughing uncontrollably.

"A Glam-Ma, you say? How capricious of you. Well, I'll be sure to let my daughters know," Dr. Angel stammered, trying to compose herself.

"Now, enough about me, Dear. Let's get down to business. Since this is our last session and you've made such lovely progress during your three years here, I would like you to use this final session to tell me what you have learned. Please tell me what you think your defining life moments were that shaped you both positively and negatively. More importantly, what will you do differently moving forward to ensure the trajectory of the progress you have attained during the past three years?"

Sheena readjusted herself in the oversized chaise lounge while massaging her stomach, let out a long sigh before asking, "Where do I even start?"

Dr. Angel opened her notebook and flipped through a few pages before saying, "It's okay, Dear. Take your time and start wherever you want when you're ready. It's your journey you're walking me through; there are no wrong answers, statements, or questions," she stated reassuringly while positioning her pen to a selected page in her notebook.

"Alright, after three years of therapy, I feel like I've figured a lot of things out," she said with a look of accomplishment.

Sheena let out a long and exasperated sigh while rubbing her tight and protruding belly before beginning, "If Neil were still here, things would be so different, probably better. Neil was my person, my best friend. He genuinely loved me for me. And that I miss. I miss it so fucking much!" Sheena stammered as her voice trembled. Tears began to well in her eyes.

Sheena sniffled, wiping the tear from her right eye. She took a deep breath and let out a long, cleansing sigh.

"I don't think anyone ever truly understood our relationship. He was beyond my best friend, this man was my family, my friend, my supporter and the biggest pain in my goddamn ass!" She chuckled while wiping away the tears forming in the corner of her eyes.

2

THE BEGINNING

"We met in the fourth grade at the Hennigan school. He was so annoying," Sheena exclaimed while throwing her hands up in the air and giggling.

"I remember this one time in French class, Mrs. Fournier would have us write messages to each other, only in French."

Sheena started with an exaggerated, "Well…. Neil and I were assigned together for the day's assignment on this particular day. So, this fool handed me an assignment written in French; I still remember it like it was yesterday. Bonjour beaute. Est-ce que tu m'aimes? Oui/Non."

"Sooooo, naturally my response was, no ugly! Non moche,

FUCK toi! Au revoir. Needless to say, my ten-year-old self was a shitty French student, so I had to improvise. As expected, Mrs. Fournier was not amused."

Sheena took a deep breath before continuing her story.

"I can still smell Mrs. Fournier's perfume like I'm back in that fourth-grade French class."

"White Diamonds," she whispered as she inhaled.

"White Diamonds by Elizabeth Taylor," Sheena continued, "Mrs. Fournier made us both stay in class during recess as punishment so we could...."

Sheena lifted her hands while gesturing quotation marks and finishing her statement, "Explain our little shenanigans we displayed in class today."

■

 "But, Mrs. F., I didn't even do nothing, I did my assignment. Curtis wrote that, he asked me to pass the note to Sheena. I'm telling you, Mrs. F., that ain't mine. See?" O'Neil asked while holding up a perforated piece of notebook paper.

 "See, this is my assignment. Look! Look at the note. It's not even my handwriting." O'Neil pleaded emphatically.

Mrs. Fournier approached him and took the notebook paper from O'Neil's flailing arm.

"Settle down, Neil, let me take a look," Mrs. Fournier says, lifting her reading glasses to her eyes and walking back to her desk. She read the notebook paper O'Neil handed her and picked up the other note she had confiscated earlier.

"Okay, Neil. Good job on today's assignment. However, you are both still banned from recess today. First of all, Neil, you know better than to pass notes in class, and secondly, Sheena, this behavior and language is unacceptable. So, today, the punishment stands for both of you. No recess, and I want a sentence of contrition in both English and French from both of you. Do the best you can with your French translation."

Sheena rolled her eyes and sucked her teeth, "Fine," she sulked.

"Come on, Mrs. F, this ain't fair," O'Neil exclaimed. "I didn't do nothing!"

"Enough!" Mrs. Fournier said sternly. This isn't up for debate. Sit here and think about what you both did."

She made it a point to look at each of them separately before finishing.

"And complete the assignment that I have just given you. I will be back in 30 minutes to collect your completed assignment," she said before exiting the classroom.

"So, you didn't write this?" Sheena asked O'Neil while rolling her eyes and her neck.

"Nooooooooo!" O'Neil retorted while drawing out a long and exaggerated denial. "It was Curtis, not me!" O'Neil bellowed while throwing up his hands in disbelief.

"Ugh," Sheena responded in disgust.

"I don't like him, so you can tell him that!" She scoffed.

"Good, I'm glad you don't like him. He's stupid," he huffed as he settled down and leaned backwards in his chair. "He's a liar and he's always claiming he has all these girlfriends that show him boobs. He's stupid, he's a liar. Don't ever like him."

Sheena snickered. "I know. I don't like him. He has special needs anyway," she said sarcastically.

O'Neil chuckled, "Good. My mother thinks he's special, too."

■

Sheena's voice cracked as she spoke to Dr. Angel.

"It was at this moment that Neil and I became best friends. He looked out for me from this day forward," she stated with pride and adoration.

"Then, eighth grade rolls around, and puberty hits us both. We were so awkward, especially me. Neil had a friend, Hakeem. I had the biggest crush on Hakeem; every girl at school did. Of course, I'm awkward, too scared to speak, and shy. All I could do was stare at Hakeem like a creep, lurking in the shadows." Sheena explained while covering both her eyes with her hands in embarrassment.

"Ugh, I was so corny," she said in disgust.

■

It was a Saturday morning, O'Neil called to ask if Sheena wanted to go Downtown to the Corner Mall with him and his cousins.

Then he added, "Your little boyfriend is coming too," he taunted.

Trying to hide the excitement in her voice, Sheena asserted, "Boy, ain't nobody thinking bout him. We'll see ya'll later. Ring my doorbell when ya'll ready since you gotta walk by my building to get to the bus stop anyways. Chrissy's already at my house."

"Chrissy's Ninja Turtle head spent the night? Tell my wife I'll see her soon. Let me go get jiggy. Peace out!" O'Neil joked as he rushed Sheena off the phone.

"Eeeewwwww, take a chill pill. My best friend doesn't want you. Bye!" Sheena yelled into the phone before hanging up.

"Chrissssssssy! You want to go to the Corner Mall with Neil and them?" She yelled from the kitchen.

"Yeah!" Chrissy hollered back from the hallway before entering the kitchen.

"I need to go to Claire's to get some earrings," she said while massaging her bare earlobe, which was missing a silver cubic zirconia stud.

"Cool, they're gonna ring the doorbell around 1 pm so we can all walk to the bus stop."

"What are we wearing?" Chrissy asked, walking out of the kitchen towards Sheena's bedroom.

"What you bring? We can match." She said, following behind Chrissy.

"I got Levi's, my grey Champion sweatshirt, and white and grey Reebok Classics," Chrissy said as she pulled the items out of her L. A Gear duffle bag and placed the clothes on Sheena's bed.

"I hope I washed that laundry," Sheena mumbled as she rushed to her bedroom closet. "Nice, okay, I have my pink Champion sweatshirt, jeans, and white Classics."

"Gimme, I'll iron,"
"Do my hair too!" Sheena stated as she handed her outfit to Chrissy.

Buzzzzzz.

Sheena looked up at the clock on the kitchen wall that read 1:17 pm.

"That's Neil and them."

"Are you ready?" She asked, as Chrissy smeared Wet & Wild clear lip gloss over her full lips.

"Ready."

Chrissy smacked her full, glossy lips together and shoved her money and lip gloss into the back pocket of her tight, dark-washed Levi jeans.

"We look cuteeeeeee!" Chrissy sang as they walked to the front door to exit the apartment.

"What up, Block Heads!" O'Neil yelled out as Chrissy and Sheena walked down the concrete steps leading to the sidewalk on Blue Hill Avenue.

"Talk to the hand," Chrissy said while sucking her teeth and playfully smushing O'Neil in the face.

"Awww snap! That's a love tap," O'Neil jokingly responded while tugging at the collar of his Polo shirt.
"Dang! My friend doesn't want you," Sheena said, annoyed.

You're so aggy, Neil. Let's go!" She demanded, rolling her

eyes.

"Awww come on, I'm just joking, relax," he said while spinning Sheena around to face the three boys shadow boxing each other and playing on the sidewalk.

"Yeah, Neil, introduce us," Chrissy whispered as she watched the three boys on the sidewalk.

"Boys! Aye, yooooooo, Boys!" O'Neil yelled.

The three boys continued laughing and fake boxing each other, unaware of Sheena and Chrissy's presence or O'Neil's attempt to get their attention.

"Dang, I can't take them anywhere," O'Neil mumbled, sticking his thumb and index fingers to his lips and letting out a piercing whistle.

"Aye, yo boys!" He yelled again.

The three boys stopped immediately, looked in O'Neil's direction, and saw him standing with Chrissy and Sheena.

"Twins, this is my home skillet, Sheena and her homegirl Chrissy."
"Sup," The Twins responded, nodding their heads in unison.

"That's Jamal," O'Neil said, pointing to the right.

"And that's my cousin Jason, but we call them The Twins."

"They don't look like twins," Chrissy said while giving O'Neil the side eye.

"We're fraternal," The Twins sang out in synchronicity.

"Hi, Jamal," Chrissy said softly.

She batted her eyes and reapplied her Wet & Wild lip gloss to her shiny lips.

"Sup, Jason," she said, quickly glancing in his direction before turning her attention back to Jamal.

"Aight, aight! Knock it off, your lips look like a Slip ' N ' Slide already." Hakeem interjected while snatching the lip gloss out of Chrissy's hands.

"Hey, Twins," Sheena chuckled as she waved at them.

"Hi Hakeem," Sheena said bashfully as she watched Chrissy and Hakeem playing tug-of-war with her lip gloss.

"Ugggh, come on Hakeem, you so aggy! Stop!"

"Let me stop before I make you cry. Here!" Hakeem said as he handed Chrissy her lip gloss back.

"What's up, She-She?" Hakeem asked in a high-pitched, exaggerated tone as he walked over to Sheena and wrapped his arms around her in a soft embrace.

Sheena could smell the Cool Water cologne on his neck as she returned a one-armed half hug, not to appear too enthusiastic, but she could feel the butterflies in her stomach as he held her close.

"Man, come on! You on her like white on rice, let's go." O'Neil joked as he pulled Sheena and Hakeem apart.

"Ain't gonna be none of this on my watch, ain't that right, Chrissy? If anybody fall in love it's gonna be me and you boo." O'Neil said while blowing a kiss in Chrissy's direction.

"Homie don't play that." Chrissy sassily replied while rolling her eyes.

"Keep it up, they're gonna get stuck like that."

"Stop sweating me, dang! "Let's go!" She said, annoyed as they walked towards the bus stop.

■

"Let's go eat," The Twins said as Jamal paid for two shirts at J City.

"We've been out here for two hours," he said while looking at his Casio G-Shock watch.
"We're walking to the food court," Jason announced to the group.

"At the Corner Mall?" Chrissy asked as she finished smearing lip gloss on her lips.

"Yeah. And you can't be serious." O'Neil said incredulously. "Chrissy! How many times are you gonna pull out that stupid gloss?"

"Mind ya business, you so aggy."

"Yeah, mind ya business, O. Shine up those pretty little lips, girl," Jamal said with a smirk.

"That's right, tell him, Mal," Chrissy said while blushing and moving closer to him.

"Oh, I see what this is. Cuzzo, you snaking my girl?" O'Neil asked in a high-pitched voice while mimicking a dramatic and flabbergasted expression.

"Nah, Bro! You frontin'. I ain't gank nobody." Jamal said with a chuckle. "Ain't that right, Chrissy?"

"Boy, please. Neil knows I don't like him. He plays too much," Chrissy responded, shooting dagger eyes in O'Neil's direction.

"See!" Jamal exclaimed.

"Homegirl said..." Jamal paused before continuing with Jason joining in, "Hasta la vista, baby!"

They all laughed as O'Neil looked over to Sheena and

tapped her on her arm.

"You see this, Sheena? It be your own people," he said while laughing and jumping onto Jamal's back.

"That's fine. You may have won this battle, but not the war." O'Neil said jokingly as he kissed Jamal's forehead before hopping off his back as they approached the Corner Mall's front doors.

"Sheena, come with me to Pagoda. Yo! We'll meet ya'll in the food court. Sit on the lower level. We'll come find ya'll. I need to stop at the Pagoda right quick." Chrissy said to the boys.

"Aight, bet. Let's go, Squad. I'm starving." Hakeem said while rubbing his stomach.

"Don't be taking all day either!" O'Neil scoffed while looking at Chrissy.

"I'm talking to you!" He said while pointing his finger at her.

"Boy, I oughta…. Right in your face," Chrissy said while balling up her fist and waving it in O'Neil's direction.

"Let's go, Sheena. Ugh, he gets on my nerves!"

She pulled at Sheena's arm and walked towards the Pagoda store entrance.

"Sheena! Look, these are so cute. Look!" Chrissy squealed as she held up two black leather bracelets with silver charms attached.

"These are cute," Sheena agreed as she took both bracelets out of Chrissy's hands and inspected them.

Together, the charms made a heart, and the words "Best" and "Friends" were on each side of the charms.

"I like this," Sheena said as she put the "Friends" bolo bracelet around her wrist, tightened it, and extended her arm to Chrissy. She twisted her wrist and showed all angles of the bracelet.

"Let's get them!" Chrissy said excitedly as she slipped the "Best" charmed bracelet onto her arm and held it next to Sheena's.

"How much for these?" Chrissy yelled to the Sikh store owner behind the counter, watching them admire the bracelets.

"Aha! Those are my last. My mother always told me it will never break if it is a real friendship. But, never seek friendship with those who are selfish," he said as he walked out from behind the counter towards Sheena and Chrissy.
"For you ladies," he said as he pulled down on his turban.
"Fifty percent off. You can have each bracelet for five dollars."
"I'll buy yours, Sheena."

"Okay, I'll get yours," Sheena said as they followed the store owner back to the register.

"Wait, you didn't buy your earrings, Chrissy," she said, holding her money in her hands.

"I like this better, I'll get them another time," she said while handing the store owner five dollars.

"You sure?" Sheena asked as she handed the store owner a ten-dollar bill.

"Yeah, I want us to have these," she replied, holding her wrist up again to admire her new friendship bracelet.

"Okay, girls. Thank you for your business," the owner said, handing back the change.

"Come again."

"Thank you," Sheena responded as they turned to leave the Pagoda and headed out to the food court.

"Aye yooooo! Sheena, over here." O'Neil yelled while wildly waving his hands in the air.
"I see them over there," Sheena said, pointing to the table farthest to the right.

"Here, we ordered your food already," O'Neil said, pointing at a tray containing two McDonald's cheeseburgers, two small fries, and two small drinks.

"Who paid for our food?" Sheena asked, surprised, while preparing to sit down.

"Who cares, I'm starving!" Chrissy mumbled while stuffing fries into her mouth before taking a seat.

"Because. That was sweet, whoever it was."

"I did She-She," Hakeem said while sipping his fountain drink. "I didn't want ya'll to have to wait for your food."

"Aww, thank you, Hakeem," Sheena said sweetly, blushing, and starting to unwrap her cheeseburger.

"No sweat."

"Yeah, thank you, Keem," Chrissy said between chews of her cheeseburger and sips of her soda. "Good looking out."

"Aight, are you Garbage Pail Kids almost ready to go?" O'Neil asked as he cleaned the table and walked to the trash can.

Once he was back at the table, Jamal said, "Let's take the Orange line to Ruggles."

"And then hop on the 28 bus," Jason added.

∎

As they stood on the train station platform waiting for the inbound train to Ruggles station, Chrissy and Sheena sat on an empty bench while they all waited for the train to arrive. O'Neil, the Twins, and Hakeem stood off to the side, listening to the music blaring from a boom box that someone was playing.

"Awww, snap, that's my song!" The Twins exclaimed excitedly.

They jumped up, turned around, and moonwalked over to Sheena and Chrissy.

"Yeah, we're doing this for all the ladies, huh. B-Town Boys kickin' it with my boy O," Jamal says seductively as he swayed back and forth.

Jason jumps in and continues, *"For the nine-trey, yah-mean, 'cause we will be bumping dem boots,"* as he rocked his hips back and forth in Chrissy's face.

O'Neil joined in with a slow Cabbage Patch dance move before beginning, *"Hakeem, Jay, Mal. We bout to do something real fresh for ya. Hey, bro-bro. Check this out."*

That's when Hakeem does a back flip, lands next to O'Neil, puts his arm on his shoulders, and starts singing.
"Last night I thought back to when I put it all on youuuuuu."

The Twins tapped Hakeem on his shoulder, got in front of him, and belted out the next lyric.

"Listening to some Tevin Campbell till the sun comes up."

O'Neil pushed the Twins out of the way and stood in their place.

"Now I want my young girl back, make these dreams come alive once again."

Then they all joined in together again while gyrating their hips and humping the air before they sang in unison.

"Good humping, body jumping, knocking Timbs all day long. Yah-mean. Taking these big ole deez to the break of dawn," before everyone burst into laughter.

"Oh my God, you're so embarrassing," Sheena said, covering her face.

"Everybody is staring. Stop!"

"Girl, who cares. They sound good!" Chrissy said as she snapped her fingers and swayed side to side, encouraging the boys' shenanigans.

Once the song was over, the boys drifted off to the side until they heard the beat drop. The four of them retreated into their own frenzy when they heard Method Man start the intro as they yelled out the song title.

"Cash rules everything around me, C.R.E.A.M."

The boys stood in a circle, like they were part of a Brooklyn cypher, joking and taking turns rapping their own lyrics.

"Get that moolah, get your dollars up ya'll!"

"Ugh, where's this train?" Chrissy sighed as she pulled her lip gloss out of her back pocket and unscrewed the cap from the tube.

"It's running on a weekend schedule, and they said a train stalled at Haymarket, so it's gonna be even longer," a deep male voice said while slurring his words.

"Mind if I sit down?" He asked while stumbling and almost falling before regaining his footing and plopping down on the hard wooden bench.

Once he sat down, he let out a long sigh. Sheena and Chrissy could smell the pungent, stale odor of alcohol coming from his breath and body. He was a big, tall, scruffy-looking man carrying a duffel bag. He unzipped his bag, pulled out a quarter pint of Mad Dog 20/20, and drank half the bottle in one gulp.

"Pretty young thangs, want some?" He asked as he shoved the bottle under Sheena's nose, moving closer into her personal space.

"No, thank you," Sheena responded, nudging Chrissy to move over to create more space between herself and the drunk man.
"I woulda took it if he didn't put his nasty wet lips all over it first," Chrissy whispered in Sheena's ear.

"Whatcho' name is, baby girl?" He asked with a grunt.

"I don't speak to strangers," Sheena replied indignantly, looking into his bloodshot, glassy eyes.

"This train needs to hurry up," Chrissy mumbled as she reapplied lip gloss.

"Can I have some? I forgot my Chapstick," she said as she rubbed her dry lips and held out her hand.

"Thank you. Sheesh, my lips feel like sandpaper."

She carefully applied the thick, sticky, shiny gloss to her lips, then pursed her lips together to even out the coating.

Sheena then heard a low grunting noise and looked over to the drunk man as he was looking at her every move while holding the half-empty bottle of Mad Dog to his wet lips.

"Mmmmm, those some sexy lips, girl. Whatcho' name is? Stop playing wit me. You a pretty young thang, huh? Umm hmmm, yeah you a pretty young thang," he moaned excitedly while licking his lips.

Sheena nudged Chrissy again so she could move closer to the edge of the bench and farther away from the dunk man as he downed the rest of the Mad Dog and tossed the bottle onto the train tracks. He then unzipped his duffel bag on the ground between his feet, pulled out a black jacket, and rested it over his thighs as he whispered.

"Pretty young thang, don't be like that. Tell me yo' name, baby. Tell me, tell me yo name baby," he continued to whisper and moan while inching himself closer towards Sheena.

The drunk man fumbled with the jacket and put his right hand underneath it.

"Come on, baby, don't be like that. Whatcho' name is, baby? Let's go party. You wanna party wit me, baby girl? Lick them lips again. Tell me, whatcho' name is, baby? Tell me whatcho' name is baby," he said breathlessly.

Sheena looked at him and saw his body jerking back and forth as he looked at her.

"What the heck is he doing?" She mumbled in Chrissy's direction as she turned to see what she was talking about.

"Is he scratching?" She asked, confused.

"What the. . . He's playing with himself!" Chrissy blurted out, stunned.

At that moment, they both froze.

"You like that pretty young thang? You like watching. Whatcho' name is, baby? Mmmmm, whatcho' name is?" The drunk man asked while grunting, moaning, and masturbating under his jacket in the train station.

Sheena and Chrissy sat in horror and disbelief while holding each other's hands. Unable to move, look away, or call out for help. The drunk man's moans became louder and faster as he rose from his seated position, stood up and let the black jacket fall from his thighs revealing his erect penis while fondling himself, stroking voraciously.

"You like that, baby? Open that pretty little mouth, yeah, open ya mouth pretty young thang," he whispered and moaned as he stepped closer before letting out a series of deep grunts.

"Aargh, Aargh, Aarrgh!"

At that point, the drunk man was standing over Sheena and ejaculated. Still in shock, unable to move or speak, Sheena looks down and sees a cloudy white-gray substance on her sweatshirt and on her jeans, dripping down the front of her sweatshirt in between her thighs. Chrissy looked, still holding onto Sheena's hand, they couldn't speak, frozen with fear.

"Yoooooo, what the fuck!"

Sheena heard a familiar voice yell out, and the sounds of a thunderous stampede of footsteps.

"Get him!"
O'Neil grabbed Sheena's shoulders to get her attention while The Twins and Hakeem surrounded the drunk man.

"Sheena, you okay?" He asked with genuine concern and adrenaline in his voice.

"I'm okay," she stammered as she looked back down at the semen dripping down her sweatshirt.

"Look what he did," she muttered, still in shock.

"Are you serious?" Hakeem asked.

"You did what?" He demanded, looking at the drunk man in his eyes.

"You getting fucked up for this one," Hakeem said while tightening his grip on the back of the drunk man's neck.

"You's a muthafuckin' pedophile, you bitch!" O'Neil spat and screamed in his face.

"You know what this means, right?" The Twins asked. "We bout to fuck you up!"
"Fuck you up real good," Jamal added so there was no misunderstanding.

O'Neil looked up from Sheena and stepped back. His fists were balled up so tightly that Sheena could see the veins pulsating.

"Y'all, let this bitch go. We shooting a fair one. But, don't let this muthfucka run away. You gonna take this ass whooping,"

O'Neil said breathing heavily while his chest started to move up and down from his erratic breathing.

The drunk man stumbled as Hakeem released the grip from his neck while he tried to pull his pants back up over his flaccid gooey penis.

"Fuck you gone do? Huh? Fuck you gone do?" The drunk man sputtered as he swayed side to side.

O'Neil set his stance by standing tall, moving one foot in front of the other, bringing both hands above his chin, tightening his fists even more, bending his knees slightly, and like lightning, he hit the drunk man with a jab, jab. As the drunk man stumbled back, O'Neil hit him with a savage uppercut to the face as he fell backward onto the ground, motionless. At that moment, the train station platform erupted into cheers.

"That's what the fuck he gets!" A man in the crowd shouted.

"You did the right thing, baby," an elderly woman with a cane said while walking past the motionless drunk man. "This muthafucka' better wake up and take the rest of this beating," Hakeem said while reaching down and going through the drunk man's pockets.

Hakeem threw the pocket contents onto the train station platform but kept the wallet, then proceeded to pick up the drunk man's duffle bag and put it on his shoulder before hacking up phlegm and spitting on the intoxicated man.

"Is, is he dead?" Sheena asked, still in shock.

The old lady looked at Sheena, extended her frail arm and thin wrinkly fingers, and lifted Sheena's chin before speaking.

"Baby, don't ever stand for no disrespect. That young man did an honorable thing here today; that's a genuine soul. Raised right, has respect and can lay a motherfucker out. Don't ever forget this moment. There's darkness and there's light. Stay in the company of light."

Her eyes were so kind and so loving before she proceeded to walk towards the drunk man.

"This dirty dick motherfucker aint' dead," she reassured them as she took her cane, lifted it and slammed it down onto the drunk man's exposed genitals.

"See, he's just a dirty drunk that got his comeuppance," the old lady chuckled as the drunk man jerked up and turned on his side, howling in pain.

"Whootie whooo. One Time, One Time!" Someone called out in the crowd.

The old lady urgently instructed, "Go on now, hurry up before the police show up, go on now."

As they turned to leave, they could hear people cheering

and reassuring O'Neil that he had done the right thing. Random people jokingly yelled out the names of the greatest black boxers.

"You did your thing, Frazier!"

"Keep knocking perverts out, Sugar Ray!"

"Keep our girls safe, Muhammad Ali!"

They ran from the platform as they tried to exit the station quickly before the MBTA cops appeared.

3

MOMMY DEAREST

"Dr. Angel, I was so scared in those few minutes with that crazy man."

Sheena slowly opened her eyes and looked up at the ceiling before readjusting and looking at Dr. Angel, holding her notepad and pen.

"Oh, my Deary, you must've been so frightened and confused. You were a child, and he stole your right to feel safe and respected. He had no right, Dear. No right at all. How do you think that moment shaped you?"

"From that day on, I knew Neil would never let anyone hurt me. He'd beat a man unconscious for me if he had to. Ever since that day, I had the utmost respect for him. But I won't lie, I did wonder if he reacted the way he did because he had The Twins and Hakeem as backup, but life is full of surprising disappointments, and he would get another chance to show me how much of a loyal protector he truly was."

"Go on, Deary, tell me what you mean by that and why it's so important to you."

"Okay, Doc, but I need a quick break. This baby is moonwalking on my bladder. I need to use the restroom," Sheena said as she struggled to rise from her sitting position.

"You'd think, all this water this baby has me retaining in my feet, face, and hands, you'd think I could retain it in my bladder instead of needing to pee every fifteen minutes."

Dr. Angel chuckled while covering her smile.

"Oh, Deary, soon you will be holding your bundle of joy, and this will be just a quick blip on the radar. Trust me." She said reassuringly as Sheena waddled out of the room towards the bathroom.

"Doc, how is it possible that I feel heavier now than when I went into the bathroom?" She asked sarcastically, plopping back into the chair, massaging her stomach, and sighing.

"Okay, where were we?" She asked, trying to get comfortable.

"You started to discuss Neil and how he proved himself to be your protector again after your sexual assault. Because let's be frank, Deary, that is exactly what that was in that train station. And it was not your fault," Dr. Angel reiterated while emphasizing it was not Sheena's fault.

"Okay, well, you know it was just my mother and I, practically no family, and my father was barely around outside of popping up once every few years to stop by and say hi," Sheena explained while making air quotes.

"My mother, Evelyn, worked at Boston City Hospital since I was young. She worked a lot and would work long hours. If she wasn't working long hours, she would work the overnight shift. So, if she was home, she was sleeping.

"That seems very isolating. Who were you with when your mom was working or sleeping?"

"Mrs. Mattie"

Sheena smiled while remembering Mrs. Mattie.

"Mrs. Mattie was our neighbor; she lived in our apartment building for about thirty years. Everyone knew Mrs. Mattie and almost all the neighborhood kids had Mrs. Mattie as a babysitter at some point. She was so sweet and so insightful. I loved her; she was everyone's grandmother. And, awwwww man! That woman could cook! Mrs. Mattie taught me everything I know in the kitchen. Her grandparents raised her in Alabama while her parents moved to Boston to find better opportunities. She told me she moved to Boston full-time to be with her parents when she turned thirteen, but would always go back to Alabama for weeks at a time until her grandparents died. Mrs. Mattie said that once both her grandparents died, there was no reason to go back; there was nothing to go back to. Once they were gone, everyone and everything she loved was here, in Boston. She said teaching us kids how to cook a good southern meal kept her grandparents' love and legacy alive. So, when Evelyn needed to work, I was with Mrs. Mattie, and that went on until I was about twelve. Once I got too old to need a babysitter, I would still go to Mrs. Mattie's every Sunday and help her cook, listen to her advice, and hear her talk," Sheena said while smiling and reminiscing on her time with Mrs. Mattie.

"It sounds like you greatly respected and adored her, Deary. What are some of Mrs. Mattie's viewpoints and principles that you can remember and use to still help guide you till today?"

Dr. Angel perked up in her seat and positioned her pen and paper to begin taking notes.

Sheena chuckled.

"There were so many, she would always start with, Sheena baby. That's how I knew she wanted me to pay close attention and learn something. Sheena, baby... don't you never, ever, ever tell another woman how yo' man is in bed. I don't care how good or how bad, cuz either way, they gone wanna try it out for themselves."

"If she saw me getting too friendly with kids she didn't think had any home training, as she put it, she would tell me... 'Sheena, baby. If you lay down wit' dogs, ya gone get up wit' fleas. One time, she saw Chrissy and me skating around the neighborhood while she was sitting in the back of the building watching the kids play on the swings and slide, and she called me over to her. She looked at me before speaking . . . Sheena, baby. She pointed to Chrissy, who was skating in the parking lot, pointed to her and said, Remember... fleas."

"And then, when I got a little older and the boys started to notice me, Sheena, baby... never depend on a man for your survival. Men are very fickle. You stay smart, independent, never make a man or anyone else, for that matter, so important you lose yo'self. People come, people go, and people can be unpredictable. Protect yourself, your heart, and ya sanity. Fortune favors the brave; don't follow the wicked or the stupid. And stay the beautiful soul you are. Pretty is as pretty does, and your heart is pretty. You're the cat's meow she said before pinching my cheeks and playfully swatting me on my behind."

Sheena let out a slight chortle.

"She made everything seem simple and did everything with love and out of love."

"She surely sounds quite insightful and full of love to give," Dr. Angel reaffirmed.

"So, once I got old enough to be home alone, I saw Mrs.

Mattie less. I knew she was busy with the younger kids, and I liked hanging out with Chrissy. As you know, Evelyn worked a lot, but she could and would make time for a man."

Sheena let out a sarcastic chuckle.

"You'd think that, with all that work she was doing, she'd at least find a man who worked too. But ooooooh no! Not Evelyn, she had a type, which was a thing for losers. More specifically, underemployed or flat-out unemployed losers. And, if that wasn't bad enough, sprinkle on some bad habits. Drinking, drugs, women, take your pick, they all usually had some issue," Sheena said while rolling her eyes and throwing her hands up in frustration.

"But the one I hated the most, Donnie! At first, he was okay. I remember he started coming around if something needed to be done because he was handy. VCR stopped working; Evelyn called Donnie. The brakes on the car start grinding, and Evelyn calls Donnie. If she needed something put together, Donnie's at the house."

"At first, he was just around if Evelyn was home. Then, I say about two years of him just coming to the house to fix stuff or hang out with her. One day, he came over, and it was like he never left. By then, I'm around sixteen, and Evelyn is still working the night or double shifts. So, I'm home a lot with Donnie when he's around. Chrissy would try to stay with me on the nights Evelyn worked overnight to keep me company and get away from all her family staying at her grandmother's house, so I never really had to be with him alone. Something about him, I just never really liked. Once Evelyn let him stay, I couldn't stand him at all," Sheena said while her lips curled in disgust.

"This particular day, it was a Friday evening, Evelyn wouldn't get home until about 7:30 am or 8:00 am the following day. Chrissy and I were in the living room watching New Jack City on the VCR that Donnie had fixed for us. We hear keys fumbling in the door and then the lock unlatching. Next thing you know, Donnie flies into the house looking like a Tasmanian Devil that just ran a marathon in 90-degree heat."

■

"Look what I got. Look what I got ya'll!" Donnie said excitedly as he opened the front door as wide as it could go, before stepping back into the hallway to retrieve a large cardboard box and sit it in front of Chrissy and Sheena.

"Look, look!" Donnie said, animatedly pointing to the box before returning to the doorway to retrieve a second box.

Beads of sweat formed on his forehead and neck as he continued emphatically, prompting Chrissy and Sheena to look into both boxes. He then ran to the kitchen and picked up the telephone on the wall.

"What is this?" Sheena mumbled to herself as she paused the movie, got up, and opened the box.

Chrissy walked up and stood beside her.

"What the. . . What on Earth?" Sheena said under her breath.

"What did he rob? A store?" Chrissy asked with confusion.
"Look at all this! You can open your own Bodega," Chrissy
shrieked.

As they looked in the box, they saw it was filled with gum,
candy, and chapstick, all packaged in bulk, stuff you see on
store shelves. There were bulk packages of Big Red gum,
Double Mint gum, Skittles, Chico Stix, M&M Peanuts, M&M
chocolates, Now & Laters, Cry Baby gumballs, Sour Punch
straws, Warheads, Ring Pops, Airheads, and Nestle Crunch
bars.

Chrissy started opening the Chico Stix package.

"Ohhhhh, I love these," she said while fumbling with the
packaging before sprinting into the kitchen to get a knife.

As Sheena watched Chrissy sprint past Donnie, she saw him
hastily punching numbers into the receiver's keypad and
slamming the phone down before immediately picking it
back up and repeating the same action.

Chrissy returned to the boxes with a knife and started to slice
open all the bulk packages in the first box. She took a Chico
Stix and stuck it in her mouth before biting.

"I love these," she said with her mouth full as she made
crunching noises while eating.

Donnie was still in the kitchen dialing numbers and hanging up the phone when it rang, startling him and causing him to jump up like a thunderbolt.

"Hello, yeah, yeah, yeah. It's Donnie, man. Where's Charlie, Charlie, Charlie, Charlie? Where? Aight, I'mma meet you now. What?! How much? Fuck outta here. Come onnnnnnn, man. Okay, okay, okay. I'm coming!"

Donnie yelled hurriedly as he slammed down the phone.

"Okay, girls! Donnie out!" He said jokingly as he wiped the sweat from his face and walked towards the door like Sherman Hemsley from The Jeffersons sitcom.

"Going to get Charlie," he squealed before slamming the apartment door after he exited.

"Ugh, God. He's so freaking weird," Sheena said as she shook her head and pressed play on the remote to resume the movie.

"Ohhhh, this is my part!" Chrissy said with delight as she focused on the television and mimicked along with Wesley Snipes.

"I wasn't born with a silver spoon in my mouth, Miss Sheena…"

"Keep it up, I'mma rock-a-bye baby you!" Sheena joked as she threw a Chico Stix in Chrissy's direction.

They ate candy and chewed Big Red gum for the remainder of the movie until about 11:30 pm when the phone rang.

"Hello. Hi. I'm good. Yeah, hold on. Yes, she's still up. Chrissy! Phone." Sheena yelled into the living room while Chrissy was on the couch watching Roc on BET.

"Awwww come onnnn, whyyyy?" Chrissy whined while sucking her teeth and rolling her eyes as she held the receiver to her ear.

"Fine! Okay, bye!" She said curtly before slamming the kitchen phone down.

"Ugh, I hate them!" Chrissy yelled as she stormed out of the kitchen and back towards the sofa in the living room.

"What happened now?"

"They want me to go home and watch them damn Bebe's kids!" She said, annoyed.

"I'm sick of being everybody's sitter, I didn't have all of them damn kids! Why they my problem?" Chrissy said as she got up and stormed into Sheena's bedroom to retrieve her overnight bag.

"My stupid ass sister and cousin about to come pick me up now so they can go hang out all night. If they didn't wanna watch they own damn kids they shouldn't of had them, better yet, they should call the daddies. I can't wait to move out!"

"Well, I can hang out with you tomorrow if you're still watching them. If not, just come back over here." Sheena said, trying to make Chrissy feel better.

"Here, take this," she said while handing Chrissy the opened packages of Chico Stix and Big Red gum before the doorbell rang.

"That's them," Chrissy said, sulking as she got up from the couch, slung her bag over her shoulders, and picked up her box of Chico Stix and gum.

"I'll see you later," she said as she unlocked the front door.

"Okay, I'll talk to you tomorrow," Sheena said as she closed and locked the door behind Chrissy.

She returned to the mess they had made in the living room, with candy and gum wrappers strewn all over the coffee table and floor.

"Yikes, let me get this up so I don't have to hear that woman's mouth," she mumbled to herself as she started to pick up the wrappers, bring them to the kitchen trash, retrieve the vacuum from the living room closet, and vacuum the entire apartment before going into the kitchen and washing the dishes in the sink. She used Pine-Sol on the countertops and stove until everything was spotless, just like her mother liked it.

Sheena looked up at the clock on the microwave.

"1:27 am? I'm tired. I'll do the bathroom in the morning," she said as she walked towards her bedroom.

Once in her room, Sheena closed her bedroom door and set her alarm clock for 6:30 a.m., talking to herself, "I need to get up before Ma gets home so I can clean the bathroom and cook breakfast. Ugh, I'm tired," she said before getting into her bed and pulling the covers over her head.

■

Sheena slowly awoke from her sleep, confused.

"Thought I heard something," she mumbled as she looked at her alarm clock on her nightstand, which read 2:42 a.m.

Sheena noticed her door was slightly ajar before she heard a voice from the darkness.

"You awake?"

"What the fuck!" Sheena blurted out in shock as she jumped up and switched on the lamp on her nightstand.

"Whoa, whoa, whoa. It's me." Donnie said while standing at the foot of Sheena's bed, wearing a tank top and boxers, looking like he just finished running around the block a few times.

"You awake?" He asked again while wiping the sweat from his brows and rubbing his glassy eyes.

"Get out! Why are you in here?" Sheena yelled out with fear dripping from each word.

"Go! Now!"

"Awww girl, come on. I see you done cleaned your mother's room and made the bed. I'm not tryna hear her mouth tomorrow. Lemme' get in bed with you." Donnie said while walking towards her bed and picking up the sheets.

"Get out! Get out of my room!" Sheena yelled as she jumped out of bed as Donnie tried to make his way into it, pulling his tank top off his sweaty body.

When Sheena looked more closely at Donnie as he flung his tank top over his sweaty head onto the floor and proceeded into her bed as she protested, she noticed his erect penis sticking out from the front fly of his underwear. Immediately, Sheena froze in familiar terror and her mind raced not knowing what to do next as she watched Donnie laying his sweaty body in her bed with just underwear on with his erect penis pointed to the ceiling.

Sheena's mind returned to that day at Downtown Crossing in the train station, and fear gripped her. Then she remembered what the little old lady had said to her: "Baby, don't ever stand for disrespect."

"Donnie, get out of my bed now!" She said more forcefully as she glared at Donnie with hatred and disgust.

"Girl, cut it out, come on and lay back down. I can't sleep in your mama's bed, you cleaned up the room. You know she's gonna come in here tomorrow with all that hooting and hollering about her room being a mess. Come on now."

"So, you're not going to leave?" Sheena asked while bending down and reaching under her bed.

"Come on now, I just told you. Your mother gonna cuss both of us out. Just get in the bed, girl."

Sheena stood tall and held a steel bat, remembering the correct hand and grip position that O'Neil had taught her. She positioned her left hand at the bottom of the bat and her right hand at the top, lining the small knuckles of one hand with the big knuckles of the other and ensuring she had a firm grip.

"I'mma take your fucking head off!" Sheena yelled as she swung the bat and made contact with the lamp and headboard, just missing Donnie's head as he jerked to the left in surprise.

The loud sound of the porcelain lamp shattering and the crack of the wooden headboard rang out before Donnie jumped up and out of the bed.

"Get the fuck out!" Sheena screamed while chasing Donnie out of her bedroom, swinging the bat in the darkness of the apartment. Before she made contact, she heard a thud, and then Donnie yelled out in pain.

"Awww shit!" He yelled before running into Evelyn's bedroom and slamming the door.

Sheena rushed back to her bedroom. The door had no lock, so she pushed her bed against the door before picking up the phone and paging O'Neil. Sheena dialed O'Neil's pager five times in a row, entering 9-1-1 after her phone number each time, praying that he would be awake.

A few minutes later, the phone rang.

"Hello."

"What's wrong?" O'Neil asked with genuine concern.

"He wouldn't get out of my bed! I had to hit him with your bat." Sheena said almost in tears.

"I'm on my way. I should be there in 10-15 minutes."

"Okay," Sheena said before hanging up the phone while she stared at Donnie's sweaty tank top and shards of the broken lamp on her bedroom floor.

Sheena jumped as she heard the doorbell buzz. She looked at the alarm clock, which read 3:20 am. Sheena stood up, moved the bed away from her bedroom door, ran to the living room with the bat still in her hand, and buzzed O'Neil into the building. Sheena stood outside the apartment waiting for O'Neil as she heard the elevator doors open and close on the ground level and approach the 2nd floor of the building before opening. O'Neil rushed out of the elevator while pushing his bike by his side.

"You okay? He's still here?" O'Neil asked while walking into the apartment with his bike in tow.

"I.. I don't know. I think so." Sheena said while shaking her head.

O'Neil walked to the primary bedroom door and tried turning the knob to open the door.

"It's locked, he's still in there."

O'Neil started banging on the door.

"Aye, yooo! Open the door." O'Neil yelled while twisting the doorknob again, trying to open the door.

O'Neil put his ear to the door.

"Is that him, snoring?" He asked in disbelief.

"Probably, let's just stay in my room until my mother gets here. She'll be here soon," Sheena said as she began to walk towards her bedroom.

"Gimme a sec, let me put my bike up," he said as he walked his Huffy Mudslinger bicycle to the living room corner and pushed down on the kickstand.

"So, what happened? Tell me everything," O'Neil prompted as he walked into Sheena's bedroom, where she was pulling out a comforter and extra pillows to make a makeshift bed on the floor next to her bed.

"I was in bed, sleeping, and woke up to him watching me and asking if I was up. Then he took off his funky t-shirt," Sheena said as she choked up and pointed anxiously to the dingy white tank top on the floor.

"Then, he got his nasty sweaty ass in my bed, in his underwear!" She said, filled with rage, as she ripped the bedding off her mattress.

"He got in my bed, and it was hard!" She said while pointing to her crotch.

"His dick was hard, Neil!" She said while tears started to form in her eyes.

Sheena wiped her eyes with the back of her hands before the tears could fall and stood up straight before continuing.

"Then I remembered the bat you left me. So, after I saw he wasn't leaving my bed, I pulled out the bat and swung and kept swinging until I hit that piece of shit, and he ran into my mother's room."

Once Sheena finished recollecting the events, she looked over at O'Neil, who was visibly upset. He was breathing deep and fast as he balled up his fists and released them.

"Nah, fuck that! Are you serious? Nah, man. Nah, he ain't getting away with this shit!" O'Neil said as he released his balled-up fists and cracked his knuckles.

"Where's your phone. Lemme call my Pop's and let him know I got here safe." He said as Sheena handed him the cordless phone from her nightstand.

"Hey, Pop's. I got here safe, I'm at Sheena's now. I'm going to stay until her mother gets home from work in the morning. No, everything is fine. She didn't want to stay by herself. I'll tell you in the morning when I get home. Okay, love you too, Pop's. Goodnight."

O'Neil hung up the phone and turned to Sheena as she put fresh sheets on her bed.

"Yoooooo, She-She. On dead dawgs, he's getting fucked up! That was a total violation, and if I can't get to him because he's locked up in your mother's room, my Pop's will definitely take care of his ass whooping for violating like this, on dawgs. I just don't want to disrespect your mother's house!" O'Neil reiterated with vitriol as he got ready to lay on his makeshift bed on the floor.

"I know you will, Neil. You always look out for me," Sheena responded with certainty.

"But I don't want you getting into trouble. Just leave it alone. I'm sure my mother will tell him to leave once she gets here, and I tell her what his nasty ass did," she said reassuringly before closing her eyes and falling asleep.

The 6:30 am alarm woke both Sheena and O'Neil up before she could hit the off button.

"Ugh, I'm so tired. Good morning. You hungry?"

"Hungry for some whoop some ass!" O'Neil said half-jokingly.

"Cut it out! I'll make breakfast. I still have to finish cleaning up, too," she said, looking at the broken lamp on the floor. She then got out of bed and bent down to pick up the shattered pieces and bring them to the kitchen trash.

"Clean up? The house is spotless, why are you always cleaning when there ain't nothing to clean?"

"You know my mother will have something to say if this place ain't cleaned the way she likes it."

"You wanna watch Don't Be a Menace?" Sheena yelled out to O'Neil as she opened the refrigerator and pulled out a carton of eggs, a package of bacon, sausage, and a box of pancake mix before walking into the living room, putting the VHS tape into the VCR, and turning on the TV.

"Yeah, put it on," he said as he picked up the comforter and pillows from the floor, folding them and putting them back into Sheena's closet before walking out to the living room and sitting on the couch.

"Dip Shit Donnie better not think about stepping foot out that room till Ms. Williams get here!" O'Neil yelled out in the direction of the closed bedroom door.

"Piece of shit," O'Neil mumbled under his breath as he could hear Sheena in the kitchen moving pots and pans to the stove as the movie started the opening credits.

"You want pancakes or waffles?"

"Oooohh, make those banana pancakes like you did that last time! Those were slamming," O'Neil said while rubbing his stomach in anticipation.

As Sheena cooked, she could hear O'Neil in the living room laughing to himself while watching the movie. She felt safe knowing O'Neil was with her, even though Donnie was still in the apartment, hiding in her mother's room behind a locked door, waiting to exit.

"Food's almost ready," Sheena said as she walked to the bathroom carrying Pine-Sol, Ajax, and a rag.

O'Neil could smell the Pine-Sol waft into the living room as Sheena cleaned the bathroom and could hear the water running and the scrubbing of the tub with the Ajax.

"Alright. I'll make your plate." Sheena said, walking out of the bathroom and back to the kitchen.

"Come eat," she squawked.

"I'm starving. Dang girl, I didn't know you were cooking like this!" He said, pleasantly surprised, while looking down at the table and his plate that Sheena had made for him.

"Banana pancakes, peppered omelet, sausage. It smells good, too! Alright, She-She." O'Neil joked as he sat down at the table.

"That's turkey sausage. I know you don't eat pork. The bacon is for my mother when she gets home. She should be here soon," Sheena said as she took a bite of her omelet.

"Aww man, that was good. Thanks for cooking, Block Head," he said as he got up and returned to the living room to finish watching the movie.

Sheena picked up their plates and washed their dishes before joining O'Neil on the couch. While laughing and watching TV, they heard the keys in the front door before Evelyn entered.

"I know one thing; this house better be clean." Evelyn declared as she looked at Sheena and O'Neil sitting on the couch.

"Morning, Ms. Williams," O'Neil said with repugnance as he rolled his eyes and watched her walk straight to the kitchen.

"Now you know good damn well I don't like my bacon like this. This ain't crispy," Evelyn said with a cynical tone.

"You gotta be kidding me," Sheena muttered while defiantly

crossing her arms over her chest and rolling her eyes before whispering. "Make it your damn self then."

O'Neil looked over at Sheena and could no longer tolerate the situation, so he decided to speak up.

"So, Ms. Williams, you're not even curious why I'm over here this early in the morning. You're more concerned about some dirty swine on your plate than the dirty swine you got in this house with Sheena, alone overnight?"

Sheena could see the anger in O'Neil's face and voice. That familiar feeling of safety and assurance he gave her that day in the train station with that drunk man was back again in this apartment, standing in defiance of Donnie and Evelyn.

"Excuse me?" Evelyn responded with flippant disdain.

"What are you tryna get at?" She asked with derision as she tossed the plate of untouched bacon in the trash.

This angered O'Neil further.

"How about asking your DAUGHTER!" O'Neil yelped with emphasis. "Ask your daughter if she's okay! And ask what happened in this house last night!"

Evelyn sneered.

"Clearly, not much. She looks fine to me," she said as she turned to look at Sheena.

"You look fine to me, so what's the problem?" She asked, without real concern.

"Ma, Donnie needs to go! Tell him to leave," she cried out in exasperation. "Tell him to leave, now!"

"You better pump your brakes, little girl. Who the hell do you think you are, telling me what to do? This is my house. Do you pay bills here? You keep these lights on? You buy this food? Because, if not, you don't get a say in what I do and who I bring in here!" Evelyn roared as she pointed her fingers in Sheena's direction.

Flabbergasted, O'Neil shook his head in disbelief.

"Wait. . . Wait, so you ain't even gonna ask your daughter why she wants that pig out the house? Are you serious!"

"Ma, that man came in my room last night when I was sleeping and tried to get in my bed practically naked!"

"With his fucking dick out!" O'Neil interjected while becoming visibly disturbed and aggravated with Evelyn and her callous regard for Sheena and the previous night's events.

"Like. I. Said." Evelyn began dramatically emphasizing each word before finishing her sentence.

"A muthafucka' that don't pay no bills in my house aint gonna tell me what to do," she said before walking to her closed bedroom door and attempting to enter.

"Ma, he scares me. Tell him to leave. He got in my bed, took off his t-shirt, and wouldn't leave. I had to get a bat and beat his ass for him to leave me alone!" Sheena said through tears.

"Please, tell him to leave, Ma."

"Donnie! Open my goddamn door!" Evelyn yelled while banging on the door and jiggling the doorknob.

"Donnie! Donnie! Get up and open the door, now!"

O'Neil stood by Sheena as they watched the bedroom door slowly open, and Evelyn stormed into her bedroom. Sheena sprinted to her bedroom to retrieve the steel bat just in case. She returned to the living room and stood next to O'Neil.

"He's not gonna do nothing to you," O'Neil reassured her.

"Donnie, what the fuck! What the fuck did you do in here. Look at my room. What the fuck is all this! Why my room smell like shit? Is that shit?! Get the fuck out, get the fuck out now!" Evelyn hollered.

Sheena and O'Neil stood there anxiously, waiting for Donnie to exit the bedroom. While they were standing there, the stench of feces permeated the living room.

"Oh my God!" Sheena shrieked, "That's disgusting!"

"Yoooooo, don't tell me last night you knocked the shit out of him." O'Neil joked as he pinched his nose.

"Baby, Baby, listen. Them lil bastards wouldn't let me leave, baby. They kidnapped me!"

Sheena and O'Neil could hear Donnie pleading with Evelyn as he appeared in the bedroom doorway, struggling to put his legs in his jeans and move out of the way of Evelyn's wrath.

"Damn She-She, you did knock the shit out of him," O'Neil said as they both looked at Donnie stumbling and fumbling in the doorway trying to put his pants on.

The back of his boxers was soiled, and watery brown liquid ran down both legs. The right side of his face was swollen twice its original size, with a deep gash over his right eye, which was swollen shut. His left eye was bloodshot, his nose was running, and he had a white powdery substance on the tip of his nose and around his lips.

"Get your shitty ass out my house, you nasty muthafucka!" Evelyn yelled as she smacked him in his head.

"Ouch, baby! Why you doing me like that? Those kids are demons. They like that Chucky doll. You remember that movie Chucky, right? That's them!" Donnie rambled as he pointed at Sheena and O'Neil.

"Baby, they crazy. They kidnapped me, I was scared, had to lock myself in the room till you got here. Couldn't even leave out to go to the bathroom." Donnie said finally pulling his pants up.

"Baby, Baby, listen. It was like Poltergeist up in here last night. She a demon! Why you ain't tell me you gave birth to Rosemary's baby? Then, she summoned that other spawn!" He said, jerking and fidgeting while pointing to O'Neil.

Evelyn slapped Donnie upside his head again before demanding, "Get your stuff and those shitty ass sheets and get the fuck outta here. You must be out your rabid ass mind. Brand new goddamn sheets and you in here shitting on em' like you a goddamn newborn!"

"Oh, Baby don't be like that, just cause I like to suck on them milk jugs don't make me no baby. You yelling at me, what about them heathens over there?" Donnie said while fidgeting and pulling at the collar of his t-shirt.

"Them two psycho."

Evelyn took a deep breath, walked over to Sheena, and took the steel bat out of her hands.

"Donnie, I ain't gonna tell you again. Get your stuff and those shitty ass sheets and get out of my damn house, or I'm gonna take this bat," she said as she raised the bat in Donnie's face.

"And I'm going to finish what she started."

"Well damn, you ain't gotta tell me twice. I know when I'm not wanted," he said while scratching the left side of his face before walking back into the bedroom with Evelyn following close behind him.

Soon after, he exited the bedroom with a trash bag full of his belongings and carried the soiled bedding over his shoulder.

"I've been kicked outta better establishments," Donnie said mockingly as he walked towards the front door before stopping abruptly.

"Aye bitch, hold on now, bitch. I ain't leaving Charlie. Charlayyyyy," he sang as he turned around and returned to the bedroom, where Evelyn met him in the doorway.

"Here. OUT!" Evelyn said sternly as she handed Donnie an envelope, then pointed the bat toward the front door.

"Yeah, yeah, yeah. Hold your horses. I'm leaving." Donnie said as he put the small brown envelope in his back pocket.

"Donnie, outtie five thousand," he said while holding up his two fingers in a peace sign, carrying his trash bag in his left hand, and draped the soiled sheets over his right shoulder.

"Don't come calling me when some shit don't work around here either. You and your daughter can kiss my hairy black ass, ya dig." He said as he unlocked the front door and opened it.

O'Neil looked at Sheena.

"He asked for it. Aye, yoooo. Repeat that." O'Neil called out while walking towards Donnie.

Donnie snorted, rubbed his nose aggressively, then snorted again, "You deaf? I said. . ."

That's when O'Neil stepped back, jumped up with all his strength, and connected with a strong roundhouse kick while his body was turned at a forty-five-degree angle. Donnie was lifted off his feet and thrown into the hallway wall as he dropped his trash bag. The soiled bedsheets covered his face as he lay slumped against the wall, dazed and confused before speaking.

"Goddamn! You ain't had to do me like that, young blood."

"Get your smelly ass outta here, don't ever come back. And just so there's no confusion, I'll be sure to tell my Pop's, Kenny, to see you." O'Neil said before turning around and walking back into the apartment.

"Whoa, whoa, you ain't gotta do all that youngin. I was just playing, come on now." Donnie tried to plead as O'Neil closed the door and locked it.

O'Neil walked over to Sheena, who was sitting on the couch.

"You alright? Dude ain't never coming back," he reassured her.

"Look at this mess," Evelyn complained from her bedroom.

"Sheena, you need to come clean this up. I'm not dealing with this shit."

"Oh my God, is she really serious right now?" Sheena asked in utter disbelief.

"Whatchu want me to do, She-She? She's your mother, so I don't wanna be disrespectful but, this right here, this ain't right." O'Neil said while shaking his head.

Sheena was finally at her wits' end and decided to finally muster the nerve to divulge her true feelings about her mother for the first time. She buried her face in her hands, mumbled, and shook her head side to side.

"No, noooo. I'm not."

Sheena took a deep breath and stood up, looked over to O'Neil before saying, "Fuck it! Now, she asked for it."

"I gotcha, She-She," O'Neil said as he got up and stood beside Sheena, waiting to follow her lead.

Sheena walked towards her mother's bedroom door and stood in the doorway with O'Neil.

"Ma, I'm your daughter, not your freaking maid. I'm sick of it. You don't act like a mother. I cook, clean, wake you up for work, wash, and iron your clothes. I'm a better parent to you than you ever been to me! You know who raised me? Mrs. Mattie raised me. Your dirty ass boyfriend tried to have sex with me last night and you didn't even care. You were more concerned about some fucking sheets from K-Mart than your raggedy ass boyfriend trying to fuck me!"

"I'm a good daughter, never give you problems, do everything you ask, and never complain. But, if you think I'm cleaning actual shit up out your room that pedophile left after he tried to have sex with me, you're crazier than him."

"I tried to tell myself for years that you loved me, but today, you proved that you don't. I tell my mother; I tell my mother her boyfriend scared me and wouldn't get out of my fucking bed. A real mother who loves her child would have immediately gotten rid of that man. The only reason he's gone is because he shit in your bed and fucked up your sheets! Sheets are more important to you than me! Fucking sheets!" Sheena screamed out between tears.

"I try so hard to make you happy so you can see me, love me. I do everything without complaining because I want you to see how hard I try to make you happy. But you don't see me. You don't care about me. I don't even think you love me. You don't act like my mother; you act like I'm your servant. Why? What did I ever do to you?"

At this point, O'Neil couldn't take Sheena's suffering anymore and stepped closer to her, grabbed her hand, and whispered, "I got you, get it out."

"You have never, ever been a mother. What could I have possibly done to you to get treated like this? Are you kidding me? You had no concern for what I told you Donnie did? Really? You hate me that much? If he didn't mess up your room or sheets, he'd still be here, right? Right? You don't care that he tried to have sex with me, do you? I have no family; I have no real mother. This, this is my family." Sheena said while pointing to O'Neil.

"You didn't teach me how to cook, you didn't talk to me about boys, you don't ask me about what I like. All you do is make demands and expect me to do things for you. You don't spend time with me. You think just because you provide and buy stuff, I should be happy. You think your money makes you a mother. Newsflash, it doesn't. You don't even know me, but you know what mothers know me and show me love? Mrs. Mattie and Mrs. Harris, you could never be half the mothers they are. You could never!" Sheena said while wiping the tears from her eyes and snot from her nose.

Evelyn stood motionless with a pensive look on her face before speaking.

"Are you finished, or are you done?" She asked with a patronizing smirk.

"You in here boo-hooing over a bunch of nothing. Have I ever beat you, starved you, or left you out on the streets? Have you ever gone cold, hungry, or raggedy? You're talking all this nonsense, sounding like you're slower than a parked car. Let me tell you something, so there is no confusion. I never wanted any goddamn kids! You understand that!? So, you're pretty fucking lucky if you ask me. I told your slow ass, janky ass daddy I didn't want no kids, we had plans, I knew a kid would fuck everything up. We were supposed to move to D.C. and open a barbershop and hair salon, together. And, you know what happened? His dumb ass couldn't keep the condom on the right way. Then had the nerve to beg me to keep you! Begged, cried, pleaded for me not to abort. He said that once we moved to D.C., his aunt could watch the baby so we could work on our business plan."

"I was so close, so close to making it out this damn city. And you wanna know what happened? Once I got all big and pregnant and couldn't travel anymore to look at storefronts for our business, that bastard would go alone. And you wanna know how that story ends? That snake ass mother fucker took his one last trip to D.C. when I was eight and a half months pregnant, with my half of the business money and opened his barbershop, got fucking married and never looked back. I didn't ask for this life! I was tricked, duped, hoodwinked, bamboozled, deceived, and double-crossed into this life of motherhood. I sacrificed my dreams, my ambitions because I trusted a fraud, a snake a mother fucking rat bastard. I sacrificed everything, being tricked into bringing you into this world when I had no desire to. I forfeited my dreams to change bed pans, wipe asses, be cussed out, spat on and change adult diapers for 50-60 hours a week so you can have, so that you can live. So, Sheena, if you have found a better mother in Mrs. Mattie or Mrs. Harris, so be it, because I ain't never pretended to be something I never wanted to be." Evelyn said before calmly turning her back on Sheena and O'Neil, walking back into her bedroom, and closing the door.

Sheena yanked her hand from O'Neil's before charging into Evelyn's room and flinging the door open.

"I didn't ask to be here, I didn't have a say in who I was born to! You never wanted me?" Sheena screamed, "I don't want you! Just like you don't want me, I don't want you! You're miserable and evil, no wonder why my father left. You deserved it!"

Evelyn broke out into wicked laughter.

"Did you forget? He left you, too. So, you're no better off than me, sweetheart."

Sheena composed herself and spoke gently. "That's where you're wrong. People care about me. I have friends. My friends are my family. I know what it's like to be loved. Do you? Who do you have? Your job, your things, this place?" Sheena asked as she waved her hands, pointing at objects around the room.

"You may have bought all this crap, but I took care of all this and, you! If you don't have me, what do you have, Evelyn?" Sheena asked with vigor.

"You don't deserve the title of mother." Sheena finished as she glared into her mother's eyes.

Evelyn's eyes began to glisten, but she quickly collected herself.

"I never wanted to be a mother; I only ever wanted to be just Evelyn. I'm glad you get it now." She said before closing her bedroom door again.

4

SOMETHING OF MY OWN

"Hmph," Sheena grunted.

"You know, Doc, that was the last time I ever called her Ma. Can you believe that? This is the first time since that day that I've ever repeated that story. Wow! And, you know what? I have no regrets. In that moment and time, I had no choice but to resign to the fact that Evelyn didn't care and could never love me like a mother loves a child. I was a constant reminder of everything she didn't want and despised."

"Sheena, Deary." Doctor Angel began. "What would be different in your life if you had a positive relationship with your

FOR THE LOVE OF YOU

biological mother?"

Sheena thought about that question and pondered extensively before speaking.

"Ummmm, good question. If Evelyn were a normal mother, I wouldn't have had Mrs. Mattie or Mrs. Harris in my life in the same way. I probably wouldn't have any of my closest people in my life like I do. So, I think Evelyn did me a favor. I feel like the options were to have a great mother and we be a family of two or, have a shitty mother and have two amazing bonus mothers, Neil, Hakeem, Chrissy and The Twins as family. I don't think I would change my life for anything because, if I did, I wouldn't have her on the way." Sheena said as she looked down at her protruding belly, massaged her daughter, and showed her baby bump some love.

"Yeah, Evelyn did me a favor. I guess my life is what it should be. I worked hard and put myself through school. I got my MSN, have an awesome nursing job at Mass General, have amazing friends, and I'm about to start my own family with Hakeem. Every day, I miss Neil; not a single day goes by that I don't think about him. But I know he wants me to move on and live life to the fullest." Sheena said with a smile.

"Oh my goodness!" Sheena exclaimed while jolting upright.

"I totally forgot to tell you. Last week Chrissy told me she's pregnant, so now me and my bestie will get to raise our kids together. My baby will have a little cousin. I'm so excited!" Sheena said as she rubbed her belly warmly.

"So yeah, Evelyn definitely did me a favor."

"Ohhh, splendid! It must be wonderful to share this journey with someone so close to you for all these years. Can you tell me a little more about your relationship with Chrissy?" Doctor Angel asked inquisitively.

"Sheesh, it feels like I've known her for a lifetime. We met in elementary school at the Mattahunt. We sat right next to each other. That girl was never prepared for anything."

Sheena chuckled as she recalled her early memories of Chrissy.

"Mrs. Dickerson would say, alright, class, pull out your pencils and notebooks. And, here comes Chrissy tapping my shoulder and whispering, you got an extra pencil and paper I can borrow? Or, the teacher would say, okay, class, pull out your textbooks. I'm going to call on you all to read a section. Lo and behold, here comes Chrissy, tapping my shoulder, whispering, can I look on with you? I forgot my textbook. That girl was never, ever prepared." Sheena said with laughter. "She was always a little firecracker, never afraid to do or say what was on her mind, complete opposite of me. I don't think many people understood or understand her like I do."

"Tell me more about that. Why do you think she's misunderstood?"
"Well, what stands out is Mrs. Mattie and Mrs. Harris. If Mrs. Mattie saw us hanging out, she'd usually make a comment,

"Sheena, baby... lie down with dogs, gonna wake up with fleas. Or she'll make a point to comment Sheena, baby. . . don't wake up wit' fleas, if Chrissy was around. I remember one time Mrs. Harris and I were talking, random talk, and I recall her telling me to make sure I'm not being more of a friend to Chrissy than she is to me. But again, I feel like they didn't understand her."

"Sheena, let's dive into this. What do you think the misunderstanding was?"

"To be honest, I think they felt that she was fast, loose, and was too grown for her age. Maybe they were scared or worried she would be a bad influence on me. But I never judged her, she was funny, wild, crazy, and I love every bit of her mess! She helped make life with Evelyn bearable, and she spent so many nights with me so I didn't have to be alone when Evelyn was working or with some man. So, if no one understands Chrissy, I do. She's always happy, sassy, and ready to have a good time. I remember this one particular day she just had enough." Sheena said as she reflected on that day.

She rummaged through her purse, pulled out a water bottle, and took a sip before beginning.

■

It was Friday evening, and Sheena was lounging in the living room watching reruns of In Living Color when the telephone rang.

"Hello?"

"It's me, can I come over? These people getting on my freaking nerves!" Chrissy yelled into the phone as Sheena could hear all the chaos in the background, with the TV blaring, kids screaming, and babies crying.

"If they think I'm staying in this damn house to watch all these damn kids, they crazier than a house of nuts!" she said with attitude.

"Yeah, come on. I'll be here."

"Okay, I'm walking over now. They think they slick. Bye, girl." Chrissy said, rushing off the phone.

"Good Lord, that house sounded like a circus," Sheena mumbled as she got up to tidy her bedroom before Chrissy arrived.

The doorbell rang.

"Hello?" Sheena asked through the intercom.

"It's me."

Sheena pressed the buzzer, walked to the front door, unlocked it, and sat on the couch. Chrissy burst into the apartment.
"Sheena, I swear to God, I need to get out of there!"

"What now?"

"There's too many people in that house. I have no peace; everybody thinks they can touch or use my stuff! My aunts and sisters think I'm the live-in nanny. I'm over it." Chrissy yelled as she walked towards the couch with her L.A. Gear duffel bag and plopped down angrily before continuing.

"Every time I complain to my mother, her only response is, 'We all had our turn growing up and watching our younger family members; now it's your turn."

"That's bullshit! My sisters and cousins need to stop having babies if they can't be the ones to watch them. Sheena, you've seen that house. Three-family house, kids on each floor, I'm so over it! Fuck them kids and they mommas!"

"Ha! No, you didn't!" Sheena laughed.

"Look, I said what I said," Chrissy replied, trying not to crack a smile. "I'm serious."

"You hungry? I made potato salad and can heat up some barbeque chicken from last night." Sheena said before getting up from the couch.

"Ohh yes! I love your potato salad."

"You mean you love Mrs. Mattie's recipe," Sheena said with pride.

"Whatever, that batty old coot can't stand me."

"Stop! That ain't true, come on, sit down and finish your story." Sheena said while pointing for Chrissy to sit at the kitchen table as she started making their plates.

"Girl, please. You don't think I hear her saying I'mma give you fleas? Or whatever the hell her old ass be saying. If I ever give you fleas, it's because I done caught them from all them damn snotty nose kids I'm forced to watch." Chrissy said while letting out a soft chuckle.

"She's just overprotective," she reassured Chrissy.

"You know you're my sister from another mister," she said, placing the two plates of food on the table before taking a seat.

"Girllllll, anyways!" Chrissy said dramatically as she stuffed a forkful of potato salad in her mouth.

"Oh, this is slamming, sis."

"You're so greedy. Finish your story." Sheena playfully interrupted.

"She-She. I can't take that house, I'm so serious. Kids are on the first, second, and third floors! Why I gotta watch all them damn Bebe kids? Stop bringing all these damn kids home. Grandparents too old to be running around and watching all these damn bad ass kids, they parents want to run the streets.

Why is that my problem? They can all kiss my ass!"

"At least you got family, grandparents, siblings, cousins, and a mother there for you," Sheena said as she picked at her barbeque chicken.

"You have an actual family; there's always someone to talk to and keep you company. You know where you come from, that's a blessing."

"Blessing?! You know what it's like to have no privacy? No peace and quiet? You know what it's like to have absolutely nothing of your own? I have to share food, clothes, underwear, a bed, and life with all my cousins, sisters, nieces, and nephews! Where's the blessing in that?" Chrissy asked, breaking out in tears.

"I can't have anything, and I don't have anything of my own. Do you know what it's like to get something and be told to share it with someone else? It sucks! I have to share my underwear, who does that?! I get my first bra, and my mother hands it to me and says that's for you and Ti-Ti. Who has to share underwear?! I don't even get to sleep alone. It's me and at least one or two of my nieces or nephews in the bed. Why? Why do I have to live like that!? My bed, my clothes, my underwear, my life! Nothing is my own. I want something just for me! That's it, that's all!" Chrissy whimpered while showing her vulnerability to Sheena for the first time.

"I'm sorry, Chris, I didn't know you felt this way."

"You complain about living here with your mother, who buys you everything and anything. It's clean and quiet. You have a full-size bed just for you, clothes, shoes, and a fridge full of food." Chrissy said while pointing to her plate.

"This, this is just for you! Do you know what a blessing is, Sheena? Your life! This! This is a blessing." Chrissy said while pointing around the apartment.

"You know what it's like to have absolutely nothing for yourself? Nothing, not even a damn bra that is just your very own. Do you know what it's like to get up every morning and step over your nieces, nephews, and cousins to get to the bathroom? Go to the store for a bottle of soda and chips, and don't even get to enjoy it without someone asking to have some. Why do you think I always want to be here, with you? I'd trade with you in a heartbeat. I can't think or breathe in that house, it's just too much. When do I get something of my own? When do I get a chance to be happy? When can I just live my own life and not worry about a bunch of kids that aren't mines or sleep in a pissy bed because someone done crawled in my bed with a full diaper that their damn mother didn't change. When do I get to be a normal seventeen-year-old, Sheena? When? I want something for myself, just mine, for me and only me." Chrissy cried while trying to eat.

Sheena got up from the table, wrapped her arms around Chrissy's neck, and hugged her.

"I'm sorry, Chris. You know you're always welcome over here and can have anything of mine you want." Sheena said as she kissed Chrissy on the cheek.

"Now, stop crying; you're getting snot in your food." Sheena chuckled as she walked back to her seat at the table.

"Girl, I was wondering why that bite tasted so salty," she joked as she wiped her nose with a paper towel.

"Seriously, I want out of that house. And, the few hours a week we get at Tello's definitely not enough to get us our own place."

"I know! And depending on who's doing the schedule, we're lucky to even get twelve hours." Sheena agreed.

"You done?"

"Yeah, I guess," Chrissy replied, looking dejected as Sheena gathered their plates and washed their dishes.

"Come on, sis, cheer up," Sheena said as she wiped the counters with Pine-Sol and returned the dishes to the cabinets.

"What do you want to do tonight? Whatever your little crazy ass wanna do, let's do it!" Sheena said with excitement, hoping that would lighten Chrissy's mood.
"Well, in that case, " Chrissy said as she stood up from the kitchen table, pulled her lip gloss out of her pocket, and slathered her lips with the thick, sticky, shiny, clear gloss. She then smacked her lips together before finishing.

"I got something for us," she said with a devilish grin.

"To your bedroom we go," she said, pointing towards Sheena's room.

"Okay, tell me. What is it? What do you have?" Sheena asked as she closed her bedroom door, went to her stereo system, and pressed play.

"Look what I goooooooot." Chrissy sang out as she unzipped her duffel bag and held up two bottles—a pint of Bacardi Limon in her right hand and a pint of Seagram's Gin in her left.

"So many goddamn people coming in and out that house they won't know who took what. It's party time, She-She!"

"No, you didn't," Sheena said, surprised. "Whose is it, your uncle's?"

"Hell, if I know." Chrissy shrugged. "It's ours now. We need cups, ice, and whatever you want to mix it with."

Sheena went to the kitchen and returned with two plastic cups filled with ice and a bottle of ginger ale.

"Which one do you want to crack open first?" Chrissy asked, holding both bottles out for Sheena to inspect.

"That one," she said, pointing to the pint of gin as she twisted the cap off the two-liter soda.

"Your wish is my command. Don't you dare complain about my bartending skills. You better drink every last drop of this, too." Chrissy challenged.

"Yeah, yeah, yeah. Cut out all that yapping. I said I would. This isn't an after-school special. No need to apply the peer pressure, you bully." Sheena joked as she held her hand out for her drink.

"Now, it's time for my magic trick. You ready? Keep your eyes on my drink. Ready?" Sheena asked as she raised her cup to her lips and chugged down her entire drink.

"Ahhhhhhh, refreshing," she joked as she unintentionally burped directly into Chrissy's face, causing them both to burst into laughter.

"Okay, now I gotta catch up with you," Chrissy said as she began to drink.

"Ohhhh snap, this is my song!" Chrissy squealed as she sang to Mary J. Blige's Not Gon' Cry and playfully made up her own lyrics.

"While all that time I was humping you. You was busy tryna hump my friend."
"I would stop messing with these other dudes if you told me to, now you're busy loving my friend."
She sang out as she swayed back and forth, snapping her fingers. Sheena got up, a little unsteady on her feet and a bit

tipsy, and joined in with her rendition.

"Well, I'm not gon' yell, I'm not gon' scream. I'm not gon' punch yo' face."

Sheena grabbed the hairbrush off her dresser and started singing into it like a microphone as she stared in the mirror. Chrissy walked over and joined in while finishing her drink. She took the hairbrush from Sheena's hand and sang louder.

"I was your girl and your chef on the daily, cooking every day of the week... cooking up those tasty pigs feet."

Sheena and Chrissy locked eyes and couldn't contain their giggling.

"I think I'm drunk already," Sheena said, laughing.

"That's the point, duh. It's time for another." Chrissy said as she returned to the nightstand to play bartender again.

"Here, bottoms up," she said, handing Sheena back her cup.

"Let's go, same time." Chrissy challenged.

"Okay, on three." Sheena agreed.
"One, two, three." Chrissy and Sheena chugged their drinks between giggles as some of Sheena's drink dribbled down her chin.
"Done!" Sheena yelled out as she held her empty cup under Chrissy's nose.

"See?"

"Of course you're done first. You're wearing half of it on your shirt." Chrissy laughed as she pointed to Sheena's shirt.

"Shut up! I won; you lost. Kiss my rass."

"What? Rass? Speak English." Chrissy joked.

"You know what I meant, girl. I'm tipsy." Sheena said as she stumbled to the bed.

"Let's page the boys and see what they're up to. Hand me the phone," Chrissy asked Sheena as she quickly punched numbers into the phone's keypad, hung up, and did it three more times.

Sheena got up from the bed, walked to the stereo, stopped Mary J. Blige's tape, and hit play on the second cassette holder.

"Awwww shit! Is this the SWV mixtape?" Chrissy asked while bopping her head to the beat before the phone rang.

"Got it," Chrissy said quickly before picking up the phone. "Hello? Nah, it's me, baby. Sheena's here, she's wasted. We're here drinking. Huh? Nah, tryna see what ya'll up to. Don't be like that. Cut it out. You know you miss me. You know you miss that thang I do that you love. Whatever!"

"Who's that? That must be Mal." Sheena said out loud.

"Stop being so scary, damn!" Chrissy said, annoyed.

"Tell Mal I said hi!" Sheena yelled.

Chrissy quickly threw an empty plastic cup in Sheena's direction, motioning for her to be quiet.

"Fine, heifer. I gotta go to the bathroom anyways. I'll give you and your little boyfriend privacy," she said as she got up and started making kissy faces and noises at Chrissy before walking out of the bedroom to go to the bathroom. When she returned, Chrissy was sitting on the bed reapplying her lip gloss.

"Girl, the room is spinning," Sheena said as she stumbled to the bed.

"I'm officially drunk."

"Sis, you're a lightweight." Chrissy teased as she got up.

"I gotta pee now," she said as she got up, tripped over her duffel bag, and fell on her hands and knees.
"Clearly, I ain't the only lightweight. But at least I stayed upright." Sheena mocked as they both laughed.

"Here, let me help you," she said as she helped pull Chrissy to her feet.

"Make sure your drunk ass pee in the toilet and not by the toilet."

"Keep it up. If you keep bothering me, I'll leave you a little Hershey surprise," Chrissy taunted as she walked out of the bedroom toward the bathroom.

The phone began to ring.

"Hello. Hey twinnnn!" Sheena sang out.

"What ya'll doing? Mannnn, Chrissy, and I are over here getting toasty. Yep. Didn't you just speak to her? Ha! Oh, my bad. I'm drunk as a skunk." Sheena laughed as Chrissy walked back into the room.

"Yeah, here she is. Here, it's your boyfriennnnnnd," Sheena goaded as she handed Chrissy the phone.

"Hey, sexy. Yeah, we wasted. Where ya'll at? Nah, we won't. I promise, we gonna save ya'll some. We got a whole bottle of Bacardi we ain't even touched yet, and didn't finish the bottle of gin. Aight, bet. We'll all party tomorrow. Don't worry about what I'm gonna wear, you like everything I wear anyways. You talking all this shit now, don't be acting all scary tomorrow either. Okay, bye." Chrissy returned the phone to the receiver.

"Girl, what you got to snack on?"
"Let me go check. I know we have chips," Sheena said as she walked to the kitchen and returned with a bag of Lay's

potato chips and Oreo cookies.

"Jackpot! Bring that bag over here."

Sheena crawled into her bed and sat beside Chrissy as they listened to music and ate chips.

"This is the life, girl. Would you really trade all this for the madness at my house?" Chrissy asked while stuffing her mouth full of chips.

"You bugging."

"Honestly, would you want to feel all alone even when your mother is in the next room and just ignores you because she blames you for her shitty existence?"

"HELL YEAH!" Chrissy shouted emphatically.

"If I was home, as soon as those crumb snatchers woulda heard the crumple of the chip bag opening they woulda ran over with their hands out crying for some. I wouldn't be able to listen to this tape over all the yelling and screaming. Do you think I get to chill out in my room, in my bed, alone? Hell no! Because I have nothing of my own. So yes, Sheena, I would rub the genie bottle, wiggle my nose, click my heels three times, and scream Beetlejuice in the mirror if that meant magically getting THIS life. Having all this, just for me? In a goddamn heartbeat."
"It's so crazy, right? Sheena asked, reflecting on the irony.

"What's crazy?"

"My Hell is your Heaven."

"And my living nightmare is your dream life." Chrissy added, "Yeah, girl, it's crazy."

"This reminds me of something Mama Mattie said to me." Sheena started by mimicking Mrs. Mattie's southern drawl.

"Sheena, baby. Comparison is the thief of joy. Don't steal your own happiness trying to secure something that's not for you. Trust me, just trust me."

"She's wrong; there's nothing wrong with going after what you want. How else are you going to get anything for yourself? See, like this." Chrissy said as she picked up the bottle of gin from the nightstand and held it up.

"I dealt with those kids all week, I deserve something for myself, and I wanted this. I saw it, so I took it, and I deserve it. I deserve to have some fun, right?"

"I mean, when you put it that way. I see where you're coming from. But, devil's advocate, you technically stole from somebody and, actually, not somebody, you stole from family."

"Stole?! How? I share everything I have, so if you say I stole, that means my family steals from me! My clothes, my time, my food, my life. Girl, it's not stealing, it's called quid pro quo."

Chrissy said sarcastically as she snapped her fingers in a circle.

Sheena chuckled.

"Girl, you can explain anything away, huh? You could sell water to a duck. Or, as Mama Mattie would say, that girl done perfected the fine art of persuasion, so keep your eyes open."

"Tell that old coot I also perfected my punani persuasion too," Chrissy said as she rolled her eyes.

"That old lady can't stand me. I know she can't." She whispered to herself.

"Anyways, speaking of punani, you give Keem some yet?"

"Whaaaat?" Sheena asked, dumbstruck.

"No! He's not my boyfriend. Just cause he says he loves me, I'm not about to just give him some. What made you ask that?"

"Girl, we've known him for how long, how many years? But hold on. He told you he loved you. When did this happen?" Chrissy asked, shocked.

"He gave me this," Sheena said as she got up and walked to her dresser. She opened the top drawer and pulled out a jewelry box and a greeting card.

"Wait! Hakeem bought you jewelry?" Chrissy asked as she flipped open the gift box lid and pulled out its contents.

"Why you not wearing it?" She asked, confused, as she held the thin gold rope chain with an initial pendant with the letter H dangling from the chain. She stood up and looked in the mirror, holding the chain up to her neck to model it in the mirror.

"So, why you not wearing it?"

"He hasn't asked me to be his girlfriend, so why would I wear his initials around my neck? If he doesn't want to claim me, there's no reason for me to walk around looking like I'm claimed, right?"

"Why didn't you tell me?" Chrissy asked as she put the gold chain back in the box.

"There was nothing to tell, I'm not wearing a man's chain if he's not my man."

"And he said he loved you? Girrrl, you didn't tell me that either."

"Chrissy, is there really anything to say if his words don't match his actions?"

"Oh, my God! You've been around Mrs. Mattie too much! I'm going to need you to step into 1997 right quick, leave that 1927 thinking to your ancestors." Chrissy joked as she opened the envelope, pulled the greeting card out, and read it aloud.

"Thinking of you. Sup She-She. I just wanted to let you know that I think you the bomb. You the smartest girl I know with the biggest heart. Everybody I know loves the hell outta ya. You all that and a bag of chips. My moms keeps telling me if I bring a girl home, it better be you or someone just like you. And, you know ma dukes don't like none of these chicks round here. I ain't gonna front, I love you She-She. So, wear this so these lames know to back off. Love your #1 dude, Keem."

Chrissy put the card back in the envelope.

"I can't believe you didn't tell me. So, everybody just loves you, huh?" Chrissy asked in a flippant tone.

"Girl, cut it out," Sheena said as she put the card and jewelry gift box back in her drawer.

"Like I said earlier, words don't match his actions. So, that will stay in the drawer until he comes correct. Enough of that. You are all up in my business. Have you given Mal some yet?"

"Stop playing, whatchu think?"

"I don't want to assume, so just tell me."

"Girl, I did, and he pumps like a rabbit! That's why I can't mess with these little boys like him." Chrissy said, rolling her eyes.

"Now, JB. He knows how to do it like I need it done."

"Wait! JB, your cousin's friend? Ain't he like twenty-three?" Sheena asked, surprised.

"He's twenty-five and can do the damn thang."

"Chrissy! He's too old, and I thought he had a girlfriend and a baby. Why is that dude messing with you?"

"They broke up a while ago. Besides, he got his own place, and you already know anything other than that house of insanity is better."

"What about Jamal? Did you tell him?"

"Girl, what about Mal? It's none of his business, I don't have to tell him nothing. I'm pretty sure he's doing his own thing with whoever he wants to. I don't need his permission."

"Ohhh, Chrissy! You're so foul. You better tell that boy you're seeing other people, just be honest. What's so hard about that?" Sheena asked, annoyed.

"We've been friends too long to be shady, come on!"

"See! This is why I didn't want to tell you. You over here judging me like Mad Mattie." Chrissy said, letting out a little snicker.

"I'm not judging you; being dishonest makes no sense. Especially with people we have been friends with for this long. First of all, who cares what you think he's doing? Just be honest about what you are doing. Second of all, I would never judge you, but I'm going to tell you if I think you're wrong. Lastly, I sure hope you never lie to me, cause there is no reason to ever keep something from me. You're my sister, no matter how you think I might feel about something, tell me. And I think you should tell Mal, what's the worst that could happen?"

"Listen, my grandma always says, better to ask for forgiveness than permission. I'mma do what I wanna do. Don't judge and don't snitch." Chrissy said while pointing her finger at Sheena.

"Promise?" She asked as she held out her pinky finger.

Sheena sighed.

"Fine. I still say you need to be honest. But it's not my story to tell, so I will keep my mouth shut. And I could never judge you." Sheena said as they interlocked their pinky fingers together. "I promise."

■

"So, Doc, I think I understood Chrissy a little better after that day. Although I didn't and still don't agree with how she handles some things, I think I understand.

"Sheena, tell me what you feel you have clarity on regarding Chrissy."

"I think she's been starving to feel special and feel like a priority. Even though she grew up in a house full of family, and I believe they all truly loved each other. I think she needed more attention, but there were so many kids and family members in that house, she just never got that one-on-one attention I feel she needed. Add on the fact that she never felt like she had anything to call her own, and felt like she was always responsible for her younger family members. I think Chrissy was always looking for something and someone to make her feel special and take her away from what she felt was chaos. Even if it meant dealing with a guy she shouldn't have been dealing with, if it meant it could get her out of the house for a few hours, days, weeks, or months, she was fine with that. That meant she was getting the attention from whomever and getting away from home, no matter how temporary it was."

Sheena let out a slight chuckle.

"Ya know, if she were sitting right here, she'd say, 'girl, stop tripping. You know my weakness is guys and gifts. Doc, she's a mess, but she's my mess. I wouldn't change our friendship for anything. We've been friends for so long, I couldn't imagine not having her around."

"It's clear that she is a very significant person in your life, and you adore and accept her for who she is, and vice versa. That's lovely, deary." Dr. Angel said as she watched Sheena readjust herself in the chair, looking uncomfortable.

"Are you okay? Do you need a break?"

"Whew! I'm fine, this little girl is doing somersaults. I think I need a bathroom break." Sheena said as she held her lower back, stood up, and waddled to the bathroom.

"Take your time, dear. Would you like a cup of warm tea? That might settle the baby down a bit." She shouted as Sheena walked into the bathroom.

"Yes, please."

Dr. Angel walked to the kitchen, poured two cups of hot water from the electric tea kettle on the counter, unwrapped two teabags, dropped them in each mug, and squeezed a dollop of honey into each mug before returning to the room.

"Thanks, Doc," Sheena said as she reached for the cup of tea.

"It smells good."

She held the cup under her nose and smelled the warm tea and honey.

"Oh my!" Dr. Angel said in shock. "Look at that! I see the baby moving through your shirt, deary. Is that a footprint? Oh my!" She chuckled. "Oh my, look at that, I see a hand!" Dr. Angel gasped as she covered her mouth and chortled. "You most certainly have a lively baby girl, deary. How precious."

FOR THE LOVE OF YOU

"Doc, it's so uncomfortable," she said as she gently rubbed her stomach.

"You're almost there, almost. Well, speaking of this active little baby's upcoming arrival. Can you tell me a little more about the baby's dad? Hakeem, is it?"

Sheena settled back in her chaise chair, rubbing her belly with her left hand and sipping her warm tea with the other before resting the mug on top of her protruding belly.

"Hakeem," she said with a smile.

"Where do I start? I had the biggest crush on him since the 8th grade. But I was always quiet and a little shy, so I never even thought he noticed me. I figured Chrissy was more his speed. It wasn't until high school, around 10th grade, that he started to pay attention to me. But I didn't really take him seriously because he was definitely a little player. But, you know, Neil was so overprotective, he definitely wouldn't let Keem play with my feelings."

Sheena smiled while recalling O'Neil's overprotective and chivalrous nature.

"He didn't play about me at all. So, Keem knew that if he was going to try to be with me and Neil knew about it, he would have to come correct. And if not, Neil was going to blow his whole spot up and snitch," she said through laughter.

5

FEAR NOT

"Girl, why you ain't tryna wear my chain?" Hakeem asked as he sat down next to Sheena on the picnic bench at Franklin Park.

"You foul girl."

Hakeem clutched his heart before finishing. "You're breaking my heart, girl."

Sheena rolled her eyes.

"Cut it out, Keem."

"Why? I gave that chain to you over a year ago. What's up?"

Sheena blushed.

"So let me get this straight. You want me to wear your chain so people think I'm your girl while you do what you want with who you want? Ain't happening, sorry. I'm sure you have someone else you can convince, but it ain't me, buddy," she said confidently.

"You're so mean! You know I love you, She-She. Stop fighting it," he said as he tried to hug Sheena.

"Whatever, Keem. You were just with Latoya last week and Keisha a few weeks before that. Cut the shit."

"But I don't want them! You the only girl I want."

"Ahhhhhh, come on, bro!" O'Neil scolded as he walked over to where Sheena and Hakeem were sitting.

"I can hear your B.S. all the way over there. So, did you hit? If you're gonna tell Sheena a story, tell her the whole story."

"Mannnnn, this dude!" Hakeem scoffed.

"Here come Spike Lee with 'Do The Right Thing,' get outta here. This between me and Sheena." Hakeem said irritated.

"I wanna hear this too, so did you?" Chrisssy asked as she walked towards Sheena, Hakeem, and O'Neil, with Jamal following her.

"We're waiting! Answer the question, Hakeem!" Chrissy demanded.

"Yooo, wassup wit ya girl?" Hakeem whispered to Sheena before yelling, "Yo, Chris, mind ya business. Damn!"

"Bro, you smash or not?" O'Neil asked again.

"You gonna keep it real or not? Cause, if you don't, you know I will."

"Damn, why all ya'll in my business?" Hakeem asked as he stood up from the picnic table, throwing his hands up.

"Cause we family and we don't fuck each other over by lying, that's why," O'Neil said before taking his seat on the picnic table's bench across from Sheena.

"Okay, but I didn't smash Keisha, she just gave me head, and technically I didn't do it with Latoya either. I stuck it in twice before her little brother started banging on the door, so I bounced. On dawgs!" Hakeem swore as he took his right hand and motioned a crossing of the heart hand gesture.

"Swear to God."

"Ewwwww, Keisha used to come to school smelling like piss and fish and Latoya reads at a 3rd grade level. You whack for that." Chrissy said, annoyed as she rolled her eyes and crossed her arms over her chest.

"Yo, Mal, get your girl. Why are you so worried about me? Sheena doesn't have a problem with it. Why are you in my business? Damn!"

"Shut up! Talk to the hand." Chrissy said as she shoved the right palm of her open hand in front of Hakeem's face.

"You see this?" She asked as she pointed to the silver charm on her bracelet that was in the shape of a half heart.

"What does it say?" Chrissy asked, not waiting for an answer.

"Best! Cause we're best friends and I'm looking out for my bestie. So, it is my business."

"Chrissy, you wildin'. You wild. Aight Chrissy. Yeah, okay. Whatever you say." Hakeem responded dismissively.

"Fucking psycho," he mumbled under his breath.

"I heard that," Sheena said as she looked in Hakeem's direction.

"Okay, ya'll chill out. It's not even that serious. Hakeem can do whatever he wants; he's not my man and has never been. What he does is not my business. So why are you two even going at it?" Sheena asked, confused.

"If Keem wants his girl to smell like a downtown back alley or needs Hooked on Phonics, that's not my business," Sheena said as she held her hands up in defeat.

"Ohhhhh snap! She gotchu' bro!" O'Neil and Jamal teased as they pointed at Hakeem and laughed.

"And clearly, you're a little desperate if you let snaggle-tooth Keisha put it in her mouth. Everybody literally calls her Count Von Count from Sesame Street." Sheena said as she rolled her eyes.

"Ugh, do better!"

"Oh Shit! Not the Count. Not Count Von Count!?" O'Neil asked while laughing uncontrollably as Jamal and Chrissy joined in the bantering.

"Aight, chill. Leave my boy alone! Maybe he like a lil' sexy saber-toothed tiger. Let him live." Jamal joked.

"Awwww, come on Keem, don't be like that," Sheena said sweetly as she touched his arm and gently rubbed it reassuringly.

"Keem, just tell the tooth, that's your girl? Come on, the tooth shall set you free!" Sheena said, barely maintaining her composure before cackling.

Hakeem couldn't even muster any semblance of annoyance any longer as he watched Sheena playfully laugh, which made him chuckle along with everyone else.
"So you're turning on me, too? You're cold, She-She. Cold as ice. But I still love you," he said as he winked at Sheena,

leaned over, and kissed her forehead.

"I mean it."

Sheena's face turned warm as she blushed.

"Whatever, Keem," she said as she smiled sheepishly.

"Yoooooooooo, misfits! Look what I got!" Jason yelled as he walked towards them, holding two brown paper bags.

"Finally. What took you so long?" Chrissy asked as she held her hand out, waiting for Jason.

"Chill out. I had to wait for Big Red to do the L.Q. run for me. Don't question me, woman." Jason said playfully as he walked over to the picnic bench after handing Chrissy one of the paper bags.

Jason pulled out a bottle of Seagram's Gin, Sunny Delight, and five plastic cups while Chrissy pulled out a bottle of Blue Raspberry MD 20/20 and a liter of Sprite.

"Jason, I knew I should have gone with you. What the hell is this crap?" Chrissy asked, pointing to the bottle of Sunny D.

"I said orange juice. Does that look like orange juice, dumbass! Don't nobody drink that fake ass O.J."

"You got one more time to talk to me like I'mma simp before I hem you up. Now make the drinks and put a muzzle on while you're doing it." Jason joked as he sat down and lined up the plastic solo cups for Chrissy.

"Aargh! You're so aggy." Chrissy complained as she stomped over to the picnic table, where Jason was starting to set up.

"Listen, this is how this is gonna go. I make the drinks and don't want to hear nobody complaining or telling me how to make them, capeesh? You get what you get. Don't start none, won't be none." Chrissy demanded as she began to untwist the caps on the MD 20/20, Sprite, and bottle of gin. She then picked up the bottle of Sunny D and walked it over to the empty picnic table next to them.

"Don't nobody drink that mess." Chrissy chided as she sucked her teeth and went back to playing mixologist as she went down the row of solo cups, first pouring equal amounts of Blue Raspberry MD 20/20 in each cup followed by Sprite and finished off with a splash of gin.

"Viola! Go ahead and try that and tell me what you think." Chrissy beamed with excitement.

"Hold on now, wait a damn minute. How you gonna treat Sunny D like that?" Jason asked as he walked over to the other picnic table.

He picked up the bottle of Sunny D and cradled it in his arms like a newborn baby.
"It's okay, Sunny boy, she's a mean ole lady, huh?"

He jokingly rocked the bottle in his arms.

"Shhhhh, Sunny boy, I love you. Remember that time I poured you in the glass with some ice cubes and we watched The New Batman Adventures together? I know, she's disrespectful, huh?"

He kissed the bottle of Sunny D.

"It's okay, I won't abandon you," he said as he put the bottle back on the table.

"Are you done, jackass?" Chrissy yelled as she started to hand everyone their drinks.

"Didn't I tell you to watch ya mouth?"

"Screw you!"

"What I tell you?" Jason questioned as he walked towards Chrissy.

"Didn't I say I would hem your disrespectful ass up?"

"Boy, ain't nobody scared of you." She said as she handed Jamal his drink.

"Oh yeah, how about now?" Jason asked, playfully putting Chrissy in a headlock and shaking his hand back and forth to mess with her hair.

Her perfectly coiffed mane looked like she had just walked through a wind tunnel.

"Alright! Alright, come on!" Chrissy pleaded.

"Oh, now you want to act right? You were talking all that trash. Say sorry, Jason."

"Get off me!"

"What I say? Say Sorry, Jason."

"Alright! Sorry Jason. Quit it!"

"And you better not talk trash once I let you go."

"I won't. Let me go! I said sorry, damn!" Chrissy pleaded.

"Is that attitude I detect? I think you need more time to settle down." Jamal teased as he tussled her hair some more.

Alright! Alright! I'm sorry. I was talking shit, I'm sorry. I won't do it again." Chrissy said, exasperated.

"Let me go, please?"

"Don't let it happen again," Jason warned as he turned her loose.

"Yo, I ain't even gonna lie, this drink is bomb," Jamal said as he downed the last of his drink while Chrissy tried to fix her hair as everyone sipped on their drinks and chuckled at her and Jason.

"See, told ya'll to trust me. I know how to make a drink."

"Sis, I ain't gonna front, this is bomb.com." Jason cosigned as he gulped down his entire drink before high-fiving Chrissy.

"You did your thing."

"Dang, all ya'll finished already?" Chrissy asked as she started to sip her drink and tried to fix her hair with her hands.

"Gimme your cups. I'll make us more," she said as she started to line the cups up again and refill them with the same order of drink ingredients.

Jason pointed to the unopened Sunny D bottle. "Did you forget something?"

"Did you like your drink?" Chrissy asked sarcastically while rolling her neck and eyes.

"So no, I didn't forget anything."

"See, Sunny, she's still trying to play you out," Jason said, clutching the bottle in jest.

"I know what her problem is."
"She needs the big D!" The Twins exclaimed in unison as they snickered and dapped each other up.

"As if!" She said as she rolled her eyes and handed Jason and Jamal their second drink.

"Don't start that twin shit," Chrissy warned.

The Twins laughed.

"Aight, sis. I come in peace." Jason said as he placed his right hand on his heart.

"Promise. We good?" He asked as he took his drink and sat on the picnic bench with Sheena, Hakeem, and O'Neil.

"Finally. Leave Chrissy alone. Jesus Christ." Sheena said as she finished her drink.

"Come on, sit down, Chris," Sheena instructed as Chrissy finished making everyone's second drink.

"Why do we even hang out with these mongrels?" Chrissy asked as she sipped from her cup.

"You know they love you," Sheena responded as she started to feel the warm tingling sensation approaching from her second drink.

"You hear back from any of your schools yet?" O'Neil asked Sheena as everyone settled into their seats around the picnic table.

"Some. So far, UMASS-Boston, Dartmouth, and Simmons. I'm still waiting on B.C."

"Boston College, is that still your number one choice for that nursing program?"

"Yep. But I still have those other three to pick from if I don't get in." Sheena said as she shrugged her shoulders.

"What about you? You hear back from the one and only school in Massachusetts you applied to? I still can't believe you didn't even attempt to pick a backup school here!" Sheena said, dismayed.

"You better get in because if you go out of state, I'm going to kill you. For real!" She said with a twinge of fear at the thought of O'Neil leaving for college out of state.

O'Neil smiled, "Oh, so you're a tough guy now? You tough and threatening my life? Sounds like I should leave the state in fear for my life."

"Cut it out! Did you get in or in? I mean, not in?" Sheena asked, slurring her words.

"Just call me mister M...I...T, bay-bee!" O'Neil yelled.

He stood up on the bench, chanting while pounding on his chest.
"M...I...T, bay-bee!"

"Wait, what? You got in? Stop playing. You did?" Sheena asked, shocked and ecstatic at the same time.

She stood up and wrapped her arms around O'Neil's neck. "Congratulations, that's so dope. I love you."

"Thanks, She-She. Wherever you end up going I know for a fact you're gonna crush it and be a dope ass nurse. I love you, too," O'Neil whispered in her ear as he wrapped his arms around her waist and returned the hug.

"That's what I'm talking about, that's my dawg!" The Twins celebrated in unison as they ran towards O'Neil and gave him dap and a hug.

"That's what I'm talking about. We're on our way!" Jamal said as he hugged O'Neil tightly.

"Twins, ya'll still going to Florida to work with your grandfather and get your contractor license?" Chrissy asked as she started to make more drinks.

"Yup! You know we got a plan to take over Boston," Jason said excitedly.

"We building Boston!" The Twins and O'Neil yelled out simultaneously.

Sheena beamed with pride as she felt the effects of her drink make her feel more relaxed and giddy.

"Go ahead, tell us the plan, and act like we haven't heard it before," she instructed.

"Aight! Boom, check it." Jamal started.

"My cuz, the brainiac of the group, is about to bust it down at M...I...T bay-bee and get that electrical engineering degree."

"And, me and Mal," Jason interjected.

"After graduation, we're about to go work for my grandfather's construction company in Florida and snatch the remaining year and a half of hours in building construction and learn all the business stuff, like the G's we are."

"Then, they come back to Boston and apply for their contractor license." O'Neil chimed in, "And our grandfather agreed to come help us start our own business. Once we have that business acumen, we're gonna be unstoppable. And, we're going to call our business, what?" O'Neil asked playfully.

"Harris and Harris Construction. And our motto is what? Building Boston!" The Twins sang out together.

"Let me run that back for the slow people in the back. Harris and Harris Construction. Building Boston!" Jamal reiterated with excitement.

"Oh, hold up! Let's not forget our boy. Keem will be the computer guy. We all know he's the techie."

"Yes, sir. I'll be in Rhode Island at Johnson and Wales. Ya'll not leaving me behind," Hakeem said while winking at Sheena as she blushed and slightly swayed as her drink began to take over.

"Chris, have you decided yet?" Jamal asked, as everyone looked in her direction, waiting for her response.

"You know that girl can't make her mind up for nothing," Hakeem yelled over his shoulder towards Chrissy.

"She don't know if she wanna be a friend or foe, good girl or hoe."

Hakeem continued with his impromptu rap as he started pounding on the picnic table, making a beat, as The Twins started beat boxing to Hakeem's rhythm, as he continued.

"Her confusion's not an illusion; the girl lost."
"Always seeking and taking, and faking, no matter the cost."
"Boston's very own Lolita, seductive temptress wit' the bubblegum lip gloss!"

"Wack! You suck!" Chrissy yelled with half a smile as she pulled out her lip gloss and reapplied it to her lips.

"At least you got one thing right about me. My lip gloss do be popping." She said sarcastically as she seductively licked her shiny lips while staring directly at Hakeem.

She walked over to Jamal, stuck her tongue in his mouth, and kissed him performatively.

"Awww, come on, get a room."

"Knock it off!"

They all yelled at Chrissy and Jamal as Jason stepped in between and separated them.

"Don't nobody want to watch this nastiness," Jason teased.

"Aye yo. Yo, yo, yo. Who's that?" Hakeem asked while pointing to a group of about seven dudes dressed in all black walking towards the park area where they were sitting.

They all tried squinting their eyes and holding their hands over their brows to block the sun so they could get a better look.

"I can't tell who that is, but it looks like something is about to pop off," O'Neil said as he stood up and tried to get a better look.

"I know that walk, that's Shizz and them," he said as he sat back down.

"Looks like something happened, though; they dressed for war."

"Yeah, they look like they're about to light something up." Hakeem agreed as they all watched the group of guys dressed in all black get a little closer. They could hear the commotion and emotion—it was palpable.

"Nah man, not my brother! Not my fucking brother, bro! They got my fucking brother, man!"

They could hear one of the men screaming through tears.

"Why, man, why? Why my fucking brother?" The unidentified male wailed.

"Ohhh shit! That is Shizz and them." Jason agreed as he started to walk towards the group dressed in all black, as Jamal, Hakeem, and O'Neil began to follow.

"Ya'll stay here," O'Neil instructed Sheena and Chrissy.

"Let us go see what's up first," he said, following Jason's lead.

"I hope everything is okay, that doesn't look too good over there," Sheena said woefully.

"Sure nuff' don't," Chrissy agreed as she moved closer to Sheena.

They both stared at The Twins, Hakeem and O'Neil, who approached the group, trying to determine what was happening.

"They all got hoodies on; I can't tell who's who over there," Chrissy added.

"Looks like they're all walking back over here now."

Sheena noticed O'Neil with both hands on his head in disbelief while Hakeem and The Twins walked with their heads down with the group of seven males all dressed in black following behind them. As they approached, Sheena and Chrissy could smell the strong odor of marijuana before the group even got to the section of the park where they were sitting. Once they got to where Sheena and Chrissy were seated, they could see their faces; some were wet with tears, some enraged, and others lacking emotion.

"Gizmo's dead." O'Neil declared sullenly before leaning his head back to keep the tears from falling down his face.

"Fuuuuuck! This can't be life right now. I can't lose my brother, man. I can't!" Shizz cried out as he collapsed onto the bench, sobbing uncontrollably.

Sheena instinctively wanted to console him and immediately rushed to his side and wrapped her arms around him as his body trembled and heaved with profound grief.

Sheena hugged him tighter and whispered, "It's okay. Let it out. We got you. We got you."

She rocked him back and forth, trying to soothe his broken spirit.
His screams got louder, and Sheena held him tighter as his voice became increasingly hoarse with each blood-curdling

cry for his beloved brother.

"I can't, I can't sit here and watch this, I can't watch my little cuz hurt like this. Yo! Boogs, we're riding. We're riding tonight. On dawgs, we airing that bitch out tonight! I can't take this shit! I can't take this shit!" The cousin shrieked as he started punching the air in anger while pacing back and forth screaming and declaring vengeance as he grew increasingly agitated to the point he began to pull at his hoodie and stripped his clothes off from the waist up revealing a 9mm Glock in his front waistband and a Colt 45 in the back.

"Fuck everybody, I'm pushing caps back for real! My cuz? My cuz? They murdered my fucking cuz, over a bitch? A fucking bitch? That muthfucka a dead man walking. Sniper, let's go," he demanded.

"Yo, cuz I love you, but I can't sit here and let my family hurt like this and do nothing while this mother fucker out here still walking. I got you, cuz," he said as he leaned down and hugged Shizz and Sheena.

Before Sniper walked away with the cousin, he spoke to Shizz.

"They call me Sniper because I don't miss. You want him gone?" He asked Shizz with a deadpan disposition.

Shizz pulled himself together, stood up, looked Sniper in his eyes and without hesitation said, "May he rest in piss. Whatever you do, don't get caught." Shizz instructed as he gave Sniper dap and a half hug.

"Have I ever?" Sniper asked as he pulled the strings on his hoodie to tighten the hood around his face and ran to meet the cousin, who was walking towards the parked car.

Chrissy handed Shizz her drink while his other friends started drinking what was left straight from the bottles and whatever they had brought with them. Shizz lit another blunt, inhaled deeply, and exhaled long and slow before talking.

"This feels like a damn dream. This can't be real."

"This shit is unbelievable," The Twins said while both shaking their heads in disbelief.

"I know you're hurting, Shizz. But I want to take the time right now to celebrate Gizmo's life. That man spoke so much life and positivity into us, I wanna take the time to respect and honor his existence." O'Neil said with respect.

"Absolutely, bro," Shizz consented as he dapped up O'Neil and hugged him.

"Mannnnnn, Gizmo would always stop by when my Pop's would be outside doing something. Washing the car, cutting the grass or just chilling on the porch shooting the shit," O'Neil said before pausing and smiling.

"Yoooo, I'd listen to my Pop's and Gizmo go round for round talking about the Nation of Islam, the Qur'an, and what we needed to do as people of color to keep gentrification from erasing us out of our own communities. I mean, Gizmo had so much knowledge and insight that my Pops would sometimes call my Grandad and put him on speaker so they could all debate social issues together. Gizmo showed everybody respect. I never once heard him say anything bad about anybody. His life, his actions, his respect, his love of life, all of this made Gizmo the epitome of righteousness. Raise your cup or bottle. As Salaam Alaikum, Gizzy! Rest easy, bro. We all love you." O'Neil said as he choked up and wiped away his tears.

"Long live Gizmo!" Jamal said as he raised his cup.

"Man, Gizmo was the homie, for sure! Shit, all this talk about the community and how all these developers and cocksuckers that never stepped foot in our hood to actually live but, buying up all the real estate and pushing us out, man that got us all thinking."

"Sure did!" Jason interjected.

"That's how we came up with Harris and Harris Construction. Man, Gizmo told us our people need to build Boston, don't let those colonizers come in and take it from us and push us out."

"Don't worry, Gizz, we're gonna make you proud!" The Twins declared.

Again, O'Neil spoke, "The jewels Gizz gave us won't be wasted."
"That's what I'm talking about," Shizz said as he walked up to everyone and hugged them.

"I'm about to go home and check on the family," he said as he turned to leave. His remaining crew, dressed in all black, mournfully followed.

Once they were alone again, Sheena, Chrissy, O'Neil, Hakeem, and The Twins gathered again at the picnic table, sitting a little closer together as the somber mood continued.

"I can't believe he's gone," Sheena said, shaking her head.

"You said it perfectly, Neil. He was such a genuinely good person, all the time, and to everybody. I can't believe someone would even think to hurt him," she said as tears began to well up in her eyes.

"I can't even think about this anymore, it's so scary. Who wants to die? I just can't." Sheena said as she shook her head no, as if she could stop herself from processing the tragedy.

"I couldn't imagine losing anyone at this table. I couldn't handle it. What would I even do?" Sheena asked as she got weepy again.

"Aww, come on, bestie. None of us is going anywhere anytime soon. Cheer up," Chrissy tried to reassure her.

"I mean, let's be real. Life is unpredictable, but one thing is certain. Whatever lives will die. That's why you make the best of the one life here on earth you are given. Be good to yourself and be good to others because, in the end, we don't know when our time here is up." O'Neil said.

"Yeah, but what is death? Are you just stuck in darkness, forever? Is there really a Heaven and Hell? It's scary if you don't know what's on the other side of life," Chrissy argued.

"I feel you on that," Hakeem agreed.

"I think everyone needs to think about the impact they leave on this world. I believe that being a good person, your soul will never die. I think it's Proverbs that says good people will be remembered as a blessing, but evil people will soon be forgotten. If I'm remembered with love, how can I truly die?" O'Neil asked rhetorically.

"I believe in life and if I believe in life and living and, I accept life. Well, I also must accept death. I can't accept one without accepting the other. So nah, I'm not afraid to die. I'm not ready to die, but I'm not afraid. As they say, the only thing we have to fear is fear itself."

Sheena looked at O'Neil and smiled. She thought to herself that he could always make her feel like everything would be okay.

■

"Doc, that was always Neil. He seemed so mature and introspective even when we were kids. As Mrs. Mattie would say, he was like an old soul who had been here before. He would always bring a calming energy and make you feel like everything would be okay. Even if we were sitting around mourning Gizmo, he found a way to be strong."

"Sheena, from all that you have shared, O'Neil sounds quite remarkable and impressive. Based on the memories you recalled in our sessions, he was most certainly inspiring. I can certainly understand how he became such an integral part of your life, deary." Doctor Angel said warmly.

Sheena sighed heavily, "Sorry, Doc, I feel like I went off on a tangent. I know you asked about Hakeem."

"Oh no, deary, that's quite alright. I want you to take me on this journey. If answering one question leads you to another topic, so be it. Just take your time. You've done all the hard work and made huge progress over the past few years. You're in control of this, don't forget that, dear."

"I know, Doc, when I wake up every morning, that's what I tell myself. I am in control, this life is mine, I am in control," Sheena said with more conviction.

"Alright, so back to Hakeem. Ummmm, it wasn't until the summer of '98 that we all graduated high school, and Keem was going to Johnson and Wales in Rhode Island," Sheena said as she sipped the last of her tea and began to get comfortable. The baby started settling down with all the strong kicks to her insides.

"It wasn't until we finished high school that I started to take him seriously," Sheena said as she remembered the conversation with Hakeem that made her fall in love with him.

"We were all hanging out at Franklin Field at our little hangout spot, celebrating finally finishing school. The Twins were getting ready to go to Florida, Keem was leaving for Rhode Island, I was going to B.C., Neil was going to M.I.T., and Chrissy decided to go to cosmetology school. One of her cousins had opened a hair salon near Dudley station and convinced her to tap into her talents. Hair and beauty were always her thing," Sheena chuckled as she reminisced.

6

I WANT YOU

"She-She, graduation night, you were wasted, do you even remember that night?" Hakeem asked.

"My girl was the life of the party that night." Chrissy laughed as she recalled that day.

"If she told us she loved us one more time, I was about to tape her mouth shut!"

"She's wholesome as fuck," Jamal added.

"I love you guys; I'm going to miss you when you leave. Thank you for being my chosen family," he continued to mock as everyone joined in laughter.

"I hate all of you!" Sheena blurted out in embarrassment.

"Was I that bad?" she asked, covering her face self-consciously.

"Why ya'll fools let me drink so much?"

"My bad, bestie, I did make those drinks stronger than an extra-strength Excedrin because..." Chrissy said as she began to twirl around in circles.

"It was a celebration!" She yelled before stopping and giving a dramatic curtsy.

"Thank you, thank you. I know, I know; my bartending skills are impeccable," she joked.

"Yup, you had us all fucked up, boo. Bring that sexy butt over here," Jamal gushed as he wrapped his arms around Chrissy's neck and kissed her.

"You gonna miss me?"

"I wouldn't have to miss you if you'd just bring me with you, would I?" Chrissy asked seductively as she applied lip gloss on her lips and purposely ran her fingertips over the front zipper of Jamal's Levi jeans.

"You know I would bring you if I could."
"Awwww nahhhh, come on now. Here goes the temptress. Don't fall for that shit, bro." Hakeem laughed while shaking his

head.

"Mind your business, damn! Stop worrying about what I got going on. You're supposed to be focused on my bestie, right?" Chrissy asked, rolling her eyes.

"You so aggy."

"Leave my bro alone! And he's right, cut that shit out. I see you over there tryna' offer some tail for a trip to Florida. Not on my watch!" Jason asserted.

"Matter of fact, break this shit up. Get away from his no-no parts," he quipped as he stood between Jamal and Chrissy.

"No girls allowed; Florida is for business. Ya heard?" Jason taunted Chrissy while getting so close to her face that they were touching nose to nose.

"No means no, Chrissy."

"Shut up! And get out of my face. Your breath stinks," she said as she slapped Jason on the side of his head.

"Ouch! You so violent," he yelled while rubbing the side of his head, then sticking his tongue out in Chrissy's direction.

"You all are always going at it. Can ya'll get along, we're about to go our separate ways for a few years. Chill out." O'Neil suggested, like a father bartering with his teenage children.

"I'm always chill, it's these dumb dicks! They like annoying me, for no reason," Chrissy said as she pointed to Jason and Hakeem.

"Always got some slick shit to say."

Hakeem waved Chrissy off. "Girl, ain't nobody worried about you. She-She, let's take a walk," he said as he led Sheena away from the group by her hand.

"What's up, girl?"

"Nothing much, same old same old. Working and getting ready for school."

"You decide if you're gonna live on campus or not?"

"I'm gonna commute. I'll save money by being a commuter. I got a decent amount of scholarships and grants, plus my financial aid package. I'd rather not run a bill up by living on campus," she said as they walked towards the empty park.

"Want to go on the swing?" Hakeem asked as he led Sheena towards the swings.

"Depends, are you going to push me?" She asked sweetly as she batted her eyes.

"Don't look at me like that. You know you give me butterflies," he said, looking down at the ground.

"Boy, stop," she said playfully, tapping him on his arm.

"Aight, come on and sit your pretty self down," he said as he held the swing steady for Sheena to sit.

"Hold on, you ready?"

"Not too high, I'm not trying to fly with the birds today," she joked.

"Relax, girl, I got you," he said as he gently pushed the swing while Sheena slowly kicked her legs in and out.

"So, do you remember anything from graduation night? Tell me what you remember," he nudged as he slowly pushed the swing.

Sheena chuckled then sighed before speaking.

"That damn Chrissy made some bomb drinks that were strong as hell!"

"Strong like Hercules," Hakeem agreed.

"We hung out for a while, just drinking and talking trash like always. Once it got late, everyone started to head home. You and Jamal walked Chrissy and me back to my house. Did Jamal put a movie on? I think we were watching Players Club or something," Sheena said with uncertainty.
"Yep, so far so good. Maybe you weren't that drunk. Keep

going."

"Well, I tapped out first. I started to fall asleep. But I remember Jamal said his cousin was coming to pick him up. I remember he left first; I think you woke me up and told me to get into bed. And I told you to get in with me."

Hakeem stopped the swing and asked for clarification.

"And what did you mean by that?"

"You know what I meant," Sheena said, almost whispering.

Hakeem walked from behind and stood in front of her, holding the swing steady.

"Look at me. What did you mean by that?" He asked sternly.

Sheena looked up and into Hakeem's eyes. She could feel her face growing hot and feeling slightly nervous before answering.

"I.. I wanted you," she stammered. "I wanted you to be my first. I wanted to be with you. I wanted to have sex," Sheena said with more certitude.

"But you clearly didn't feel the same way. And I'm okay with that," she said as she looked down at the ground.

"Nah, don't do that. Look at me," Hakeem said as he took his hand and lifted her chin up to look at him in his eyes again.

"You want to know why I didn't take it there with you that night? You were drunk, and I never want you to feel like I took advantage. You were in no condition to make a decision like that. When I make love to you, I want you to be completely sober. I need you to tell me you want me and mean it; I don't want the alcohol to talk to me. I'd never take advantage of you or hurt you like that. If it's meant to be, it will be, and it will be done the right way. You're a princess, and I want you to be my princess, and I'll wait for you if I have to," he said as he walked behind Sheena and slowly pushed the swing again.

Sheena smiled as she relished in the familiar warm feeling before identifying her feelings. It was that familiar feeling of protection and care that O'Neil had shown her over the years. Sheena's eyes dampened as she placed her hand on Hakeem's left hand, holding the metal chain of the swing. Then, she guided his hand towards her lips and kissed the back of his hand.

"Thank you, Keem."

"Anything for you, princess. You ready to get out of here?"

∎

"Thanks for walking me home," Sheena said as she unlocked the lobby door to her apartment building.

"Do you want to come up?"

"Yeah, I'll come hang out. What you got to eat? I'm starving."

"I can make dinner," she said with a smile as they walked up the stairs to her second-floor apartment.

"Awww shit! She-She about to throw down in the kitchen? Oooooo weeee!" Hakeem sang out as he clapped and rubbed his hands together in anticipation.

"Whatchu' plan on chef-ing up, boo?"

"Something quick," she responded as she turned the key to open the apartment door.

"Fried chicken, yellow rice, and green beans?"

"Yooooo! That's what I'm talking about." Hakeem said as he slapped Sheena's butt as they both stood by the doorway and took off their shoes.

"Ouch! Quit it. Want to watch a movie?"

"Why not? What you got?"

"Did you see How Stella Got Her Groove Back, yet?"

"That chick flick? Nah, but you can put it on."

"You want to watch in the living room or my room?"
"I don't need your moms showing up and rushing me out. I'll stay in the living room."

"Oh, please. Go to my room. You know Evelyn works nights, and she could care less. The only thing she's concerned about is this house being cleaned when she gets here, and the food not being burned," she said as she rolled her eyes.

 "Go!" She said as she pushed Hakeem into her bedroom.

"Ohhh, I like it when you get rough. Go ahead, put the chick flick on," he said as he plopped down on Sheena's meticulously made bed.

She turned on the television, inserted the VHS tape into the VCR, and pressed play.

"Hurry up so we can watch it together."

"I'll be back. Let me get this food together," she said as she rushed out of her bedroom and into the kitchen.

As Hakeem watched the movie, he could hear the pots and pans clinking and the rustling of wrappers and water running. Sheena was in the kitchen preparing her food just as Mrs. Mattie had taught her. Once the chicken was cleaned, Sheena put the boneless chicken breasts in a large mixing bowl and got another large bowl to mix the ingredients of garlic powder, onion powder, paprika, pepper, Sazon, Old Bay seasoning, and seasoned salt, then mixed in the flour. She whisked two eggs and buttermilk in another bowl while heating oil in a cast-iron frying pan.

Sheena checked the boiling pot of water, then dumped a

cup of rice, adding Sazon seasoning and chives before putting the lid on and turning the heat down to low. Pressed for time, Sheena heated frozen green beans instead of using Mrs. Mattie's recipe. Sheena then put the chicken in the frying pan, and once all the food was actively cooking, she grabbed two glasses out of the cabinet, opened the freezer, pulled out the ice tray, and put three ice cubes in each cup. She opened the refrigerator, pulled out a liter of Coca-Cola, and poured two drinks before walking them into her bedroom.

"Here."

She handed Hakeem a glass of soda.

"She-She, that food smells bomb. I'm starving like Marvin," he said as he rubbed his stomach.

"I'm almost done," she said, returning to the kitchen to flip the chicken and stir the rice.

"Perfect," she mumbled to herself as she put two plates on the kitchen table as she turned the knobs off on the stove for the burners that the green beans and rice were on. Sheena rechecked the chicken by flipping it for the third time before turning off the burner and using tongs to take it from the cast iron pan and place it onto a cookie sheet pan lined with paper towels to soak up the extra oil.
Sheena began to clean up the countertops with Pine-Sol, poured the used oil from the pan into a mason jar, and ran the cast iron skillet under cold water in the kitchen sink as she

watched the beads of water hit, jump, and sizzle as the skillet began to cool down. Sheena scrubbed the skillet with dish soap and a Brillo pad until it was clean and then wiped down the stove before making both plates. She ensured Hakeem's plate was made with a generous amount of food before placing the leftover food in Tupperware and placing it in the refrigerator. Once satisfied with the kitchen clean-up, she took both plates into her bedroom.

"Here you go." She handed Hakeem the bigger plate of food.

"Damn girl, who you think you're feeding, Fat Albert?" He asked teasingly as he took the plate.

"This looks good, girl. Gimme a kiss. Thank you, baby," he said appreciatively as he kissed Sheena on the lips.

"You're welcome. Hold this," she said as she handed him her plate.

She then pulled two bed trays from underneath her bed and set one over Hakeem's thighs. He placed both plates down, and Sheena set her bed tray over her thigh before retrieving her plate.

She watched Hakeem put a portion of each food group onto his fork before putting it in his mouth. Hakeem immediately started pointing to the food on his plate.

"This is bomb, the bomb diggity!" He said with a mouthful of food.

"My baby can cook."

Sheena smiled with satisfaction.

"I'm glad you like it," she said as she slowly ate her food and watched the rest of the movie with Hakeem.

"Well damn! Hey, hey, hey!" Sheena mocked.

"I guess you are Fat Albert," she wisecracked as she picked up his empty plate.

"You left nothing, not even a crumb."

"I was hungry, and that food was the shit, girl."

"Do you want anything else?" She asked before bringing both plates to wash and putting them away in the kitchen.

"Nope, just you back here in my arms."

"Still think it was a chick flick?" She asked as she walked back into the bedroom, where the movie credits rolled.

"I mean, yeah. But it was cool. Come here."

Sheena climbed into her bed and lay beside Hakeem as he snuggled closer.

"Can I ask you a question?"

"What's up?" Sheena asked.

"What do you think about me?"

Sheena was confused.

"What do you mean?"

"I want to know how you feel about me."

"Hmmm, I think you're smart, funny, and attractive. I feel safe with you and love being around you. I also love the way you care about your mother. It's sweet. You're also loyal to your friends and even though you and Chrissy fight like cats and dogs," Sheena said as she let out slight chuckle and sucked her teeth.

"I know you look out for her and will make sure she's okay if you needed to because you're a big softy," she said as she poked Hakeem in his belly before climbing out of bed.

"Where you going?"

"I'll be right back," she responded as she left her bedroom and returned with two cold Coronas.

"Here."

"Aight, just this one." Hakeem conceded.

"No getting faded tonight, deal?"

"Just the one, promise. There's no more anyway. Chrissy brought them over the other day when I made tacos."

"I should've known, Chrissy is trying to make us all alcoholics so we can't leave her. Goddamn demon."

"Aht, aht, ahhhh. No name-calling, especially my bestie." Sheena said as she raised the Corona bottle to her lips and took a long sip.

Hakeem watched her wrap her lips around the mouth of the bottle.

"So, question for you. What do you think about me?" She asked as she got out of bed, went to her stereo, and pressed play.

The sound of Xscape's album Traces of My Lipstick played softly as Sheena climbed back into bed.

"She-She, that's easy. I've been crushing on you for years. You're smart, caring, beautiful. I don't even think you know how beautiful you are. You take care of the people you love, and you're not a follower. You're not scared to be yourself. You make me want to be a better person. And I always knew you were going to do something big with your life, and I knew I'd have to be able to match your drive to get your attention. You know, to get you to take me seriously and to keep you."

Hakeem paused before finishing his beer and then continuing.

"She-She, look at me. I'm being real with you. I love you; I want you to be my girl, on dawgs," he professed as he leaned in and kissed Sheena softly on her lips.

Sheena pulled away slowly, "I love you, too, Keem."

They both smiled passionately at each other.

"Gimme that," he said as he took the nearly empty Corona bottle from Sheena's hand and placed it on the nightstand.

"Open your mouth," he whispered as he stuck the tip of his index finger in Sheena's mouth as she gently sucked and circled her tongue around the tip of his finger. He pulled it out and traced his wet finger around her lips.

"Now, gimme a kiss," he demanded passionately.

Sheena obliged as she parted her lips and let Hakeem take control as he slowly and methodically explored Sheena's mouth with his tongue as he held her face softly with both hands before lightly sucking on her bottom lip and slowly moving one hand down toward her neck as he applied slight pressure.
Sheena purred as her breathing increased, and the music played in the background. Xscape sang "The Arms of the One Who Loves You," affectionately singing about finding

true love with someone and creating a safe space to be who you are, free of judgment and abundant in pure love.

"You like that?"

"Mmm hmm," Sheena moaned.

"Nah, I want to hear you say it," he instructed.

"I....I like it." Sheena panted as she started to lift his shirt.

"You want me to take it off?"

Sheena nodded her head, yes.

"Say it."

"Keem, take it off," she said with a little more authority as she leaned in for another kiss.

"Can I take yours off?" He asked between kisses.

Sheena nodded her head, "Mmm hmm."

"She-She, you gotta say it."

"Yes, you can take it off." Sheena agreed, lifting her arms over her head to help Hakeem remove her T-shirt, revealing her black lace bra.

Hakeem lay flat on his back and guided Sheena on top of

him and repositioned her; she straddled him as she pulled both straps down off her shoulders and unhooked her bra as he watched her every move.

"Damn," he moaned as he seductively grabbed her waist and ran his fingers down her neck, in between her breasts to her belly button and stopped at the top of her jeans at the zipper.

"How are you feeling? He asked as he ran his fingers back up to her belly button, in between her breasts, back up her neck, as he wrapped his hand gently around her neck.

Sheena moaned as she looked down at him.

"Ohhh, you like that, huh?"

Sheena giggled and covered her face; he pulled her hands down from her face.

"I asked you a question, do you?"

"No. I love it." Sheena said as she looked into Hakeem's eyes.

Hakeem felt himself grow harder as he pulled Sheena down to him and kissed her long and hard while he positioned her back onto the bed as they both looked into each other's eyes.
"I never felt this before," Hakeem said as he looked at Sheena, moved the hair from her face, and smiled.

"Like what?"

"I can't explain it. I want you so bad. But at the same time, I'm fine with just laying here with you and doing nothing, just kissing and talking. I don't want to rush you into anything. I never want to do that to you."

"You're not doing anything, Keem. I want you to be my first. I want you, I do," she reassured him.

"Keem! I'm eighteen; it's time," she said impatiently.

"I want you. Am I being clear enough for you?" She asked as she tugged at the waist of his jeans.

"Take them off," she said as she unbuttoned his jeans and unzipped them.

"You sure?"

"What I say?" She asked with sass.

"I'm ready, I'm ready to be with you," she reiterated as she leaned down and gave Hakeem another slow and sensual kiss as he delicately unbuttoned and unzipped her jeans, then lovingly laid her on her back.

At the same time, he continued to kiss her and tell her how much he loved and wanted her. Sheena melted in his arms as he touched her. He reached his hands down her pants and massaged her inner thighs while he continued to kiss her neck before asking, "Can I take off your pants?"

Sheena didn't speak; she promptly lifted herself and pulled down her jeans as Hakeem began to massage her breasts. She tugged at his pants, prompting him to take them off.

"This is what you wanted?" Hakeem asked as he held his jeans up and tossed them on the bedroom floor.

"Or is this what you want?" He asked as he took Sheena's hand and guided it down into his boxers as he put her hand on his erect penis.

"You sure you want it?" He asked again as he breathed heavily into her ear.

Sheena pulled her panties to the side and placed Hakeem's hand between her legs as she slowly massaged him with her other hand. Hakeem hurriedly pulled down her panties and began to massage her inner thighs again before slowly moving his hand up between her thighs as he slowly and methodically played with the wetness between her thighs. She gasped as she felt him massage her clitoris.

"You okay?"

He whispered with concern.

"You want me to stop?"

"No. No, don't stop." Sheena begged as he inserted a finger

into her pulsating vagina as he massaged her insides slowly while rubbing his thumb over her clitoris.

Sheena never imagined anything could feel this good as she moved her hips in sync with Hakeem's internal massage.

"Goddamn," Hakeem moaned as Sheena massaged him harder.

"Ahh, no. No, stop," he demanded.

"Am I doing it wrong?" Sheena asked, confused.

Hakeem chuckled.

"No girl. You're doing everything right. I don't want to finish before I can even give you this hammer, damn."

They both laughed.

"Aight, She-She, let me take care of this. I got you. This night is for you," he said as he began to kiss her lovingly, as he continued to massage her clitoris.
"Don't worry about me, this is about you," he reiterated as he inserted two fingers deep inside her as she writhed around in bliss.

"You okay? Does it hurt?"
Sheena shook her head no as she moaned.

"You sure?"

"Yes, I'm good," she moaned as she pulled Hakeem's hand back inside of her.

"Ohhh, you like that?" He asked as he reentered her with three fingers, using his thumb to massage her clitoris.

"Yes, yes, I like it."

"Shit! You got condoms?"

"Ummm, check the bottom drawer of the nightstand, if there's a makeup bag in there, check inside. If not, I'll check Evelyn's room."

Hakeem leaned down and opened the bottom drawer of the nightstand while fumbling around, trying to look for a makeup bag as Xscape's "My Little Secret" played in the background. They sang unapologetically about exploring lustful betrayals and hiding love affairs while those around them question the possibility of infidelity.

Hakeem pulled an item from the nightstand.

"This it? Wait, isn't this Chrissy's hoe bag?" He asked, annoyed, as he unzipped the bag.

Sheena laughed.
"Yeah, that's Chrissy's. What's the problem? I know she usually keeps condoms in there," she said, shrugging her shoulders.

Hakeem pulled out two Magnums before throwing the bag back into the nightstand and closing the drawer.

"Come here," he said, pulling Sheena closer as he laid her flat on her back.

"Relax. You okay?"

"I'm good. I think you need to relax," she said jokingly.

"I'm fine. I know what I'm doing. Stop worrying." Sheena tried to reassure him.

"You sure you want to do this? Are you sure, sure?" He reiterated as he straddled Sheena as she lay on her back while he reached behind and slowly inserted four fingers into her.

"You're so wet," he said as he slowly moved his fingers around inside of her.

"Yes, I'm sure."

Hakeem opened the condom wrapper as Sheena watched him grip the tip of the condom and roll it onto the shaft of his penis.

"Is it even gonna fit?" She asked as she watched Hakeem reposition himself between her legs.

"Relax, I'll go slow. If you want me to stop, just tell me," he said as he began to kiss Sheena's neck as she held onto his waist.

"Put it in."

Hakeem grabbed his penis and rubbed it on the outside of Sheena's labia until he felt the opening.

"You okay?"

"Yes."

"I'm gonna put it in real slow. Okay?" He said as he rubbed the head of his penis up and down the opening of her vagina.

"Do it, go ahead. Do it." Sheena moaned in anticipation.

Hakeem slowly inched himself into Sheena with each slow thrust, continuously asking if she was okay.

"Yes, I'm fine. You can go harder."

"You sure?"

"Yes," she reassured him as she began to thrust her hips to match his rhythm until she felt a very subtle rupture that then allowed Hakeem to penetrate deeper.
Sheena let out a slight yelp.

"Oh shit! Did I hurt you? You okay?" Hakeem asked as he

stopped mid-stroke to check on Sheena.

She continued to gyrate and pump her hips, and the yelping continued to escape her throat.

Hakeem grabbed her face to get her attention.

"What's wrong? You okay?"

Sheena stopped immediately and began to chuckle.

"Boy! I'm fine. I think I was about to come," she said shyly, covering her mouth to stop laughing.

"Oh snap, so I messed it up?" Hakeem asked, surprised.

"My bad. I thought I was hurting you," he said, relieved as he began to slow stroke Sheena again while kissing her.

Sheena laughed.

"You're supposed to be the pro, you over here acting like you're in bed with a porcelain doll with Faberge eggs stuffed in my vagina. Newsflash, I'm not going to break," she chuckled.

"Ohhh! Nah, nah, nahhhh. You're over here laughing at me? Nahhh, I can't have that," Hakeem joked as he pulled Sheena closer.
"I got this, girl," he said as he gently grabbed her by the neck.

"You like this, huh? You ain't laughing now, huh?" He said as he thrust himself deeper inside her.

"Can't talk now, huh? You love this shit, huh?" He asked as he began to thrust harder and faster, as his breathing increased.

"You love it?" He asked again as he looked into her eyes.

She let out slight moans while trying to speak in between thrusts.

"Yea... yes." She stammered as he continued to question her.

"What's my name? Huh, what's my name? I asked a question, huh?"

"Keem. . . Ha. . . Hakeem."

"Ahh, ahh, I'm about to come. Ahh, argh," Hakeem exclaimed as he collapsed onto the bed.

"Whew, I ain't gonna lie. That was bomb," he said as he motioned for a high-five from Sheena, then kissed her on the cheek.

They lay there in silence as Xscape continued serenading them.

Hakeem broke the silence.
"How you feeling? Does it hurt?" He asked with concern.

"I'm good, I feel fine. Honestly, it wasn't like the stories I've heard."

"But does it hurt?" He asked again.

"Oh my God, no! I'm fine. I need you to relax."

"Aight, aight. So, next question. And don't lie. Did you come?"

Sheena chuckled nervously, "Nooooo, I think I almost. But your scary ass stopped before it happened, I think."

"Damn! I messed that up for you." Hakeem said as he held his forehead in disappointment.

"Damn. . .but, wait!" He said with excitement as he snapped his fingers.

"I got you. You trust me?" He asked as he looked at Sheena with a mischievous smile.

"Go on, what?" Sheena asked, confused.

"Aight, I'm about to do something I ain't never done before, with no girl. Alright? I want to do this for you. You trust me?" He asked again.

"Okay?" Sheena more so asked than stated.
"Nah, you gotta say it. Do you trust me? Yes, or no?" Hakeem asked more specifically.

"Yes. Yes, I trust you."

"Okay, if you want me to stop, just say stop. Okay?"

"Okay. Yes, I will."

Hakeem proceeded to get on top of Sheena before playfully singing.

"Do, Re, Mi, Fa, Sol, La, Ti, Do. Fa-la-la-la-laaa," as he then playfully blew raspberries and pursed his lips as they made a smacking noise before taking a deep breath and announcing, "Alright, I'm going in."

He laid a trail of kisses down her neck, between her breasts and on her belly button before pulling the sheets over his head and continuing to kiss her inner thighs before licking the inside of her vagina. He then pulled the hood of her clitoris back and took her into his mouth as he gently sucked and inserted one finger inside of her. Hakeem continued to lightly suck as Sheena moved her hips slowly as he sucked and fingered her.

"Ahhhh, I think you need to stop!" Sheena said with urgency.

"Why?" Hakeem mumbled from underneath the covers before he went back to pleasing her orally.
"I think I'm gonna pee. I have to pee!" Sheena screamed as she tried to push Hakeem's head away.

"Trust me, just relax. You don't have to pee," he assured her, chuckling and continuing.
"Oh shhh. . . Oh my. . . Keem, Keem. Ahhh, Ahh. Oh my God!" Sheena heavily breathed.

"Okay, okay, okay. Okay, stop. Stop. Stop!" She said as she pushed his head away.

Hakeem scooted himself back from under the covers and looked down at Sheena, who had sweat beads forming on her top lip and brows as she lay there breathing heavily.

"How was it? Did you come?"

"Oh my God, look at me," she said breathlessly.

"Yes, yes, I came."

She looked over in Hakeem's direction and then burst into laughter as she pointed to his face.

"Look at your face! You look like it was dipped in baby oil and egg whites. Ewwww, get out of here!" She teased as she tried to push him out of bed.

"Yo! Cut it out. You're about to make me throw up. Egg whites?" Hakeem asked with a disgusted look on his face as he heaved.
"Ewww, go! Go to the bathroom. You better not throw up in my bed. Gooooo!" Sheena yelled.

"I'm good. I'm good," Hakeem said as he wiped his face with the back of his hand.

"Ugh, it's just hanging off your chin," Sheena said between laughs.

"Go wash your face, go. Get out of here."

"What?" Hakeem asked, confused, as he began wiping his chin.

"What the fu . . . What's this?" He asked, confused.

A cold, wet, slimy trail was connected from his chin to his hand as he pulled his hand away from his face.

"Yoooo!"

Hakeem jumped out of bed, began to dry heave again, and ran out of the bedroom to the bathroom.

Sheena lay in bed laughing hysterically.

"Baby girl, I love you, but I wasn't expecting that," Hakeem announced as he returned to the bedroom and got back into bed.

"Next time, tell Chrissy she needs to pack a bib in her hoe bag for a brotha."

"Ha! Boy, cut it out," Sheena said as she rolled her eyes.

"I'm just playing She-She. Anything for you. Did you like it?"

Sheena snickered.

"Yep."

"So, how would you say I made your first time?"

"Honestly? It was perfect," she said as she nestled into the crook of his arm.

They dozed off to Xscape, singing "The Softest Place on Earth" like a lullaby, taking Sheena and Hakeem on a journey through spaces of love, wonderment, and passion as they drifted off to sleep.

7

DISCERNMENT

"Sorry for all the bathroom breaks. I never knew a human could use the bathroom this much. Even nursing school couldn't prepare me for this pregnancy," Sheena joked as she walked back into the room, as Dr. Angel waited patiently for her as she packed the remaining books on the bookshelf.

"Aww, Doc. I still can't believe you're leaving me," Sheena said, pouting and waddling back to her seat.
"Oh, now, come on, Deary. Why the long face? You've done the work; you've got this, Dear. You have the necessary tools, support, and insight to get through life's challenges," she reminded her as she returned to her chair to resume their last session.

Sheena sighed, "I know, I know. I just hate feeling like I'm losing someone."

"Don't look at it that way, Deary. You're gaining, you've gained so much. You've learned how to work through your grief, have a keen sense of emotional intelligence, built an amazing and successful career helping others, maintained positive and loving relationships, and you're about to start your own family. Sheena, you have lost nothing. And, although O'Neil has passed, his absolute love, care, and loyalty to you live on beyond this world, and it never dies. There is no true loss here, Deary." Dr. Angel emphasized before continuing.

"You are resilient. And truth be told, Dear, I was supposed to pack up and be on my way a few months ago. But I wanted to stay here and see this through until you were ready," she said with a smile.

"And, oh boy, are you ready," she smiled warmly.

"Oh, my goodness! Really? You stayed longer, just for me?" Sheena asked, shocked.

"I... I don't know what to say. Thank you, thank you so much." "There's no need to thank me, Dear. It was my pleasure. Now, let's get back to it. You lead the way, your story, your triumph," Dr. Angel said supportively.

"Hmmm, I think I left off with how Keem and I finally got together. Well, shortly after our hookup, he was on his way to

Rhode Island for school. All of us were going our separate ways to do different things, but we kept in touch and kept each other on track. Before Keem left for Rhode Island, we had an honest conversation about the relationship and the fact that we'd both be focused on school and didn't want to hold each other back from experiencing life because we knew distance and time were huge roadblocks to a new relationship. Neither of us wanted to hold each other back, but we knew we loved each other and would put in the effort to work on being together once the timing was right."

"So, summer of '98, we left off knowing we loved each other; we were still great friends... with benefits. We understood that while in college, we were free to do what we wanted, if we got into a relationship with anyone, we had to be honest and tell the other person if we were getting serious with someone else. But the caveat is that we would never mess with anyone we knew, or each other's friends. We figured that would be too messy and just downright disrespectful."

■

"Last semester, She-She, you ready?" O'Neil asked excitedly.

"Heck yeah, I'm so ready to be done. I feel like I deserve a double degree. How many papers I write for you?" Sheena asked sarcastically as she and O'Neil sat in the backyard of O'Neil's parents' house, eating Flames and sipping Hypnotiq.

"I like how you conveniently forget how many of those damn math classes I helped you with. Algebra, calculus, statistics, and let's not forget the chemistry I also helped you with. So, I guess I'm walking across that stage with a BSN, too."

Sheena laughed.

"Damn, I forgot about all those classes. You didn't have to say it like that. What's a little help amongst family?" She asked as she shrugged her shoulders and chuckled.

"Yeah, you better change your tune," he joked as he crumpled up a napkin and threw it in her direction.

"On to other news, you know my parents are talking about packing up and going to Florida? My father is talking about wanting to help my grandfather with the business so he can retire once me and The Twins start our business up here."

"Noooooooo! Whyyyyyy? I love your parents, they can't leave!" She said, disappointed.

"You know your mom and Mrs. Mattie are like my chosen mom's."

"Nothing is set in stone right now, but they want to move in the next couple of years, like in the next two or three years. My mother keeps talking about being a snowbird and says they'll come back for a few months in the summers."

"Whew! That makes me feel a little better. So, they're not leaving, leaving?"

"Nope, just turning into old folks and semi-retiring to Florida because they're sick of these cold Boston winters and want to be closer to my grandad."

"I mean, I get it. They deserve to retire and do what they want. They've raised their kids," she said as she slowly accepted the news.

"So... that leads me to the next topic. You know my parents love you like a daughter. So, they wanted me to talk to you to see how you felt about it first."

"How I felt about what?" Sheena asked, perplexed.

"Alright, so when my parents decide to move to Florida, they talked about selling the house to me for the low. Well, correction, sell the house to you and me for the low. I'll have to finish the basement with The Twins and make it into a decent little apartment for them when they come back up here for the summers."

"What?!" I'm shocked. Are you serious?"

"You know my parents. They won't feel comfortable making the move until they feel like we're set. And, you know, Ma Dukes already know you're the only woman that's gonna take care of this house like she does." O'Neil said as he playfully rolled his eyes and took another sip of his drink.

"Why are you making that face? Don't hate me because your parents think I'm the better child." Sheena said jokingly.

"But seriously, what about doing it with one of your family members, like The Twins or your brother? Are they sure?"

"You are family! And yes, they're sure. They wouldn't have proposed the idea if they weren't. Think about it. You don't have to decide now, but deal of a lifetime," O'Neil said as he leaned back into his chair and finished his drink.

"They sell to us for a hundred thousand, where else are you getting a two-family in Dorchester for that price, well-maintained two-family at that?"

Sheena smiled, "I don't have to think about it. Of course I will! You know I love it here. I can't believe your parents would think about me in this way. I mean, I can believe it, but it's still unbelievable at the same time. You got the best parents ever. This is unbelievable. When do they get back from Atlantic City? I have to thank them in person."

"I think Friday, they said they would stop by and visit some friends before heading back. You know they stay on the move. But I'll let you know when they're back."

"Sounds good. I'll come over and cook dinner for everybody when they get here."

"And you already know Mom and Pops want your fishcakes, cook some lasagna too."

"Done and done," Sheena agreed.

"I think Keem should be here next weekend, too. Soon the whole squad gonna be back together," O'Neil said as he clasped his hands together.

"Let the shenanigans begin," he joked.

"Speaking of, what's up with you and Keem?"

Sheena chuckled and smiled bashfully.

"You know I can't wait for him to return here full-time. You know, we always talk and see each other when he can get back here. But it was hard because you know, with school and him working out there, he couldn't visit as much as we would have liked. But we'll take a real shot at it once he's back here after graduation."

"So, you're sure? Do you think he's ready to settle down completely? A man going from being able to do what he wants with who he wants, while knowing he can return to his girl, is a total change to being fully committed. So, do you think he's ready?"

"I would hope if he weren't, he would just say that. We've been real with each other from the beginning, so he should feel comfortable enough with me to be honest. I've asked him and I've been pretty clear. If he just wants to be friends or if he does want to settle down once he's back, it's okay. I'm not forcing anything; he's the one who says he's ready. So, if he's ready, I'm ready."

"Well, I don't think he's done partying and doing what he wants. And. I've told him that too. And, I'll say it to both of ya'll together."

"Oh yeah?"

"Yup! He's young, smart, and has a good job lined up. I don't think his ass ready to settle down now. Temptation is a motherfucker and just because a man is well intentioned, doesn't mean he can resist temptation. And that's just the honest truth. A man could love the shit out of you but still, he will always love his own pleasure and happiness more."

"Are you trying to tell me something?" Sheena asked while raising her eyebrow.

"If so, just spit it out already."

"Put that damn brow down. I said what I said. I'm not talking to you in riddles. If I had something specific to say, you should know me by now, I'm saying it. If I had any information that anyone I care about has, was or will be fucked over, I'm telling. You know this. So, to answer your question, am I trying to tell you something? Yes, always use your discernment when it comes to people, especially relationships. Discernment in relationships with your friends, family, and men. That's all I'm saying. That gut feeling, that little voice in your head, listen to it. You know, as long as I am around, I've got you. You know I will always have your back. Matter of fact, the entire Harris family will always look out for you."

"Awww, you know you and the rest of the Harris clan are my favorite people," Sheena gushed.

"But dude! I see that MIT degree taught you a few things. When you start using words like discernment?" She cackled.

"Maaaan listen!"

O'Neil started chuckling.

"You know, I had a fleeting dalliance with that exquisite AKA Soror from Howard for a few months. Needless to say, her voracious reading created a multitudinous lexicon which my black ass had to keep up with! All that work I had to do to keep up with her bourgeois ass just to talk to her, man I should have a minor in English."

"So, would you say that you practiced discernment in that situation?" She asked sarcastically.

"Indubitably! Ms. Thesauraus had stupendous gluteus maximus. A fatty, a fatty for sure!"

O'Neil and Sheena burst into uncontrollable laughter.
"Boy, you ain't right. Not right at all," she said as she tried to compose herself from laughter.

"I can't wait until we can all hang out together again, at the same time. I miss those days; they were the best."

"Just focus on your last classes Nurse Ratchet. That's what I need you to do."

"Stop worrying about me and mind ya business. I'm good, this final semester is easy peasy. I'm just counting down the weeks," Sheena said excitedly.

"Now I just need to get ready to apply for my RN license and study for the NCLEX, so I'm laser-focused right now. Translation, worry bout yo'self."

"Girl, I can tell you never got ass whopping's as a child; it shows."

"I can't stand you, boy. Shut up." Sheena quipped before the cordless phone on the foldable card table rang.

"Hello. Yooooo! What up, bro? Chilling, what's up with you? When are you coming up to chill for a day or two? Man, you ain't working that hard. Me? Nothing much, wrapping up the last semester and working. Matter of fact, I'm here chilling and shooting the shit with your lil' girlfriend. Aight, hold on," O'Neil said as he pressed the speaker on the cordless receiver.
"What up She-She?"
"Hey Keem! What's up with you?" Sheena asked as she sat closer to O'Neil, who was holding the phone.

"I'm not even going to lie. Fucking annoyed!"

"Why? What happened?" Both Sheena and O'Neil asked

simultaneously.

"That damn Chrissy came up here with that fucktard Keisha, running game on these simps," Hakeem said, clearly annoyed.

"Wait, what? What are you talking about?" Sheena asked bewildered.

"Keisha? You mean Count Von Count, Keisha?"

"Yup! Bird-brained, snaggle-toothed Keisha."

"I didn't even know they hung out like that. What the heck are they doing in Providence? This is news to me. I'm lost, so what happened?"

"So, what I found out, Twiddle Dee and Twiddle Dumb been up here running through these drunk simps at the dorm parties and then telling these dumb fucks they knocked up and they need Planned Parenthood money."

"Get the fuck outta here, bro! Are you serious? Yooooo! That's wild. Yo! Chris is tripping. How did she even get involved with Keisha, of all people?"
"So, what I'm hearing so far, it was definitely Keisha doing the fucking and tricking. But Chrissy definitely helped her collect the money. Either way, I'm pissed. So last night I heard they were trying to get some cash from some dummy. Come to find out, he starts talking to his man's about it, then they start trading stories, and lo and behold, like four or five dudes in the

dorm been scammed by them two. But of course, there always gotta be a King Simp out the bunch. Well, King Simp was talking bout Keisha his girl, blah, blah, blah. So, King Simp ready to go to war over his girl. A full-blown fight in the residence hall. Why? Fucking Keisha and Chrissy with the ghetto hot mess!"

"Are you serious? You can't be serious," Sheena asked, befuddled.

"She-She, I kid you not! And to top it all off, I got people talking about they're my friends and I brought them here, yada, yada, yada. False! I invited them two broads to one party, one party! And that was so long ago. Whatever they did or got into after that one party is on them. Fucking floozies ain't getting me caught up in their bullshit when I'm about to graduate. On dawgs, I'm pissed off, royally. Sheena, tell Chrissy don't bring her ass back up to this campus on her tricking shit until I'm out of here with my degree in hand. I swear, she's the type of bird-brained bimbo that'll cause a person to lose everything. Old simple minded ass chick."

"I mean, I'll talk to her. But I'm shocked; this is the first I'm hearing about any of this. I didn't even know she was going out to Providence to hang out with you."
"That's the thing, we weren't even hanging out. I invited them once to a campus party. And I didn't even get to go to the party because I had to work. So, whatever they got into after that one invite, don't got shit to do with me," Hakeem said sternly.

"Alright, bro. We'll talk to Chrissy," O'Neil said as he looked directly at Sheena.

"Just focus on staying out of other people's mess and finish your classes. We'll make sure those two don't go back up there while you're there. We got you, bro. Yo, that's some wild shit though," O'Neil taunted.

"Yeah, we will talk to her, Keem. I'm still shocked she's even hanging out with Keisha. That's breaking news for me. I'm so confused," Sheena added as she rubbed her temples.

"Absolutely insane."

"Aight, ya'll, I'll talk to you both later. I'll be home next weekend, I'm gonna start bringing stuff up little by little so I'm not stressing once the semester ends, and they kick us out of these dorms. Bro, I'll hit you. She-She, love you, and I'll call you tonight. Peace."

"Alright, love you too, Keem. Talk to you later."
"Peace out, bro," O'Neil said as he disconnected the call.

"Sheena! What the hell is up with ya girl? That's bananas. Now, we all know Chrissy nuttier than a fruit cake, a few cards short of a full deck, crazier than a rat in a shit house and a basket case all rolled into one. But this shit right here takes the cake. What type of shit is she on?"

"I'm just as shocked as you are. Why is she even hanging with Keisha? Of all people, I'm still stuck on that one. Welp, Chrissy laying down with dogs and waking up with fleas. I can hear Mrs. Mattie now," Sheena said as she shook her head in disappointment.

"Get her ass on the phone," O'Neil said as he handed Sheena the cordless receiver.

"Hey girl, what's up? Where are you? What are you doing after? Cool, I'm at Neil's, come over when you're done. You're always hungry. Yeah, we got Flames and some Hypontiq. I figured that would pique your interest. Alright, see you when you get here. Yeah, just come to the back. Bye."

"What did Cuckoo for Cocoa Puffs say?"

"She's at Marshalls in South Bay with one of her cousins. She'll have her cousin drop her off here when they're done."

"I can't wait to hear this one," O'Neil said sardonically, as he and Sheena returned to discussing their after-college plans while eating chips and drinking.

■

"Ain't no party like a Chrissy party, cause a Chrissy party don't stop. Whoot-whoot!" Chrissy sang out as she walked into the backyard dancing and shaking her butt.

"Why are you always the loudest person in the room? And quit with all that ass shaking, don't nobody want to see all that!" O'Neil goaded.

"Yeah, right. Let me remind you about ALLLLLLLLL this!" Chrissy said that while she attempted to shake her butt on O'Neil while he was seated, she sang in a Jamaican accent, mimicking the beat to Patra's Pull Up to the Bumper.

"Touch all on my dumper, baby."
"Which ya long black pee-pee, ohh ohh."

Chrissy turned around and tried to shove her crotch in O'Neil's face.

"Why are you like this? No home training, I swear."

O'Neil laughed as he pushed Chrissy away.

"Get out of here, have a damn seat. Psycho."

"You know you love me; give me a hug," Chrissy said playfully.

She hugged and kissed O'Neil on the cheek before taking a seat, pulling her lip gloss out of her purse, and applying it to her lips.

"Can you two get along long enough for me to go inside and make a plate?" Sheena asked rhetorically as she walked towards the back door.

"Nooo, don't leave me with her. Take her with you," O'Neil playfully yelled out.

"Neil, shut the hell up! You know you miss me."

"Here," Sheena said as she walked back to the yard with Chrissy's plate of food and drink.

"Ohhh, I love you, girl! I'm starving. Cheers," Chrissy said, holding up her cup.

"To good food and good friends."

"Hurry up and scoff down that food like the feral beast you are."

"Would you leave her alone, good grief. She's been here all of ten minutes," Sheena said in Chrissy's defense.

"At least let her eat before you two start going at it."

"Thank you, bestie. See, that's why you're my favorite," she said while finishing her plate of food.

"Alright! Enough of this beating around the bush. What the hell you got yourself into out in Providence?"

Chrissy choked on her drink and started to cough uncontrollably between laughs.

"Ha! So, what did you hear?" She asked as she wiped the spilled drink from her face.

"Cut the shit, answer the question," O'Neil demanded.

"I didn't do nothing. I just didn't snitch and went along with the story. That's all."

"Girl! Quit playing, tell the story from start to finish. You got my boy hotter than fish grease. Why are you up there showing your ass and acting stupid when he's a few weeks from graduating?"

"Ha! Oh, Keem's mad? That's a joke."

"Stop stalling, what happened?" Sheena asked irritated.

"Well, what did Prince Hakeem say happened?" Chrissy asked while rolling her eyes.

"Grow up, we're trying to give you a chance to explain. Don't be a twat." Sheena said while giving Chrissy the same amount of attitude.

"Ugh, okay," she said while sighing dramatically.
"Months ago, I can't even remember how we even got on the conversation of college parties, but I remember asking Keem to hook up one of my cousins with a college dude. One day, he called, like, yo, there's a party at a hotel down here, one of his boys got, and asked if my cousin and I wanted to come through. When he had called and told me, I was doing Keisha's hair, and she was all in the convo and was like, I got my mom's car for the weekend, I'm down to roll. So, me and Keisha went to the party. I'm like, bet, maybe I'll find me a college dude too. You know I'm trying to elevate too, I'm sick

of these block boys, let me see what these college boys are like."

"So, me and Keisha go to the party, Keem is MIA because he said he had to work, so me and Keisha mixing and mingling, she goes off and does her thing, I talked to a few people, they were cool. Exchanged numbers with a few people. Whatever Keisha did and with who she did it with ain't none of my business. She hooked up with a few people, and after that, I would ride with her back out there so we could hang out. We supposed to be out there partying and having a good time, and this numbskull ends up knocked up."

"I don't even think she knows who got her knocked up, so I guess she just starts telling whoever she hooked up with she's preggers and needs Planned Parenthood money. I know she was pregnant because I saw the pregnancy test when she took them; she took two and both came back positive. So that's how I got roped into it. Whoever she told, and they didn't believe her, she told them to ask me if she was really pregnant. So, I just confirmed, yeah, she's knocked the hell up!"

"I know at least two dudes just gave her money, no hesitation. I know one dude was trying to avoid her because he claimed it was impossible. That dude was cool with the dude I was chilling with, so Keisha asked me if I happen to see the dude that was dodging her to tell him to run his pockets for her appointment. So, I did. So that's the story. Happy now? But I'm real curious what Keem's side of the story was though," she said with a smirk.

"Pretty much the gist of what you just said, minus the specific details only you and the Count would have. So, when did you start hanging out with Keisha? Curious minds want to know." Sheena asked.

"Awww, my bestie is jelly? Don't worry, she ain't got nothing, she can't take your place."

"You're insane. I'm not worried about any of that. You already know that girl is always into some shit and pissing somebody off. It's only a matter of time before her nonsense catches up with her, and it's not going to be pretty. Why would you risk it by hanging with her? Look at the crap she got you into already, not to mention it has the potential to affect Keem too." Sheena said while rolling her eyes.

"Fuck all that" O'Neil interjected.

"Don't ya'll bring your narrow asses back up there while my boy is trying to finish school and graduate. That doesn't make no goddamn sense, you two running back and forth up to that school to wild out and extort people," O'Neil said trying to keep a straight face.

"If that ain't the most raggedy shit I've ever heard! Come on, Chrissy, you're better than that. Seriously, I know we joke with you and give you a hard time, but stay away from these chicks that don't have self-respect and don't have shit to lose. That's not you, sis."

"So, this is why you two called me over here? To scold me like a child?" Chrissy asked as she folded her arms across her chest.

"It's not even that serious, if Prince Hakeem has such a problem, nobody has to worry about me going back to that campus," she said as she sucked her teeth and rolled her eyes before mumbling.

"That motherfucker got some nerve."

"What? I didn't catch that." Sheena asked for clarity.

"Nothing, tell your cornball ass dude he's lucky I'm not that kind of shady, he doesn't have to worry. No more Johnson and Wales trips for me."

8

CLOSING DAY

Sheena pulled two granola bars from her purse. She tore open the wrappers, bit off a huge chunk, and rubbed her belly.

"Doc, O'Neil's parents were so supportive of us. I'll spend my entire life trying to pay back so many wonderful people who were put into my life. It was about four years after graduating and saving money, his parents were finally ready to make the move to Florida and sell the house to us. I mean, Neil and I worked and saved every extra penny we got our hands on, so when they were finally ready to move, we were able to write a check for a total of one hundred and twenty-five thousand. They only wanted one hundred thousand, but we both worked hard and wanted to give them as much as possible. So, we both ended up writing them checks for an additional twelve and a half thousand dollars to show our appreciation for what they did for us. Because of his parents, we officially became homeowners at twenty-six and twenty-seven years old."

Sheena smiled as she recalled their closing day.

"I'll never forget July 14th, 2006. Neil and I walked into that attorney's office with his parents to make it official."

Sheena readjusted herself in the chaise and unwrapped her second granola bar before continuing.

■

"She-She, are you ready?"

O'Neil excitedly asked Sheena as he opened the front door to Dickerson's Law and Title office, holding it open for his parents and Sheena to enter.

"I got all the feels! I could barely sleep last night. I don't even think there's a word for what I am feeling right now." Sheena responded as she walked into the office lobby behind Mr. and Mrs. Harris.

"Well, I can tell you what you're feeling. Fifty thousand dollars poorer!" Mr. Harris joked as his wife slapped his arm.

"Kenny! Leave her alone, at least save your comments until both their checks clear!" Mrs. Harris said in jest.

"Mom's and Pop's got jokes? Well, y'all two jokers go have a seat over there and don't touch anything either. Yeah, I'm talking to you." O'Neil said as he playfully pointed at his mother.

"I see you eyeing that flower arrangement in that vase. Don't even think about it."

"You hear this boy?" Jodi asked her husband as they approached the waiting room chairs.

"Guess he told you," Kenny taunted as they both took a seat.

"Good morning, we're here to see Lamar Dickerson," O'Neil announced as he and Sheena approached the reception desk.

"Sure, I'll let Attorney Dickerson know you have arrived. May I have your name, please?"

"Yes, Sheena Williams and O'Neil Harris. Thank you."

"Perfect. Feel free to have a seat, and he will be right with you," the receptionist said as she pointed to the waiting area.

As Sheena and O'Neil walked back towards his parents, O'Neil stopped abruptly.

"You gotta be kidding me, look at what she did," O'Neil said to Sheena as he pointed to the vase holding the flower arrangement on the coffee table in the waiting room.

"Ooooooo, she did that?" Sheena asked, laughing.

"Mama Harris, you did that?" Sheena asked as they both took seats opposite of O'Neil's parents.

Pollen and fallen flower petals were scattered around the vase, on the coffee table, and on the floor.

"Me? Why do you think it was me? Aaaah choo! Atchoo! Aaah choo!"

Jodi erupted into a sneezing fit.

"It wasn't you, huh? Look at you, can't take you two nowhere."

"It wasn't me," Kenny said, raising both hands in the air.

"Talk to Jodi," he said, pointing to his wife.

Jodi playfully gasped.

"You traitor! Aaaah choo! You're a snitch, I married loose lips. Clearly, we're not ride or die. Aaaah choo!"

"Ma! Go wash your hands. You're so embarrassing, can't take ya'll nowhere," O'Neil whined.
"Ride or die? Baby girl, sound like you're dying now."

Mrs. Harris stood up to walk to the restroom.

"Aaaaah choo! Whew, look at that mess. Someone should clean that up," she said as she walked past the table, half covered in pollen and flower petals.

Jodi returned with wet paper towels and began cleaning the table and the flower petals from the floor before dumping them into the nearest waste basket and returning to her seat.

"Good morning, Harris family, you can come back with me. We're just going to head down to the conference room on the right," Attorney Dickerson said as he guided them all to the conference room.

"Feel free to take a seat anywhere you like."

"Lamar, how's the family? And your mom, how's she doing?"

"Jodi, everybody is great. My mother was just asking me about your uncle. We haven't seen him in a while."

"Scooter? He's in Florida working with my father-in-law. He should be home in a few weeks. I'll tell him to stop by."

"Speaking of Florida, you two ready for the move? Cool Cat Kenny, you ready, bruh?"

"Time for a change, brotha, me and my old lady starting to hate the winters here. My dad needs help with his business in Florida before he sells it. The kids are grown, and it is time for us to enjoy our life now."

"I hear that, well, congratulations on making that move and having the capacity to do what you want. That's the black man's dream, my brotha."

Attorney Dickerson turned his attention to his laptop and opened his manila file folder.

"Alright, let's get to the business at hand," he said as he started typing on his laptop.

"Okay, sellers, I have just confirmed that the wire transfer in the amount of one hundred thousand dollars has been received. Buyers, I have confirmed the mortgage payoff, the title has been confirmed clear, and I have the deed here for signature along with the purchase agreement," he said as he pushed some documents and a pen towards Sheena and O'Neil.

"Alright, I will walk you all through the signing of the documents," he said as he got up and walked towards Sheena and O'Neil.

"Okay, your parents have already signed, so Neil and Sheena sign here. This is the purchase agreement. Okay, Mr. and Mrs. Harris, sign your names here to turn over the deed to Sheena and O'Neil. Nice, perfect. Okay, Neil and Sheena, sign here. This is the deed. Also, sign here for the Homestead Protection Act. The homestead declaration is a legal document that protects homeowners from losing their homes to creditor claims. Alright, family, we're all set. Congratulations to you all."

"Are you serious? That's it? We're homeowners now?" Sheena asked in utter disbelief.

"Absolutely. I have to leave here and go straight to the registry of deeds to make you both the official owners on record. Once that's done, you will be official homeowners."

"Wow! We did, it She-She," O'Neil said as he raised his hand to high-five Sheena.

"I can't believe it. Thank you, Mama Jodi and Pops. Thank you so much. I can't thank you enough," Sheena said as tears rolled down her face.

"I appreciate everything you have done for me over the years, including treating me like a daughter. You've done more for me than my own mother, and for that, I could never repay you in a million years. No words could ever express my gratitude and love for this entire family. Thank you for being great stand-in parents to me. I truly love you both," she said as she hugged Mr. and Mrs. Harris.

"You will always be family, Sheena. And we are glad you will help keep that house a home," Mrs. Harris said, kissing Sheena on the cheek and hugging her back harder.

"You're the best daughter any parent could ask for. Never forget that. You hear me?" Kenny said sternly.

"I hear you, Pop's. I hear you," Sheena smiled warmly as she wiped the tears from her eyes.

"Thank you," she said again as she embraced Mr. Harris.

"You truly and always will be family," Mr. Harris reiterated as he pulled the house keys out of his pocket and gently placed them into Sheena's hands.

"And don't you ever forget it," he said as his eyes got misty.

"Now, let's get out of here so Lamar can go file that paperwork and make it official with the man."

"Alright, Harris family. As always, assisting you today was a pleasure. If you need anything else, don't hesitate to call me," Attorney Dickerson said, shaking Kenny's hand and hugging Jodi before they all walked out of the conference room.

■

Sheena beamed with pride as she reminisced about their closing day and expressed her gratitude for O'Neil and his family.

"Doc, we had so much fun remodeling, decorating, and hosting. It took us four years to perfect the house and make all the changes we envisioned. His parents loved everything, especially what we did for them in the basement. Their basement apartment turned out perfectly. I'll never forget their faces when they finally saw the finished work. They both cried; giving back to them was an amazing feeling."

9

RECIPROCITY

"Your parents get in next weekend. Is everything painted down there?" Sheena asked as she walked into O'Neil's apartment, carrying a plate of food and placing it on the kitchen table.

"Neil, I know you hear me, boy!"

"He's still asleep."

Sheena heard a familiar female voice as the person entered the kitchen.

"Krystal? Ahhhhhhh! Why didn't you two tell me you were coming?" Sheena asked excitedly as she rushed over to hug Krystal.

"We wanted to surprise you. Surprise!" Krystal yelled as she leaned in for a second hug.

"I missed you!"

"When did you get in?" Sheena asked, still surprised.

"I got in yesterday. Neil said you were pulling a double, so I figured I'd wait to surprise you after you got a good night's sleep. How are you? You don't even look like you pulled a double yesterday."

"Girl, you know this nurse life all too well. Come downstairs, I made breakfast." Sheena said as she led Krystal through the door in the kitchen, which led to the back hall and the stairs leading to the door into Sheena's kitchen.

"It looks great in here! You all did all this? This looks great."

"Girl, go ahead and look around while I fix your plate," Sheena said as she opened the kitchen cabinet to retrieve a plate.

"This all looks like a West Elm catalog. I love it!" Krystal yelled.

"I can tell you decorated Neil's place, too," she said as she walked back into the kitchen.

"Sure did, you know these fools would be content with a mattress on the floor, big screen, and Xbox. I had to, girl,"

Sheena said as she placed Krystal's plate on the table.

"Mmmm, it smells good. Sit, relax." Krystal prompted Sheena to take a seat.

"Have you even eaten yet? I'm sure the first thing you did after you cooked was bring Neil a plate. Come on, sit down, and eat," she instructed.

"Ha! Don't be in here trying to read me. But yes, I need to eat, too," she said as she began to make herself a plate and sit down with Krystal.

"Alright, so the last time we talked, you were in the process of transferring to labor and delivery. How's that going?"

"Sheena! I love it, I think this is where I'm going to stay. You know, we need more people of color in those spaces, too. I know I don't have to tell you that black women have the highest maternal mortality rate in America. I want to do my part to make sure that the women who look like us have a fighting chance to live and raise these beautiful babies to be great."

"I'm glad you found your happy place. I'm still trying to figure it out and find my specialty. I mean, being an E.R. nurse, I'm learning so much and I am grateful for all the experience I'm getting, but I don't think I've found my thing yet. I enjoy the E.R., but if I'm being honest, I don't love it."
"No, I get it. I felt the same way. I guess one thing to ask yourself is, out of all the experiences you've had so far, what

area do you feel you have a strong desire to help or change, or feel like you would have the greatest impact in? Once you can answer that, then maybe you'll be closer to finding your niche."

"Hmm, you gave me something to think about," Sheena said as she gathered their empty plates.

"Sheena, if you don't sit your butt down. Let me get the dishes, relax." Krystal said as she took the plates from Sheena and walked them to the sink to wash.

"You don't have to do everything you know."

"Oh God, you sound like your damn boyfriend. Cut it out. Don't you try and lecture me too," Sheena said as she playfully rolled her eyes.

"No lecture, it's just okay for you to relax, chill out. You don't have to constantly care for people. That's all I'm saying."

Krystal held both her hands up.

"No lecture at all. You know Neil worries about you, which means I worry about you."

"Worried? About me? Why?" Sheena asked incredulously.

"I'm fine, seriously. What could you two possibly be worried about?" She asked, confused.

"We know you're fine. I think Neil's biggest concern is that you do things for others before you do for yourself. You're always giving and doing, and you know Neil is overprotective about the people he loves. He doesn't want anyone taking advantage of your kindness and generosity."

"You two don't have to worry about me. I'm not stupid; I've never let anyone take advantage of me, ever. I do things for the people I care about, and I do these things because I can. I have the capacity to do them. What's the point in being able to help if you're not going to actually do it? That's just not me, just because I like to look out for people doesn't make me gullible, naïve, or stupid. Never that!" Sheena said with conviction.

"Oh no, I didn't mean to offend you, and I'm definitely not implying that you're naïve. And stupid, would never even be a word I would use in the same sentence when describing you. You know I respect you and our friendship. I don't want you always to be the one giving. You deserve reciprocity, too! You deserve to have people look out for you, also. I've learned that givers usually attract takers. That's all I'm saying, and that's what Neil worries about too, and I agree with him. You have a big heart, and you want to take care of everybody. Don't get into the habit of being everything to everybody and not getting the same in return. That's all, reciprocity." Krystal sang as she finished washing the dishes and sat at the kitchen table with Sheena.

"For instance, take Chrissy. I know you all have been friends for years. You always come to her rescue, and she relies on you a lot. But can you depend on her when needed? I want you to think about that. You don't even have to answer me. Just think about it."

Sheena chuckled.

"Listen, I know Chrissy is a hot mess express, but we've been friends for years, and I don't doubt that she has my back. That girl is all over the place and can't get out of her own way. So, in reality, yes, I can do more for her than she can do for me at the moment, but that's okay. It doesn't take away from the friendship. Hell, that's my sister, and I know she's still getting herself together and gets no judgment from me. We both rely on each other. And, I have never once doubted if she had my back," Sheena said as she began to fidget with her black leather bolo bracelet with the half silver heart charm with the word 'friends' engraved on it before speaking again.

"I mean, I get it. Chrissy isn't always people's favorite, but she's always been my friend, she's never done anything to me, and we've both looked out for each other for years. I get her, and that's all that matters. I also understand that she rubs some people the wrong way, but that's Chrissy. She's a goddamn handful, I know," Sheena said as she let out a slight giggle.

"A bitch be cray cray."

"Girl, please. You don't have to tell me twice. I've noticed, for sure. But I'll keep my mouth shut out of respect for you," Krystal said as she gave a sly smile.

"Yooo! Where the food at?" Jason yelled as he burst through the door leading into the kitchen.

"She-She, where my food at, woman?"

"Oh God, here we go. Jason, get out! Take your ass downstairs and finish that basement. You know Jodi and Kenny will be here next weekend," she said as she got up and started to fix his plate.

"Come on, man, you know we don't play around. Stay in a woman's place, girl."

"I can't stand you, here!" Sheena said, annoyed as she placed his plate on the table.

"That's what I'm talking about. Wait, I don't see no steam coming off this plate, woman!"

"Oh no, he didn't!" Krystal said as she laughed.

"You must have a death wish."

"I don't see any steam coming off my plate," Jason demanded again, slapping the kitchen table with his hands and taunting Sheena.

"Oh, I'm sorry," Sheena said sweetly.
"Would you like your meal warmed up, your majesty?"

"See, that's what I'm talking about. Hakeem trained you well, I see. Take it away, ma'am." Jason said as he waved his hands dismissively at the plate.

"I said, take it away, ma'am."

"Yes, sir, right away, sir," Sheena said as she walked towards Jason and picked up the plate of food.

"And, you'd like this heated up, piping hot and steamy, right? I think I can handle that."

Sheena began to rub Jason's back reassuringly.

"Just sit back, relax, and I'll get this ready for you."

"See, Krystal, take note. You better be giving my boy Neil the same treatment," he said smugly.

"Chop, chop, She-She. Chop, chop!"

"I'm on it, boss man," she said lovingly as she began to massage the top of his head with one hand while holding his plate with the other.

"Just relax. Is there anything else you need?"

"The King just requests his royal breakfast."

"And the royal breakfast is what you shall receive," Sheena said as she grabbed a fist full of Jason's hair and pushed his face down into his plate of food as she yelled at him.

"How's your food now? What? I can't hear you. How does the plate taste, your highness? What? What? I can't hear you," she taunted as she gripped his hair tighter.

"Owwww, I'm sorry. I didn't mean it! I was joking. I'll eat my food cold. I'm sorry. Owwwww! Lemme go, lemme go! Krystal, help! Krystal, help. Ain't ya'll nurses, aren't ya'll supposed to serve and protect? Owww, that hurts!"

"Boy, you're so stupid. Protect and serve is for cops. Guess you're shit out of luck," Krystal said laughing.

"Serves you right."

"Apologize, now!" Sheena demanded as she continued to shove his face into his plate of food.

"Damn girl, when did you get the strength of a chimp? Owww! Come on, that hurts! I'm sorry. I'm sorry, I was just joking. It was a little jokey joke. Come on. Owww! Come on, we're family. I love you. Owwwww! Stop, nobody wins when the family feuds. Owwwww!"

Sheena let her grip on his hair go and slapped him on the side of his head.

"Stop messing with me, next time I'm gonna kick your ass. Now eat that food before I shove that plate down your throat."

"Yes, ma'am." Jason agreed as he rubbed his head and wiped the eggs off his face before picking up his fork.

"Owwww, damn that was a mean grip," he said as he rubbed his head again.

"Medic! I need a medic, my head hurts."

"Ha-ha! Good!" Krystal antagonized.

"Who's trained now?"

"Oh Lord, let me hurry up and eat and get my ass back down to that basement, too much estrogen in here," Jason said as he mumbled with a mouth full of eggs and turkey bacon.

"Ya'll are evil. You hear that, toots? Pure evil." He scoffed as he pointed to Sheena and Krystal.

"Quit all that jibber jabber and hurry up and get out my house and take your butt down to that basement and finish whatever ya'll are working on."

"I've been kicked out of better places!" Jason said as he grabbed the rest of his bacon and walked towards the door to the hallway that led to the basement.

"And I'm telling. Watch, you damn battleaxes!"
"Get out!" Sheena yelled as she chucked a near-empty carton of orange juice at Jason's head, hitting him on the

side of his face.

"Ouch! Damn, you're getting violent in your old age." Jason yelled as he slammed the door closed and ran down the steps towards the basement.

"You see what I have to deal with? Those jackals are annoying as hell."

Krystal laughed, "I don't know how you do it. Maybe we need to put sedatives in their food. I see this is going to be an eventful week."

"Come on, let's go relax in the living room," Sheena said as she got up and finished putting the dishes back in the cabinets and wiping down the counters.

"Alright, let's go."

■

"I love it here; you all did such a good job. Taking that wall out made such a difference," Krystal said, admiring the open space of the living room and dining room.

"Yeah, it makes it look so much bigger. I like the openness of it."

"I need you to come decorate my place! You definitely have a good eye for interior decorating."
"I'll let you in on a little secret. Most of this stuff comes from Goodwill, estate sales, and yard sales."

"Shut up! Come on, no way."

"Swear to God. You know, Neil and I are all about saving coins and snagging deals. Why do you think it took so long to get this house together? Soooooo, can you see yourself living here? You know, we have the best hospitals here. Hint, hint, nudge, nudge, wink, wink."

"Awww, come on! Don't do this to me, Sheena," Krystal said as she covered her face in embarrassment.

"Look, we're taking it slow. No pressure, we're not putting pressure on each other. For now, we're fine with hopping on a quick flight to visit each other. I mean, we're okay with our current setup. I love my job at Johns Hopkins and my townhouse in D.C., Neil's growing his business, and working on this house. Right now, we are content, and neither one of us is thinking about uprooting our lives for the other. We'll see what the future holds," Krystal said as she shrugged her shoulders.

"Okay, I won't bring it up," Sheena said while pouting.

"I understand, what's meant to be, will be."

"Don't make that face! So dramatic." Krystal said as she laughed and threw a decorative sofa pillow in Sheena's direction.

"Whatever happens between Neil and me will not change anything between you and me, okay?"

"Better not," Sheena said as she rolled her neck and eyes.

"Where y'all at? She-She! Krystal!"

"In the living room," Sheena yelled, hearing the kitchen door close and footsteps walking towards the living room.

"If you're up here, that means you're done down there, right?"

"Yo! What's her problem?" O'Neil playfully asked Jason as they both sat down on the sofa.

"Picking up them bad habits from Chrissy, that's her problem." Jason retorted.

"When you are in the presence of greatness, don't act like a peasant. Have we not taught you anything, woman?"

"Jason! You got one more time to mess with me. Sit there and keep your mouth shut, dang. You already got checked. Do you want to try me again? How's that head feeling, sucker?"

Jason and O'Neil began to howl with laughter.

"Yo! Sheena, I need you to stop hanging out with Mrs. Mattie. She got you talking like an actress in a blaxploitation film," O'Neil laughed.
Jason joined in.

FOR THE LOVE OF YOU

"You jive ass turkey! I'mma get you sucka! I'm gonna let 'em know Dolemite... I mean, Beantown Brown is back on the scene! Beantown Brown is my name, fucking up motherfuckers is my game!"

"Shut yo mouth fool, you ole jock-jawed motherfucker!" O'Neil joked as they all began to laugh.

"Hold on, bro, hold on. What y'all know about this?" Jason asked before continuing in a deep baritone southern drawl.

"Way down in the jungle deep. The bad ass lion did what?"

"Awww shit. I know that one," O'Neil interjected.

"Stepped on the signifying monkey's feet!"

"Oh my God! Cut it out." Sheena whined as they all laughed.

"Not the blaxploitation, oh my word! Hilarity at its finest." Krystal laughed as she cuddled with O'Neil on the sofa.

"Leave my friend alone, not her fault she got an old soul. Y'all over here being plumb fools now."

"Ahhhh, nah. Don't start with the old-timey sayings either. Take that mess back to backwoods ass Virginia." Jason teased.

"I live in D.C., thank you very much," Krystal said, pointing at Jason.

"Get it right; respect my roots."

"Remember when you used to be sweet and innocent? Now you're turning into another slick-mouthed dame that we need to tolerate. Stop following behind that damn Chrissy and Sheena; those two chicks gonna get you in trouble. I see my bro ain't taught you how we get down in the Bean, huh? This is the 617."

Krystal perked up and lifted her head off O'Neil's chest.

"Oh, I see how you all get down in the Bean, alright. I see how you just got checked by my girl Sheena earlier, had you running out the door, ran so fast I could see your red lace panties, sis."

O'Neil covered his mouth, trying to contain his snickering while Sheena cheered Krystal on.

"That's right, Krystal, don't let him mess with you, get him," she egged her on.

"That's okay, I think I'm done. I don't want him to start crying. Are we good, Jason? Or do you want to keep going? Full disclosure, I haven't even begun to be mean yet."

"Damn sis. Why you want to do me like that? I thought we were cool; I don't want no smoke. Bro! Call your pit bull off." "Aye! That's between you two." O'Neil said as he held his hands up.

"Krystal can handle her own. You better stop messing with her."

Jason sucked his teeth and threw his hand up and waved O'Neil off.

"Awww man, I see what this is. Power of the pussy. Aight man, can we get to the reason why we even came up to this estrogen cesspool in the first place? The longer we sit here, the faster your nuts gonna shrink. You ole dainty ball sac motherfucker."

O'Neil laughed.

"You wild boy, knock it off! She-She, downstairs is officially done. Jamal's on his way to bring the last of the furniture from storage now."

"Yes, finally!" Sheena said while clapping her hands in excitement.

"Let us get the furniture in and set it up. Then you two can come down and see it and rearrange everything we did."

"Sounds like a solid plan Pooh butt," Krystal said as she leaned in and gave O'Neil an Eskimo kiss.

"Ugh, cut it out. Unhand my brother, you jezebel!" Jason joked as his cellphone rang.

"Yezzir, aigh't we coming. Yeah, she cooked. Aight, one. Loverboy, let's roll, Jamal's pulling up now."

"Gimme a kiss, call you in a few," O'Neil said as he kissed Krystal and stood up to head downstairs to meet Jamal.

About an hour later, Jamal walks into Sheena's apartment.

"Yo, Sheena! Where's my plate at, woman?"

"Is this Groundhog Day?" Krystal asked Sheena in disbelief.

"See what I deal with all the damn time?" Sheena asked as she got up from the couch.

"Coming, gimme a sec!" Sheena called out as she got up from the couch and headed to the kitchen.

"Why my plate not ready? Girl, I've been hustling all morning loading furniture, and you can't even have your boy's plate warm and ready? Girl, you're slacking."

"You and your damn brother are working my last damn nerve!" Sheena said as she walked into the kitchen to fix Jamal's plate.

"Appreciate you! You know I love you!" Jamal said as he walked over and kissed Sheena on the cheek.

"You better show her some appreciation!" Krystal threatened as she walked into the kitchen.

"Ohhh shit! When did you get into town?" Jamal asked, surprised.

"What up, sis? I didn't know you were flying into town," he said as he walked towards Krystal and gave her a loving embrace.

"Hey Mal, how are you?"

"I can't complain, things are wavy and gravy. How about yourself?"

"Everything is awesome, just working and trying to live my best life."

"As you should, queen," he said as he sat down at the kitchen table, tucked a paper towel into the collar of his T-shirt, grabbed a fork and knife in each hand, and banged them on the table while demanding "Feed me, Seymour, feed me now!"

"Unbelievable," Krystal said as she laughed and shook her head.

"You all are assholes, every single one of you."

"I need food! Get in my belly. Feed me, Seymour, feed me now!" Jamal continued yelling as he banged on the table with his fork and knife.

Sheena warmed his plate in the microwave and placed it on the table in front of him.

"Here!" She said, clearly irritated.

"Is it even hot? I don't see no steam She-She. Where's the steam woman?"

"Hmph! You want steam?"

Sheena mumbled under her breath as she went to the kitchen sink, turned on the faucet, and wet the dishrag before wiping down the countertops. As the water continued to run, steam began to rise. Sheena held the dishrag under the steamy water before turning off the faucet. She then twirled the dishrag, so it wrapped around itself multiple times before she held the steamy, soaked dishrag like a slingshot, walked behind Jamal, and quickly snapped the wet, hot dishrag on the back of his neck.

Jamal squealed like a hurt puppy.

"Ahhhh, ouch! What the hell, woman, are you crazy?"

"Was that steamy enough for you? Boy, get your plate and get out! You and your brother, keep it up. I'm gonna kick your ass. Go! Go! Bye."

"I didn't even do nothing, crazy!" Jamal pleaded.
"Damn, you're violent," he said as he hurriedly picked up his plate and rubbed the back of his neck which was stinging.

"Ahhh, damn, that shit hurts."

"No shit fuck face. Go! Out! Bye. You so aggy. Say sorry, Sheena. I won't do it again," she demanded as she held up the dishrag again and snapped it like a slingshot as a reminder.

"Ahhh, sorry! Don't hit me. Sorry, it won't happen again." Jamal yelled as he tried to rush out of the kitchen towards the door to exit as he held his plate.

"Damn girl, chill. I'm leaving. I'm leaving. That shit hurts," he whined as he ran out the door.

"Come back when you have some manners!" Krystal yelled out behind him as she snickered.

"This is my life with these boys! I'm so glad you're here. You see the nonsense I deal with on a daily?"

"You have the patience of a saint," Krystal said as her cellphone rang.

"This is Neil. Hey babe? Okay, we're coming down."

"Are they all set down there?"

"Yes, ma'am. Are you ready for the big reveal?" Krystal asked excitedly.

"Yes, those imbeciles are annoying as hell, but they do phenomenal work. Their business is actually doing really well, I'm so proud of them. Come on, let's go see how they did."

10

KARAOKE

"Whoa! This looks insane!" Sheena shrieked in delight.

"Your parents are going to be absolutely shocked. This doesn't even remotely look like the same space! Un-freaking believable."

"Babe, this is beautiful!" Krystal gushed as she held O'Neil's hand while he walked them around the remodeled space.

"Did you ever doubt us?" The Twins asked in unison.

"Alright, so pay attention to the floors. There's ceramic tiling throughout. We removed the unnecessary wall to open it up." O'Neil said as he continued to lead them through the space. "Check this out."

"Wait! What? Did you build or buy that?" Sheena asked once she saw the bar in the corner.

"We were pressed for time, so that's purchased. But we thought having an entertainment slash living room would be cool. That's called a Belvedere return home bar set. The original color was walnut. We painted it grey."

"Oh my God, this is so sick!" Sheena said while admiring the progress.

"Alright, so the bathroom is definitely on the small side, but that's okay. So, you're looking at a frameless hinged standing shower with glass shelving and polished chrome with the white and grey color scheme. Let's go back out and take a look at the kitchen. The kitchen has everything except a stove. The parents will have to use one of our kitchens if they need a stove. Low ceilings mean no stove, but they will be fine with this setup. So, we got two rooms over there." O'Neil said as he pointed towards the far end.

"Y'all go check it out."

Sheena and Krystal walked back to the living room where O'Neil and The Twins were setting up furniture, packing up their tools, and putting trash in plastic bags.

"Absolutely speechless, babe. Everything is perfect," Krystal said as she approached O'Neil.
He grabbed her around the waist and pulled her toward him.

"Thanks, boo." He said as he gave Krystal a quick kiss on the lips.

"Boys! You did good. This is insane. I never would have imagined it would look this good down here. Y'all are definitely the shit!" Sheena said, still in awe.

"Now that I've seen this space, you all should already know what I want in my dining room, right?"

"The Belvedere Bar." The Twins said simultaneously as they continued to clean up.

"Yep! You got it." Sheena said as she snickered.

"You already know."

"Man, listen, I'm just happy this is finally done. So, you know what we have to do, right?" O'Neil asked with a sly smile on his face.

"Christen the place." The Twins responded jointly.

"Ya know it—party time fellas. Let's get the squad together tonight. Twins bring your ladies. She-She, hit up Keem and Chrissy. Everybody bring a bottle or two to help stock the parental's new bar, aight?"

"Say no more, bro. Your wish is my command." Jamal said as he gathered the trash bags and headed to the door.

"Bro-bro, go take another look around and make sure we didn't miss anything before I put the tools in the truck," Jason said as he pushed the stainless-steel refrigerator into the built-in enclosure and removed the plastic wrapping from the inside shelving.

"We're good, Jay. I appreciate you. We're done in here." O'Neil said as he walked towards Jason and dapped him up.

"I'll see y'all tonight. Come on, babe," he said as he grabbed Krystal's hand and led her to the door leading to the back hallway staircase.

"Hey, what are you two about to go do, make sex? Y'all can do that tonight, damn." Jason yelled out as he faked disgust.

"Boy, leave them alone! Don't worry about the rest of this; I'll get it up," Sheena said as she started to pick up the last of the trash and cardboard in the kitchen.

"Go home, relax, and get ready for tonight. And before you even ask, heck no! I am not cooking."

"Goddamn! If you're this mean at thirty, what's it gonna be like in five or ten years? I'mma pray for you, sis. You so mean, damn! Ohhh, wait! You're menopausing? Sheena, why didn't you tell us? I'm sorry your vagina is broken, but stop being so damn evil."

Jason chuckled, then sang. "Broken poo-say."

Sheena finished shoving all the leftover trash into the garbage bag, then lifted it and swung it around her head, hitting Jason in the back with it.

"Get out! Stop being so aggy you asshole. Get out!" She screamed as she hit him again.

"Owww, stop. Why you keep abusing me?" Jason screamed as he gathered up his toolbox and ran towards the door, yelling. "I forgive you and your dry poo-say!"

"Asshole!" Sheena screamed as Jason slammed the door shut to escape her.

∎

"Sheena, are you dressed?" Krystal yelled out as she walked through Sheena's apartment towards her bedroom.

"Yeah, girl, come in. I'm just trying to throw some makeup on. Ohhhh, you look nice. Check you out."

"Thank you, I tried. Your overprotective bestie keeps telling me I will have a nip slip in this shirt. Dramatic ass negro! I look good." Krystal said as she sucked her teeth.

Sheena laughed.

"Don't listen to him. He sounds like someone's grandfather. That shirt is fire!"
"I know, right?" Krystal asked as she twirled around in a circle and playfully pushed her breasts up.

"Okay, okay, let me stop. You need help with your makeup? You know I have some skills."

"Do your thing then," Sheena said as she sat in her vanity chair to let Krystal apply her makeup.

"So, is Hakeem coming?"

"Of course, he should be here now if he's not already."

"Oh, cool. So, are you two going to move in together?"

"I'm not pressing that issue; things will happen when it's time."

"Understood. Your girl Chrissy still coming?"

"That girl never misses a party, so yes."

"You know she doesn't like me, right? I'll do my best to ignore her little shady comments. But if she crosses the line, all bets are completely off the table. I already gave Neil the same speech. That girl has become too comfortable getting out of pocket with me, I think she feels she can be disrespectful. I'll have to remind her otherwise, if needed. I never start it, but I definitely don't have any qualms finishing it."

"I wouldn't let anything disrespectful go down in my presence. If you feel uncomfortable with something, just pull me to the side and I'll fix it. If I see Chrissy being messy, I'll stop it. I won't let anyone feel uncomfortable, especially in my house. Your family too, and we all will respect you like family."

"Alright, done. Tell me what you think." Krystal said, returning the red lipstick to Sheena's makeup bag.

"Okay, you do have skills. It looks good," Sheena said, looking in the mirror at all angles of her face and puckering her lips.

"I love it. See, this is why you need to be here permanently. But you didn't hear that from me."

"We will see what happens, but right now, it's not happening. Neil and I are okay with our current setup. Just like you and Keem are fine with how things are."

"You have seen firsthand what I have to deal with, with these damn knuckleheads. I need you here! But no pressure. I understand. If it's meant to happen, it will happen, and you will be living upstairs soon enough." Sheena said as she winked at Krystal.

"Cut it out! You're as bad as these negros. Let's go downstairs." Krystal said as she turned to leave the bedroom.

"I'll see you downstairs. I'll go set the food and games up. Take your time."

"See, that's why I need you here! You actually help," Sheena yelled.
"Guilt trips don't work on me!" Krystal yelled back.

■

"Mmmmm, it smells good down here," Sheena said as she walked into the basement apartment.

"Oh wow, you set up everything. You didn't have to do that. I would've helped," she said as she walked towards the aluminum food trays to peek inside.

"Mac and cheese, wings, collards, fried fish. This looks like Slade's."

"Yeah, Neil didn't want anything else. So, drinks, salad, and dessert are in the fridge."

"Is that a cheese plate? Girl, you know these damn Harris boys can't do dairy like that, right?"

"I know, but Neil wanted it, don't ask me why."

"Oh Lord, you may want to hide out at my place once he starts complaining about his damn stomach."

"Ya boyz in da house! Where y'all at?"

"See! They bring chaos, constantly. Damn Twins."

Krystal laughed.

"At least they keep you on your toes."

FOR THE LOVE OF YOU

"I'm a nurse, I'm on my toes damn near twelve hours every shift. I need peace when I get home, girl."

"Wassup ladies, you missed me?" Jason asked as he walked into the kitchen and gave both Sheena and Krystal a kiss on the cheek.

"Let me introduce y'all. This is my homegirl Maritza, and that's her cousin Jennifer. Ladies, this is the fam, Sheena and Krystal. If y'all need anything, ask the women of the house."

"Hi Maritza, we definitely met before, it was a few months ago. You and Jay stopped by Keem's house."

"Oh yeah! She-She, now I remember. How are you, Mami?" She asked as she leaned in for a hug.

"I'm doing well. It's nice to meet you, too, Jennifer. Alright, we plan on having fun tonight. We have karaoke, Uno, Spades, food, drinks, and music. Let's get this party started."

"Si, chica! Let's party." Jennifer said in agreement.

Sheena plugged O'Neil's iHome speaker dock into the kitchen outlet and set his iPod in the dock insert before pressing play. The songs from the album My Beautiful Dark Twisted Fantasy thumped from the speakers.

"Have no fear, Chrissy is here! Are y'all ready to part-tay?" She yelled as she walked through the door.

"Goddamn! This shit is nice. Those bozos did this. Shieeeet, well I'll be damned," she said as she walked into the kitchen with a cardboard box filled with various bottles of liquors and drink mixers.

"Hey Chris!"

"She-She, what it do boo? Look, I came prepared." Chrissy gleefully announced as she placed the box on the kitchen counter.

"Chris, there's only two things you never forget."

"And what's that?" She asked snidely as she started to rummage through her purse.

"Liquor and lip gloss!"

"Ohhhh girl, you're being shady boots, honey!" Chrissy said as she pulled lip gloss from her purse and applied it to her lips.

"Shady like a palm tree. Been in forests less shady than you. Will the real Slim Shady please stand up? Where's my umbrella, it's raining shady bitches tonight."

"Are you finished, or are you done? Do you want to see the bar, or do you want to keep talking?" Sheena asked, her hands on her hips and her neck rolling.

"A bar?! Why didn't you lead with that? And stop standing like that and doing all that extra shit with your neck, looking like a damn chicken head. Cluck, cluck you bird, bring me to my bar," she joked.

"Between the boys and you, I'm so done. Let's go, grab your box."

"Oh shit! This is tight. Oh, tonight, it's on!" Chrissy said excitedly before looking up.

"Wait, who's this? Where these people come from?" She asked with a snarky tone.

"Chrissy, this is Maritza, Jay's homegirl, and that's her cousin Jennifer. And, you already know Krystal."

"Hola, Mami. How you doin'?" Maritza asked pleasantly.

"Hey girl," Chrissy responded dryly.

"Soooo, if you're Jay's friend, you're here for Mal?" Chrissy prodded as she looked in Jennifer's direction.

"Me?" Jennifer asked, confused.

"No, chica, nope. I'm just here with my cousin," she clarified.

Seemingly satisfied with that answer, Chrissy continued to set up the bar by lining up liquor bottles and stacking Solo cups.

"When are you leaving?" she asked Krystal with a pompous tone and cynical smile.

"Never!" Krystal replied with an equally curt tone as she rolled her eyes.

"She-She! Where's my baby at?"

"Keem, we're in here. Hi Boopie," Sheena said lovingly as Hakeem walked into the living room and gave her a long hug and kiss.

"Hi, Love, you look beautiful. I missed you. How was your day?"

"It was cool. I hung out with Krystal and finally got to see this place!"

"It looks good, right?"

"I was shocked!"

"I got some ill before and after photos to add to the website. Have you checked the reviews recently? Man, business is going ham. I'm so proud of them."

"I checked the website today. I see you made a bunch of updates, and it's fire. Oh yeah, I meant to tell you I gave your business card to two people at work. One wants help with building a website, and the other wants some quotes on potential computer work. She said her husband buys a lot of goods in bulk and has some desktops and laptops that need refurbishing. I'm wondering if you're interested in buying some of the inventory."

"Bet, all that sounds cool. I'll be on the lookout, and I'll let you know if they reach out," he said as he kissed her forehead.

"That's why I love you, always looking out. You're so dope. You know, I never met anyone like you except my momma."

"Uh oh, are you sweet-talking me? Nope! What did you do?"

"Me? Nothing. I'm good, I never do anything, Love." He said with a boyish grin.

"The guests of honor have arrived." The Twins announced as they walked into the living room with O'Neil behind them.

"Hey boo," O'Neil said as he hugged Krystal from behind.

"Alright, you degenerates. I whipped up my own twist on a Lemon Drop cocktail. It's vodka and lemon juice because I forgot the lemons, a dash of orange liqueur, and my little spin, some Sprite. The Sprite makes it pop, like there's a dance party in your mouth." Chrissy said as she put Solo cups filled with her Lemon Drop cocktail on top of the bar.

Krystal and Sheena started handing everyone a drink.

"Mmmmm, bueno. This is good, Mami."

"When it comes to making drinks, Chris don't miss," Jamal said as he playfully winked at Jennifer.

Chrissy became visibly annoyed but continued to make everyone's second drink.

"I'm starving, let's eat," Jamal suggested as he rubbed his stomach.

"Y'all know Chrissy pours heavy, we all gonna be fucked up in a few minutes if we don't eat. Jen-Jen, we don't let our people drink and drive, so you can always crash with me here if you need to," he said, purposely flirting.

"This motherfucker." Chrissy mumbled as she sucked her teeth and finished her second drink and started making her third.

"Okay, food is ready, let's all say grace before we eat and have fun, is that okay?" Krystal asked as they all started to walk towards the kitchen.

"Oh, here we go with this shit. Ain't nobody got time for all that. Let people eat the damn food, weirdo." Chrissy mumbled loud enough for others to hear.

"Awww shit, Chrissy on that rah-rah steez tonight."

"I'm just going to ignore that. I'm not contributing to any bad vibes in this new space."

"Blessed are you, God of all creation. Thank you for the food before us, the family and friends beside us, and the love between us. Lord, protect us from those with evil in their hearts, protect us all from the hands of the wicked. And give me the strength not to choke that chick out tonight. Amen."

Chuckles could be heard around the kitchen.

"Let's eat," Krystal said as she passed plates to everyone.

Sheena began removing the foil from the pans.

"Don't let her get to you, that's misdirected anger, she's annoyed because Mal keeps giving Jennifer the googly eyes," Sheena whispered to Krystal.

"Stop making excuses for her, she's mean and nasty for no reason. I'm ignoring her, but she won't get too many more chances to disrespect me."

"I get it, let's just enjoy the night. I'm trying to convince you to stay, not run you off."

"She-She, I love you. I just can't stand your friend. And I'm using the word friend very loosely here."

"Ladies, the food was delicious! Come on, now let's do karaoke." Maritza said with exhilaration as she grabbed both Sheena's and Krystal's hands and led them back to the living room.

 Once in the living room, everyone started to feel the effects of their second and third Lemon Drops.

"Aight, ladies, we do karaoke a little differently. You gotta make up your own lyrics but you gotta make sure you do this shit right and make it funny. Ya heard?" Jamal teased as he watched Jennifer scurry to the front of the karaoke machine.

"Aye, Papi. I got it. Maritza, look," Jennifer yelled as she bent over and pointed to her butt.

"Lo entiendes?"

"Si, chica," Maritza said while laughing.

Jennifer held the microphone, waiting for the music to begin and the lyrics to flash across the flat screen television. The song title of the music selection flashed on the screen.

Bidi Bidi Bom Bom by Selena.

"Aye, mi amor, that's my song!" Maritza announced as she jumped out of her seat and stood with Jennifer, who was holding the microphone.

The music started, and they both began to sing their newly created song.

"Culo culo bang bang."
"Culo culo bang bang."
"Culo Culo Culo bang bang."
"Culo culo Culo bang bang."
Then Jennifer started to roll her body seductively as she sang out while looking at Jamal.

"Esta noche."
"Esta noche, cuando vi a Mal."
"Mi vagina se volvio loca."
"Y empiezo a gotear."

Once the song concluded, The Twins stood up and gave a dramatic standing ovation.

"Good God almighty. I need to know what that song is about. I think it's my new favorite song, ain't that right, Jay?" He asked while tapping his hand on his brother's shoulder.

Jennifer chuckled and stumbled closer to Jamal.

"Basically, she's saying every time I see you, my heart goes crazy. But my version said tonight Mal makes my vagina go crazy," she said while winking.

"Mmm, I think I like that. How does it go crazy? Show me again." Jamal said as he licked his lips.

"Oh, Papi," Jennifer said, pushing him back onto the couch and straddling him.

"Mira, mi amor. Culo culo bang bang," she sang, shaking her breasts in his face. Then, she threw her head back and laughed.

 O'Neil, Jason, and Hakeem looked over to Chrissy simultaneously.

Jason whispered. "Shorty must have a death wish. Chrissy is definitely gonna go WWE SmackDown before the night ends."

Chrissy was still at the bar, making drinks and looking enraged.

"Damn Chris, what number drink you on?" Jamal asked out of curiosity, knowing she appeared close to her limit.

Chrissy rolled her eyes and stuck up her middle finger.

"Aight, I pick the next song," O'Neil said as he got up and gave Krystal his plate of macaroni and cheese to hold.

"I'm going to need my background dancers for this one," O'Neil said as he selected his song before the beat dropped.

Krystal shouted. "Go ahead, baby, do your thing!"

"I'm just a young man."
"I'm looking for my baby."

"Awwww shit!" Hakeem yelled as he stood up and ran behind O'Neil.

The Twins got up and followed, and they all began to sing their rendition of the chorus while gyrating and pulling up their shirts.

"If you're my home girl, let's do it."
"Ride it, my pogo."

Jamal began to walk towards Jennifer while he moved side to side and began to thrust his hips and crotch in front of Jennifer's face.

"Si, papa, si! Yesss, show me what you're working with!"

Jennifer drunkenly cheered him on as she swayed side to side on the couch, her arms up in the air.

Chrissy huffed as she rushed from behind the bar. She stopped at Jamal and shoved him out of the way as she walked to the kitchen. Jamal stumbled and then caught his footing, chuckling and shaking his head. Jennifer was too busy swaying from side to side, her eyes half closed, and singing along to notice Chrissy's behavior.

Sheena got up and followed Chrissy into the kitchen.

"Hey girl. Are you good? What's up?" She asked as she noticed Chrissy was visibly intoxicated.

"Super good, damn good, hella good, living the muthafuckin dream." She slurred as she picked up the serving spoon from the tray of macaroni and cheese and began to eat from it.

"Cut it out," Sheena demanded as she removed the serving spoon from her mouth and put it in the sink.

I'll get you something to eat. Sit down and relax," she said as she began to fix her plate and replaced her Solo cup with a bottle of water.

"Here, do you need anything else?"

Chrissy shook her head no, shoved food into her mouth, and waved Sheena off.

"I'm good. Go."

"Stay on your best behavior tonight, please." Sheena urged before returning to the living room.

Everyone was sitting around, talking, laughing, and enjoying each other's company.

Sheena walked over to Hakeem.

"Hey, Love, let me guess, she's in there spiraling?"

Sheena sighed.

"She's fine. I took her drink away. She's in there eating. Hopefully, she will pull it together and not get belligerent tonight. I'm not in the mood to babysit."

"Don't worry about her; she'll be fine. Come here," he said, pulling Sheena close and turning her around. Standing behind her, he started to kiss her on the neck and held her waist.

"Okay, okay. My turn." Krystal announced as she giggled, stumbled to the karaoke machine, and searched for her song.

"This song is dedicated to my boo thang! Hi Boo." She playfully waved to O'Neil.

"You ready?"

"I'm always ready. Show 'em what you're working with, girl. But don't hurt 'em."

The music began to play, and Krystal began to sing.

"Must not have been paying your light bill."
"I stepped right on in the darkness."
"Didn't even notice how dark it was . . ."

"Girl, you can sing! You've been keeping secrets?" Sheena asked, pleasantly surprised while laughing at her made-up lyrics.

"Sing, Mami, sing," Jennifer and Maritza encouraged as they tried to sing along, and Krystal continued to belt out her soulful, flawless notes.

"Now I've got bugs all over me."
"Baby, these bugs touch every part of me."

Hakeem danced with Sheena and twirled her around as Krystal playfully sang her heart out to O'Neil, who sat admiring Krystal. Jamal and Jennifer were busy clumsily two-stepping with each other as Jason and Maritza looked on while clapping and encouraging Krystal to keep singing. Chrissy walked into the living room with her arms folded across her chest, stone-faced as she rolled her eyes at everyone.

Once the song finished, Krystal sat next to O'Neil, kissing him. Everyone applauded as Chrissy continued to shoot daggers at Jamal and Jennifer.

"Enough of this whack shit!" Chrissy said as she went to the karaoke machine and searched for a new song.

"And I do mean whack!"

Chrissy focused her attention on Krystal.

"We ain't at church, right?"

The intro to the song started to play.

"All you ladies pop your puss. . ."

"Whoa, whoa! Ain't nobody trying to watch you pop nothing up in here." O'Neil interrupted as Chrissy was bending over and popping her booty in the air.

"Do it now."

"Lick it good, suck this puss . . ."

"Aww, come on now, turn it off!" O'Neil yelled.

"Ain't nobody trying to watch you get freaky!" He said as he walked over and changed the song.

"Hater! You know you want to see all of this, you all do." She slurred as she pointed to all the boys.

"Fine, you lames don't want to see me drop it like it's hot? Since y'all want to act like some old heads, what y'all think about this?" She asked as she selected another song while smirking.

The song began to play, and Chrissy's contemptuous smile grew more diabolical as she started her sultry dance, purposely trying to entice as she sauntered towards Hakeem and Sheena, singing.

"Yes, I've stolen a boyfriend."
"But I always bring them back."
"If it's not me, it would be someone else."
"Ain't my fault, they give it away."

Chrissy then walked towards O'Neil and Krystal, kneeling between O'Neil's legs, still singing.

"As we play, girl, we forgot all about you as we play."
"As we played, I didn't think about you as we played."

She continued as she began to rub his thigh as O'Neil kept trying to push her off. Krystal stood up abruptly and turned the music off.

"You're taking it too far now. Get your ass up and keep your hands to yourself."

Chrissy laughed.

"Chill out! So that means you don't want to share?" She asked as she licked her lips and stood to her feet.

"You're way too uptight. Neil must not be fucking you right."

"Chrissy, why do you always have to mess up a good time? Chill the fuck out. Your problem is not with my girl, so I suggest you tread lightly. You're pissing me off now!" O'Neil said, clearly upset.

"Babe, that's okay. I got this." Krystal reassured him.

"Chrissy, let's get some things clear once and for all. Just because I respect my man and Sheena does not mean I respect you. You may think that just because you have gotten away with your rude comments and bad behavior, I'm someone you can walk all over. Sweetheart, that is far from the actual truth. I tolerate you out of love and respect for my man and his best friend. You may have them fooled, but I see right through you, baby girl. Your soul is ugly, you take, but you never have anything of value to give, you're self-centered, resentful, insecure, and spiteful."

"Sweetheart, no matter how much makeup you put on, how nice your hair is laid, how many designer names drape your body or how many horny and stupid men fall for your broken spirit, you will never feel whole. Ya know, I said a prayer for you last night, and a message kept playing back in my mind almost on repeat. Chrissy, we will all have to answer for our sins, there's no question about that. But you, you Chrissy, you will see the greatest downfall. I suggest you repent and get right now before it's too late. And one more thing…" Krystal said as she walked up to Chrissy and stood face to face with her.

"If you ever disrespect me, my man or anyone else in my presence, I will fuck you up and that's on my life, you hear me?"

O'Neil rushed to Krystal's side, leading her away from Chrissy to prevent fisticuffs.

Chrissy let out a nervous laugh.

"Damn girl, you can't take a little jokey joke? My bad, I thought we were cool. But you over here walking around with a mouthful of scriptures and a heart full of hate, so how am I the only sinful heathen here, huh?" She asked as she continued laughing nervously.

"Chrissy, I'm not entertaining your B.S. anymore, but I'm going to end this useless interaction with one question for you. People inspire you or destroy you. Which person are you?"

Krystal looked over to Sheena and Hakeem.
"Word of advice. Pick and choose your people wisely. That goes for all of you."

She then pointed to O'Neil and The Twins before leaving the basement.

"Damn! Why ya' girl being so sensitive? I was just playing Neil. You know I didn't mean nothing by it. Tell her she's gonna need thicker skin if she wants to hang with this crew."

"Never. Chrissy you're too disrespectful, you get too drunk and act like an asshole. I'm sick of your bullshit. Get your shit together and don't ever disrespect my girl again. You disrespecting my girl is the same as disrespecting me. And in my book, disrespect will permanently shut doors that apologies can't reopen. Remember that."

"Come on, it wasn't even like that. Stop being so uptight, my bad, Neil." Chrissy attempted to backpedal.

"Aight y'all. I'm out, party's over. Ladies, thanks for coming, we enjoyed your company. Get home safe." O'Neil said as he looked at Maritza and Jennifer.

Maritza and Jennifer began to gather their belongings.

"Thank you, we had a fun time," Maritza said as they approached the door.

"Gracias, amigos. Thanks for the invite." Jennifer added as they exited.
"I'm calling it a night. My stomach doesn't feel right." O'Neil said as he held his side.

"Go get some rest. I'll clean up down here. Don't worry about it." Sheena reassured O'Neil as she cleaned up.

"We told you not to eat that mac and cheese. You're so hardheaded," she scolded him as he began to walk upstairs.

"You knuckleheads go make your plates before you leave."

"Already done." The Twins announced as they walked out of the kitchen with a pan of food each.

"You two are so greedy! Did you leave anything for us?" Chrissy asked, annoyed.

"Nope, you mad?" Jason taunted as he walked towards Sheena and kissed her.

"She-She, goodnight. See you later. Let's go, bro."

"Coming. Love you, She-She. See you later." Jamal said as he leaned in and hugged her.

"Keem, work out tomorrow, be ready."

"Night, Twins, love you," Sheena responded.

"Wow! So, I'm not standing here, I get no love?"

"Girl, you're on punishment for acting up tonight. So, cool your jets and relax." Jamal said as he walked out, annoyed.

"Can I get a ride home?" Chrissy yelled out after him.

"Hell no!" Jamal yelled back as he slammed the door.

"Since when did all of y'all become pansies? Sensitive asses, softer than some damn Charmin. Are y'all serious?" Chrissy asked, pretending to be confused.

"Chris, it's late. I don't feel like rehashing what happened tonight. Just let it go. You offended people, you were wrong, so you need to make it right," Sheena said as she continued cleaning.

"Take the rest of this food home, it's going to just get trashed if you don't."

"Well, I need a ride, shit!" Chrissy said curtly as she began to pack up the remaining food and a bottle of gin.

"Keem, can you do me a favor and drive her home? I need to finish cleaning down here, and I'm tired."

Hakeem sighed and sucked his teeth.

"Ugh, come on, girl, hurry up. And don't be getting on my nerves either."

"Ohhh, come on! Be nice." Chrissy said sweetly.
"I'm on my best behavior."

"I'll be back, Love," Hakeem said as he kissed Sheena on the forehead.

"Let's go, blockhead! And don't even try cracking that bottle open in my car either."
"Sir, yes sir!" Chrissy said sarcastically as she saluted.

"Any other demands, Captain Killjoy?"

"Girl, bring you narrow ass on," Hakeem demanded while growing impatient and walking out the door.

"Wait for me! She-She, I'll talk to you tomorrow. Don't be mad at me, too. You know I was just playing. You know how I am. I love you. Let me get outta here before your man leaves me stranded, " she yelled as she rushed out the door.

11

INTROSPECTIVE

Sheena became emotional, and her eyes became misty.

"Wow, Doc, I just realized that was the last time we were all together, carefree and unaware of how things were about to change." She sighed, and a tear fell from her eye as she crossed her hands over her belly.

"What I would give to go back to that night, to be blissfully unaware, was a gift. None of us would have ever imagined what was to come."

Dr. Angel stopped taking notes and looked at Sheena.

"Life is unpredictable and at times unexplainable. We cannot control the unexpected, and I know that can be very hard for so many of us, Deary. But this is something that you will always grieve. And that's okay, just remember you don't have to work through these things alone, you've become stronger and more resilient, and you have self-awareness, you know when you need to reach out for help if you need it."

"Dr. Angel, just watching the person I cared about the most be ripped away from me, I never want to feel that pain again. I can't do that again, I just can't. I know I can't!"

Sheena cried out as the memories began to flood back to her.

"Sheena, dear, I understand it can feel like a rollercoaster of emotions, but what you feel is normal. Allow yourself to feel, express, and acknowledge your feelings and needs. Communicate; don't shut down. Talk to your loved ones. If you need more support, you will have the contact information of a few of my trusted colleagues, and you can always reach out to me if needed. You are not alone, Dear."

"I know, but just thinking about that time is difficult. It just keeps replaying in my mind, and I try to see where I failed him and what I could have done differently so I could have changed the outcome. I'm a nurse for fucks sake, how did I miss it, how did I miss all the signs? How could I be so fucking stupid? With him, of all people, the person that never complains about anything."

Sheena cried as Dr. Angel let her express her frustrations and sorrow.

■

"She-She, what you got going on today?" O'Neil asked, walking into her living room as she lounged on her couch watching reruns of Martin.

"I picked up an extra shift today, 3 to 11 tonight. Other than that, I'm laying on this couch and being lazy. Why, what's up?"

"Not much, me and the crew are about to hit the gym in about an hour, wanna roll?"

"I'll pass; today's my lazy day."

"Keep skipping gym day, those hips are going to be as wide as that flat screen you're watching," O'Neil joked.

"That means I'll have more ass for you to kiss. Boy, don't play with me!"

"I'll leave all that ass kissing for Keem, move your feet," he said as he swatted Sheena's feet off the couch so he could sit.

"Excuse you, don't you have your own couch?"

"I came up here for some prunes. You got some prunes or prune juice?"
Sheena chuckled.

"When have you ever seen me with prune anything? Why do you need prunes, you need to poo?"

"Oh my God! Yes, it's been like three days. Look at this, I'm all bloated." He said as he rubbed his belly.

"Ha! I always knew you were full of shit." Sheena taunted as she got up from the couch and walked out of the living room.

"Here, take that," she said, handing him two laxative tablets, a bottle of water, and two bananas.

"Good looking out."

"You might want to rethink the gym or bring a change of clothes. Mess around, and take a squat, and leave something behind. Once that laxative gets you going, you'll have three-days worth of poop sliding on out."

"It's leg day too! I'm not skipping that, shoooot, clean up on aisle three, bay-bee. I'm going to the gym. You know what's better than a Shitty McShitster?"

"Dare I ask?" She said as she rolled her eyes.

"What?"

"A brolic Shitty McShitster with buns of steel. Trust me, nothing is escaping these tight cheeks unless I want it to. I'm good." O'Neil stood in front of Sheena and pulled down one side of his sweatpants. "Look, look at that," he said as he slapped his right buttock.

"Buns of steel, you can bounce a quarter off these cheeks."

"If you don't sit your narrow tail down. Move out of the way! I'm supposed to be having a relaxing morning, not deal with your obnoxious crap."

Sheena pushed O'Neil's exposed buttocks away with her foot.

"Move!"

O'Neil sat back down on the couch.

"What's up with Chrissy? I haven't seen her wild ass in like two weeks. Is she good?"

"I talked to her last night. She's fine. She'll be over this weekend." Sheena said as she started looking for something new to watch on TV.

"Yay! Beaches. I love this movie," she said excitedly.

"Chick flick?"

"Come on, stay. Watch it with me, please," she whined as O'Neil sank into the couch to get comfortable, and Sheena laid her feet across his lap.
"Quit your bellyaching and turn the volume up."

"It's a good movie, I promise," Sheena said excitedly as she turned up the volume and got comfortable.

"Ugh, this part always gets me. I love this song." Sheena sniffled as she sang along to "Wind Beneath My Wings."

"Are you crying?" O'Neil asked flummoxed.

"What in the heck?"

"Come on! You didn't find this sad as hell? Could you imagine losing your best friend of thirty-plus years? Could you imagine losing me? It's a tearjerker and you know it is," she said as she playfully kicked him. "Stop pretending that you don't have emotions."

"I have emotions, but I think I see things a little differently than you. Yeah, losing people you love is hard, sad, and can be tough. But how I see it, death is part of life. If I can accept life, I must also accept death. I believe we all have a purpose, and when a person is tapped into their spirituality and the understanding that we are all here for something greater than our own self, death can never be feared or sad. I understand it's sad for those left behind but when my time is up in this realm, I hope everyone I love and those that may have met me can say I was compassionate, empathetic, a protector, honest, had integrity, was loving, wise, considerate, helpful and did something no matter how big or small that had a positive impact on their life. If that can be said about me when that last grain of sand runs out of my hourglass, that means I lived a full life filled with purpose and intention. And I find no sadness in that. It's a life well lived, no matter the duration." He said with a satisfied smile.

As the credits continued to roll, tears continued down Sheena's face.

"I swear, you've always been so introspective and insightful, even when we were kids. Sometimes you just have this ability to find beauty and solace in the most difficult situations, and I'm always in awe. How do you do it? Teach me your ways, teach me!" Sheena chuckled as she wiped away her tears.

"I've been tryna teach your blockhead ass since the fourth grade, girl! I'm yo daddy! Say it with me, come on. Teach. Me. Daddy."

"Don't make me kick you in your bloated gut. Cut it out. Matter of fact, how can a man that can't take a poop teach me anything? You're full of shit, literally and figuratively."

"Damn She-She, that's a low blow. I come down here sharing my innermost secrets with you, and this is how you gonna do me? I'll be sure to use your bathroom when these shit tablets start working."

"Oh yeah? Well, I'm PMS'ing bad, I think it's time for a tampon change. You don't mind if I use your bathroom, right? You know I love your toilet; it hugs my buns just right."

"Ewwww, why you gotta take it that far? Stop hanging with

Chrissy. If you're wearing a lady diaper, you're not allowed in my domicile."

"A lady diaper? You fool! God, you act just like The Twins, ya'll need to be called the triplets."

Sheena laughed. "I can't stand you. Go home, psycho!"

"You're lucky, I hear Mal's loud ass music now, let me go. I'll see you later," he said as he got up from the couch, threw a decorative pillow at Sheena, and began to walk out of the living room, looking back at her with a pensive gaze before speaking.

"Sheena, you think we're gonna be friends for life?"

"Friends for life? No, not at all. We're family. You're my family for life, and I love you to pieces, you weirdo."

"Just checking, you passed. Carry on," he said as he walked to the kitchen door leading to the back hall, yelling, "I love you too!"

12

O'NEIL "MOTHER FUCKING" HARRIS

"Hey, you. You eat yet?"

"Nah, not yet. Whatchu cook?"

"Cajun salmon, rice, beans, and broccoli. Come down." Sheena instructed as she tapped the end button on her cellphone.

A few minutes later, O'Neil opened the back door that led into Sheena's kitchen.

"Hey She-She," O'Neil said breathlessly as he sat at the kitchen table.
"What were you doing down there, running? Why are you out of breath?"

"You see this, right? I went to my doctor like two months ago. He said everything was fine, probably allergies. It keeps happening off and on, then I'm fine."

"Are you experiencing any type of discomfort? Do you notice it happening during certain activities?" Sheena asked as she began to prepare his plate.

"Nah, it doesn't hurt. The few times it happened, I was at the gym, or I was walking the steps, or to the car, nothing strenuous. And see, now I'm starting to feel fine," he said as he began to eat.

Sheena sat down with him as they both enjoyed dinner.

"I talked to Krystal earlier today, and she said she might be coming down next week. She said she wants to plan a couple's vacation. That sounds fun."

Sheena got up from the table, walked to her guest room, returned to the kitchen with her medical bag, and placed it on the kitchen table.

"What's this for?"

"Just checking you out, the unexplained shortness of breath has piqued my interest. I'm just going to check you out. Is that okay?"
"Uh oh, Nurse Ratchet is about to pull out her bag of tricks on me. Wait, I was nice to you today! If you have anything sharp

in that bag, remember, I was so nice to you today."

"Shhh," Sheena instructed as she inserted her stethoscope in her ears and listened to O'Neil's breathing.

"Deep breath in. Good. Now, let it out."

Sheena moved the stethoscope around his chest.

"Okay, everything sounds good and clear. Put this on your finger." She said as she clipped the pulse oximeter on his index finger.

"What's this for?"

"Measures the oxygen saturation level, essentially how much oxygen is in your blood. And your level is perfect, 98%. Alright, rest this under your tongue for me. No talking once it's in," she said as she placed the thermometer in his mouth and proceeded with her examination, starting with feeling for lymph nodes around his neck as the thermometer began to beep.

"Okay, let me see. 98.4 degrees. Perfect. There is no temperature, so there is no infection. That's good."

Sheena pulled out her penlight.

"Alright, I'm going to check your pupillary response as well as your throat, eyes, and ears, okay?"

"Do your thing, Nurse."

"Okay, everything looks good, no concerns. Did they do this exam when you went to your doctor last time?"

"It was a quick visit. They listened to my breathing and put the clip thingy on my finger."

"Hmm, okay. It's time for a new PCP. How's your stomach been doing? Have there been any changes in bowel movements or appearance?" She asked, placing the stethoscope back around her neck.

"It keeps hurting off and on, especially on this side," he said, pointing to the lower right side of his stomach.

"Alright, let me listen to it." She said as she started to put the stethoscope back in her ears.

"I had diarrhea this morning, now my stomach is all bloated again and hard as a rock."

"Hard? Okay, let me listen." Sheena said as she placed the stethoscope's diaphragm in the center of O'Neil's stomach.

She immediately stopped and looked up in distress.

"O'Neil, how long has it been like this?"

The sense of urgency was undeniable in her voice.

"About two or three days."

"Get your stuff, we need to go to the E.R. now!"

■

Sheena and O'Neil sat in the waiting room of the Hematology-Oncology unit at Massachusetts General Hospital, anxiously waiting for O'Neil to be called for his 10 a.m. appointment.

"You doing okay?" She asked as she reached over and grabbed his hand.

"I'm okay. You?" O'Neil asked as he gently squeezed her hand.

"Of course," she replied as worry dripped from each word.

"Stop worrying, She-She. It'll be fine," he said with a half-smile.

"I just need to hurry up and get the okay to get back in the gym. You know a brother's not trying to lose his sexy muscle definition," he said as he held his arm up, attempting to flex his bicep.

Sheena rolled her eyes.

"Ohhhh God. You are soooooo conceited. How about you just chill out, relax, and focus on your healing. You just had surgery two minutes ago. Rushing your recovery too soon can slow down your progress."

O'Neil began to mock her as she spoke.

"Boy, don't make me punch you!"

O'Neil gasped dramatically as he playfully clutched his chest.

"But I'm disabled. Would you really hurt the wounded and infirm?" He asked melodramatically.

"Boy, I will beat you so hard, I'll beat you till your flaccid."

"Wait, what? Ha, ha, ha! Whattttt? You'll beat me, what?" O'Neil asked as he laughed uncontrollably.

"Who says that? Whew, damn girl. Don't make me laugh too hard, ooowww," he said as he grabbed his side.

"Stop making fun of me," Sheena whined.

"Aww, did I hurt the whittle baby's feelings? Fine, you can beat me flaccid. But you'll have to ask Krystal's permission first and bring the good lube too, not that cheap stuff."

"Keep playing with me, you must want to walk home."

"Empty threats," he said smugly.

"I just noticed, what the heck is up with all these damn flower arrangements? Good God! I feel like we're waiting in the Upper Room, Upper Room." O'Neil sang.

"Shhhhhh, you're so embarrassing." Sheena chuckled.

"They did go overboard, though," she agreed.

"Are they all real?" O'Neil leaned over and touched the flowers on the small end table between the row of chairs.

"Okay, Mama Jodi, stop touching stuff."

O'Neil started laughing.

"Awww damn! I am my mama's child. Remember that stunt she pulled at the lawyer's office?" O'Neil laughed and shook his head.

"Yep! Sure do. Pollen and petals everywhere while she's trying to dust the evidence off her hands and clothes."

Sheena giggled as she reminisced.

"Sniffing and sneezing like she just did a line of that premium stuff, talking about, what did I do? That woman is a mess. Always into something, just like a little kid," he snickered.

"Mr. Harris." The medical assistant called into the waiting room.

Sheena stood up and grabbed both their belongings.

"You got it?" Sheena asked as O'Neil slowly rose from his seat.

"I'm good, let's go."

"Good morning. Sorry for the delay. Follow me, and I'll take you to room 143 to take your vitals. Alright, you're all set. Just sit tight, and Dr. Zac will be in shortly," she said as she exited the exam room and closed the door.

A few minutes later, there was a knock on the door before it opened.

"Good morning, Mr. Harris. I'm Dr. Zak," he said before shaking O'Neil's hand.

"Nice to see you again. I'm not sure if you remember, but I met you while you were an inpatient after your surgery."

"Nice to see you again, Doc."

"Nurse Williams, it's nice to see you again. Okay, Mr. Harris, take a seat on the exam table. I want to peek at the surgery site to ensure things are healing properly, and then we will go over the scans and other testing."

O'Neil slowly rose from his seat, stepped up, laid on the exam table, and lifted his shirt.

"Okay, nice. Healing looks great. How does this feel when I press?"

"A little sore, but not too bad."

"It looks just how I want it to. Please keep doing what you're doing; it's healing perfectly. I'm sure having your own personal at-home nurse helps. Great job, Nurse Williams," he said, smiling warmly at Sheena.

"I see you over there making googly eyes at Nurse Ratchet."

Dr. Zak laughed.

"What you witnessed was a professional smile of approval. I've worked with Nurse Williams in the E.R. on multiple occasions, and she's an amazing nurse who did an excellent job with your post-op wound care."

"Dr. Z, pay no attention to this one; he lacks social etiquette."

"Duly noted. Glad to see he has a good sense of humor. Okay, Mr. Harris, feel free to take a seat, and we can discuss the scans and additional test results."

Dr. Zac began typing on the computer and then turned the monitor toward O'Neil and Sheena.

"So, you're both looking at the MRI before and after surgery. Right here, you see this. That was the tumor that was near your appendix area, as you know, we were able to remove the entire malignant tumor. Now look here at the after scan. You see, the mass is gone, which is fantastic. However, we've identified an additional issue."
Dr. Zac paused and looked at both O'Neil and Sheena as he leaned back in his chair and crossed his legs.

"Just give it to me straight, don't sugarcoat anything. What are we looking at?" O'Neil asked bluntly as his body stiffened.

Dr. Zac continued with a subdued tone.

"Although we were successful in removing the mass, unfortunately, cancer cells have been found in your stomach. There are cancer cell deposits found in these areas." Dr. Zac said as he traced the areas with his pen across the image of the scan.

An inadvertent gasp escaped Sheena as she tried to quickly reel in her emotions to appear strong for O'Neil. Sheena grabbed his hand and held it tightly. O'Neil looked over to Sheena, whose eyes were misty.

"It's okay, I'm okay. It will be okay. So, Doc, what's the next step to fixing this?"

"Chemo, we want to destroy the cancer cell deposits in your stomach to prevent potential metastasis. Four to six rounds of Chemo over three to four months to see how the cells respond."

"When do I start?"

"We can start your chemotherapy treatment in about two weeks."

Dr. Zac continued to discuss the treatment plan, side effects, duration, survival rates, etc., as Sheena clung to O'Neil, drowning out everything in the room except O'Neil.

"Do you have any questions or concerns? I know this isn't the news you expected or wanted to hear."

"No, no questions right now. Just ready to start treatment and get this over with so I can get back to the gym and living life."

"I understand. We all want that for you. So, if you have no questions now, I'll have my nurse come in and set up your treatment schedule. As always, if any questions or concerns arise, don't hesitate to reach out. I want to assure you that we share your same goal, getting you back to your healthy life." Dr. Zac said as he exited the exam room.

Sheena continued to sit in silence as she clutched O'Neil's hand. He looked at her before wrapping his arm around her neck.

"Don't worry, stop worrying. It's gonna be okay. Look at me," he said sternly.

Sheena looked into his eyes, and two tears fell down her face. She stared at him in complete silence, concerned.

"Quit these tears," he said, gently wiping her tears away.

"I'm strong, I'm in good shape, I have faith. The odds are in my favor. I'm going to be okay. Whatever happens, it's okay. Okay?" He asked with a reassuring smile.

Sheena gathered her emotions together before beaming with a huge smile.

"Of course it is, because you're O'Neil Motherfucking Harris! You got this, and I got this with you. I love you so much," she said as she leaned over and hugged him.

"You are absolutely my favorite person," she said as she kissed his cheek. "Don't you ever forget it."

13

HOURGLASS

Sheena slowly pushed O'Neil up to the check-in desk in the Hematology-Oncology unit.

"Hello, checking in O'Neil Harris to see Dr. Zak."

"Good morning. Dr. Zak is running about fifteen minutes late. Have there been any changes in insurance, address, or primary care physician?"

"No, no changes."

"Okay, have a seat. The medical assistant will be with you shortly."

"Thank you," Sheena said as she began to push O'Neil to the farthest side of the waiting room, away from the other patients.

"I don't feel good," O'Neil said with a strained whisper as he struggled to keep his head up.

"You feel like you're going to vomit?"

"Yeah."

"Hold on, let me get you something," Sheena said as she rushed toward the reception desk. Then, she ran back to O'Neil with a plastic emesis basin, placing it under his chin as he began to heave and vomit his vanilla Ensure, which he had tried drinking earlier in the morning.

Sheena dug in her bag, pulled out a baby wipe, and cleaned O'Neil's face. A medical assistant walked over and offered to dispose of the soiled basin.

"Someone will be out now to bring him to a room. Do you need anything else?"

"No, we're fine for now. Thank you," Sheena responded as she sat next to O'Neil and held his hand.

O'Neil was riddled with exhaustion. He placed his head onto Sheena's shoulder. Sheena pulled his thin and frail hand up to her lips and gently kissed the back of his hand.

"I love you; I got you," she said, fighting back tears and trying to remain strong.

The medical assistant walked over.

"I'll bring you to a room now," she said as she walked behind O'Neil's wheelchair and began to push him towards the hallway leading to the exam rooms.

"Thank you, I'll follow," Sheena said as she quickly gathered her and O'Neil's belongings.

"Dr. Zak will be in shortly; do you need anything before I go?"

"No, thank you. We're all set."

"Knock, knock."

Dr. Zak opened the door to the exam room.

"Hello, Mr. Harris and Nurse Williams. It's nice to see you both today," he said as he walked in and took a seat.

O'Neil was slumped over and resting his head on Sheena's shoulder as she held his hand tightly.

"Mr. Harris, I understand that you're not feeling well today. From your labs, I can see that you are very dehydrated. Because of that, we will get you some IV fluids today. I'll also go over your scans and other testing."

Dr. Zak sat at the exam room desk and logged onto the desktop.

"How's your food intake?"

"Not well, the past two weeks he hasn't been able to keep much down. For the past three days, he hasn't taken any solid foods. So, at this point, I've been trying my best to get him to drink Ensure, but he's unable to keep that down." Sheena replied with angst.

A look of despondency washed over Dr. Zak's face.

"Mr. Harris, from the moment I met you after your surgery, you asked me to be straightforward with you. And, I have been completely blunt, just as you requested. It's been a long ten months, a very challenging ten months, two different chemotherapies, and from the current scans and testing, unfortunately, the cancer continues to spread. Tumors are pushing on your organs as they continue to grow. At this stage, we've run out of options except for a clinical trial we can apply to."

Sheena let out a muffled yelp. She felt like she was gut-punched with a steel fist, but she tried to maintain her composure as she hurriedly tried to hold her emotions at bay.

"No. Doc, I'm done. No more, take the port out. I can't do this anymore. I want to enjoy my days; I don't want to spend them in the hospital being poked and prodded and sick from the poison called chemo. I tried; we tried. Now, it's time to accept that it's not working."

O'Neil looked over to Sheena with absolution in his weary eyes before continuing.

"She-She, it's time to stop. I can't do this anymore, can't eat, can't sleep. I can't enjoy anything. I'm tired. It's time for me to live the best way I can till that last grain of sand passes through my hourglass," he said as his eyes welled up and he attempted a smile.

Sheena could no longer hold back the tears as she began to sob.

"I know, I know, Neil. It's okay," she said, holding him tightly.

"Dr. Zak, O'Neil, and I discussed his wishes a few months ago when he started the second chemo treatment. Since he's opting to forgo research treatment, he would like to pursue hospice care and remain at home when it's time."

"That's what I want, Doc," O'Neil whispered in agreement as he attempted to hold his head up.

"Absolutely, we can definitely make this happen. First, I'm going to send you to the infusion department so we can get you hydrated. I'll set up the referral for palliative care, and someone will reach out to you by the end of the business day today to finalize everything." Dr. Zak said, his voice beginning to crack.

"Doc, it's okay. You did your best. My family and I appreciate you." O'Neil said as he strained his voice to talk.

"Keep doing what you're doing. This place and the patients need you. You care about the people and the cure; it shows. But the reality is, you can't save us all."

Dr. Zak stood up and approached O'Neil.

"You're a remarkable man, O'Neil. I believe I'm a better doctor and man for having met you. Thank you," he said, reaching out to shake O'Neil's hand.

O'Neil lifted his frail hand and attempted a firm shake.

"Thanks, Doc," O'Neil whispered.

"Alright, let's get you some fluids. I'm sure that will help a little. Okay? I'm still here if you have any questions or need help, okay?"

"We know." Sheena acknowledged.

"We'll let you know if he needs anything or if he changes his mind about the clinical trial option."

"Doc, I won't. Thank you for everything."

Dr. Zak looked into O'Neil's eyes again as a tear fell.

"Enjoy your family and friends, savor every moment of every day, okay?"

"Will do, Doc," O'Neil said as he managed to complete a two-finger salute in Dr. Zak's direction before he exited the exam room.

■

Sheena and O'Neil pulled up to their house.

"How are you feeling now?"

"Better, I'm hungry. Whatchu' cooking?" O'Neil asked as he looked at Sheena as she pulled into the driveway.

"What do you have a taste for?"

"Hmmm, how about Teriyaki salmon and broccoli? Mmmm, that sounds so good," O'Neil said as he closed his eyes and imagined Sheena's cooking.

"Well, today's your lucky day, kiddo. I have all that upstairs."

"Can I go in your place?" O'Neil asked with a serious tone.

"Yeah, we can have dinner at my place."

"No. Can I stay in your place? I want to go with you there. Okay?"

"Of course! Yes, absolutely. You don't even have to ask, absolutely." Sheena said as she held his hand and looked into his eyes before she opened the car door and helped him up the stairs to her apartment.

■

"Dinner's ready," she said, walking O'Neil's plate on a tray into her bedroom where he was resting.

O'Neil turned over and attempted to sit up straight.

"Thank you, She-She," he said, exhibiting more strength than earlier.

Sheena placed the tray in front of him.

"Need help?"

"No, I got it," he said as he picked up his fork and ate small bites.

"Where's yours?"

"I'm getting it, I hear both of our phones blowing up. I'll be back."

Sheena returned to the bedroom with her plate of food, a bottle of Pedialyte under her arm, and two cellphones in the other hand.

"Here," she said, placing O'Neil's cellphone on the serving tray.
"I don't feel like talking to anybody, not right now."

"I have to respond and say something; people are worried. I'll let everyone know that you were dehydrated, got IV fluids, and are feeling a little better. You ate, and now you're resting. You'll check in with everyone tomorrow. Is that okay?"

"Yeah, that's fine," O'Neil sighed as he slumped back into the pillows.

"Here, drink as much as you can tolerate," Sheena instructed as she handed O'Neil a cup of Pedialyte.

Sheena began replying to all the texts she had received since the morning, updating everyone that O'Neil was feeling better and was resting. However, she called his parents to speak with them directly.

"Hey, Pops, you're on speaker. Sorry for not calling you earlier. Hi Mama Jodi," she greeted as she heard Mrs. Harris in the background on speakerphone.

"How's my baby?" Jodi asked with stress in her voice.

"He was extremely dehydrated and couldn't keep food down. He got IV hydration, so we were at the hospital for a few hours. He's feeling a little better and has an appetite. He asked for salmon and broccoli."

Sheena looked at his plate and noticed he had finished most of his dinner.
"So far, he ate about two ounces of salmon and two broccoli florets, which is great considering the past three days. So far, so good. He seems to be tolerating his food right now. He drank a little bit of Pedialyte, and now he's trying to nap. He said he wants to get some rest and plans on talking to everybody tomorrow. But you're on speaker, so he's listening."

"Hey, baby boy, I know you need your rest, but we just want

to tell you how much we love you and that we will see you in a few days. I know you told us not to worry, but we will be there in about two days. So, get your rest, son." Kenny said, trying to hide his concern.

"Love you, baby boy, and we will see you in a few days. Inshallah."

"Father God, we pray that your hands will guide our beautiful baby boy away from this illness, away from pain, and restore his healing. Amen," Jodi prayed as she choked back tears.

"Love you, Ma, love you, Pops. Thank you." O'Neil responded softly.

"See you both in a few days. Allahu Akbar."

"Alright, baby boy. Sheena, please keep us updated and reach out. We don't care what time it is or if he tells you not to worry us. We can be out there sooner than Thursday if needed. Okay?"

"Absolutely. You and your husband will be the first to know if anything changes, I promise," Sheena assured.

"I love you both. See you Thursday."

"Love you both, goodnight," Mr. and Mrs. Harris said before disconnecting the call.

"You look exhausted. Let me get this stuff out of your way," she said, removing the food tray from his lap and returning it to the kitchen.

"You want to use the bathroom before you fall asleep?"

"Yeah, make sure your hands are warm, and you shake it three times," he joked as he slowly tried to move out of the bed.

"Keep it up, I'll throw your ass in a diaper and call it a night. You better stop playing with me," Sheena joked back as she helped him stand and slowly walked him to the bathroom.

"Is this a number one or number two?"

O'Neil rubbed his distended stomach.

"I think I'm working on a number three right now."

"You enjoy torturing me, huh?"

"You know it," O'Neil replied as he half-grinned.

"You need help, or you got it?"

"No, I'm good."

"I'll be back in a few minutes to check on you," Sheena said as she heard her cellphone ringing in the bedroom.

"Hey Keem! I know, I miss you too. He's feeling better now. He just wants to rest. I know, it's tough, he's strong. But he's going to talk to everyone tomorrow after he gets some rest. Stop by tomorrow, let him get some sleep. Okay, love you too, see you tomorrow."

Sheena walked back to the bathroom.

"You okay in there?"

"Yeah, you got lucky. False alarm."

"Lucky me or lucky you? I planned on bringing out the hose and hosing you down before putting you back in my bed!"

"Hardy har-har-har," O'Neil mocked as he held onto Sheena's arm, and they slowly walked back to her bedroom.

"Another blanket." O'Neil requested as Sheena settled him into the bed.

"Are you cold? I'll get the heated blanket," she said, taking the blanket from her closet, plugging it in, and covering O'Neil with it.
"Alright, anything you want to watch?" Sheena asked as she climbed into her California King bed and snuggled up to O'Neil.

"You know you want a chick flick, so go ahead and put one on," he said, looking at Sheena and giving her a dramatic eye roll.

"Don't threaten me with a good time," she giggled as she flipped through the channels on the remote.

"Keem called while you were in the bathroom. They'll all be here tomorrow," she said as her mood grew more despondent.

O'Neil sighed, "I really didn't want to see everyone go through this. I never wanted to disappoint anyone."

"Awww, come on. You could never disappoint any of us. I promise you. It's your life and your decision, and we all know how hard you're fighting to be strong for all of us. But we will all support your decision, no matter how hard it is for us to imagine what's to come. Remember, faith and love are powerful."

"I know what I want to do, I want all my family and friends together for one last gathering, an early Thanksgiving—lots of music, food, spades, everything. I want to be able to thank everyone I love, one last time," he said with a slight smile as he looked over to Sheena.

"She-She, I'm not going to make it to Thanksgiving, so we need to make this happen soon," he said softly as he looked into her forlorn eyes.

"No, I don't accept that. Don't say that, don't!" Sheena pleaded as she shook her head no.

"Please, please don't say that to me," she sobbed.

O'Neil gently grabbed her face and leaned into her before hugging her neck.

"It's okay, I'm going to need you to be strong, please. I'm counting on you; you're the only one I know that will let me do this how I want to do this. Please."

"I know, I know it's going to happen. I just can't say it, I can't. But you know I got you, Neil. I could always count on you, so you don't have to worry. I just can't say the words."

"Friends for life?" O'Neil asked as he wiped away Sheena's tears.

"Hell yeah, you're stuck with me forever and ever." Sheena smiled as she wiped her runny nose with the back of her hand.

"Are you serious?"

"What?" Sheena asked confused.

"I suffer from cancer, not blindness. Soooo, you're just gonna wipe your boogers on your hands and just sit here like I can't see you?"

"Stopppppp! But I'm sad," she said in a baby voice as she batted her eyes and feigned innocence.

"Girl, that shit don't work on me. Go wash your hands, nasty."

Sheena huffed as she hopped out of bed.

"You got some nerve! Better be glad I don't slap you with it," she said playfully, waving her hand in his face before running out of the room.

"Hey, the nurse called. She'll be here tomorrow at 8 a.m. Are you ready to let everyone know tomorrow? I can't keep this from your family after tomorrow."

"Yes, everyone can know tomorrow. And everyone needs to get ready for my Thanksgiving, I want it to be epic," O'Neil said with a slight smile as he nodded off to sleep.

14

INSHALLAH

"You feel comfortable with your nurse?"

"Yeah, she was pretty cool. She had a sense of humor, so she's a keeper."

"Someone will be here soon to deliver the homecare bed. I'll have them set it up in the guest room. I know your energy level is low today, so I'm thinking you should tell everyone at the same time. We can FaceTime your parents, family, and Krystal. What do you think about that?"

O'Neil nodded in agreement.

"Are you hungry now?"

"Eggs, scrambled," he replied as he nodded off.

"Coming right up, your majesty."

"Love it when you talk dirty."

"I see those pain meds are kicking in. You can barely keep your eyes open."

O'Neil slowly opened his eyes and gave a thumbs up before nodding off again as Sheena left the bedroom to make his scrambled eggs.

"Hey, bestie, your lunch is ready," Sheena announced as she walked into the bedroom with scrambled eggs and wheat toast.

"Wake up, you need to eat something," Sheena said gently as she set the tray on the bed.

"Wake up, boopie, wake up," she said as she gently rubbed her knuckles up and down his sternum until he roused from his sleep.

"Here, I got your eggs and some toast."

O'Neil opened his eyes and gave a mischievous grin before opening his mouth wide.

Sheena chuckled.

"Ohhh, so this is what we're doing now? You're forcing me to feed you? Last time I checked, your arms worked."

"Less talk, more action," O'Neil joked as he opened his mouth wide again before taunting, "I'm waiting."

"The nerve, you better be glad I like you today," Sheena joked as she began to feed him tiny morsels of scrambled eggs.

"Mmmm, tastes good."

"Want a piece of your toast?

"No, I'm full."

O'Neil dozed back off to sleep. Sheena picked up the tray and returned to the kitchen to clean up when she heard her text message alerts repeatedly chiming.

"This has to be the knucklehead squad," Sheena said to herself as she picked up her phone and checked her messages.

"Oh, good. They'll all be here before 6 p.m., enough time to clean up," Sheena mumbled as she put the dishes away.

Once Sheena straightened up and cleaned to her satisfaction, she sat on the living room couch and looked at the clock.

"5:15 p.m." She whispered to herself.

"Shoot, I forgot to tell them to bring food."

Sheena picked up her cellphone and texted the group chat.

"Sorry, I forgot to tell you all to bring food. I didn't cook. See you when you get here. Love you."

Hakeem texted back immediately.

"No worries, Love. Took care of it. We'll see y'all in a few minutes. Unlock the door."

Sheena got up, unlocked her front door, and went into her bedroom to check on O'Neil, who was still sleeping. She rubbed his head and kissed him on the cheek.

"Love you." She whispered before readjusting his blanket.

Sheena heard her front door open and all her favorite voices as she walked out of the bedroom towards the kitchen.

"Chrissy don't start no shit tonight. You hear me?" Hakeem demanded as he began to unpack the Styrofoam take-out containers from the paper bags.

"I'm not, I promise," Chrissy whined.

"I just wanna see my bro," Jamal said with concern.

"You and me both." Jason agreed.

"Hey everybody," Sheena greeted with a forced smile.

"I missed y'all," she said as she walked into the kitchen and hugged and kissed everyone.

"I can see it in your face, Love. What's up?" Hakeem asked, giving Sheena another hug and holding her hand.

"I'm okay, y'all eat? I'll go and get Neil," Sheena said as she started to walk towards her bedroom.

"Wait! Sheena, I'm scared," Chrissy blurted out, quickly covering her mouth and becoming tearful.

Sheena turned back around and embraced Chrissy.

"It's okay, Chris. It's okay." Sheena tried to comfort Chrissy without becoming emotional herself.

"Alright, I'll be back. He'll be out in a few minutes, and everybody needs to be in a better mood when he gets out here!" Sheena demanded, attempting to lighten the mood.

"Oh, I almost forgot. Everyone has a job to do. We'll need to FaceTime some people. Twins, get his brother and your cousin on your phones, I'll FaceTime Krystal from Neil's phone and his parents from mines. Hakeem, you get his grandfather on the line, and Chrissy, get his uncle. Okay?"

"Roger that, we're on it." The Twins said in unison as Sheena walked towards her bedroom.

"Hey, you, you up?" Sheena asked as she entered the bedroom and walked towards the bed.

"The terror squad is here."

O'Neil turned to face Sheena.

"I'm up. Ready or not, here I come." O'Neil playfully teased as he slowly started to pull back the comforter.

"You need help?"

"I think I got it, hand me my pimp robe," O'Neil instructed as he pointed to the closet.

"It's in there."

"Jesus Christ! You gotta be kidding me. It's too long, you're gonna trip over it. Leave it to you to want to wear this damn thing today, of all the days Neil, today?" Sheena asked while shaking her head and smirking.

"Well, if not now, when?"

Sheena went to the closet to retrieve the extra-long, fluffy, red polyester robe with gold trim and a long train. She laughed out loud as she helped O'Neil put this monstrosity on his thin frame.

"Happy now? Is this the look you were aiming for? Goddamn you don't take anything seriously, huh?" She asked as she laughed at O'Neil as he tied the gold belt around his waist and began to rub the fluffy, polyester faux fur up and down his chest.

"Don't hate on my version of dress for success. Now, let's go get this done," he said as he leaned on Sheena's shoulder for balance.

"Do you need your walker?"

"Walker?"

"Hospice dropped off your bed and some other supplies when you were sleeping. Everything is in the guest room. Do you want it?"

"No, no, I got it."

They ambled into the living room, with O'Neil holding onto Sheena for balance. As they entered, Hakeem was the first to see O'Neil.

"Awww man, I missed you, you sexy mother fucker!" Hakeem shrieked as he jumped up, rushed to O'Neil, and hugged him.

"Goddamn I missed you. I love you, bro."
"I missed you, too. But dude, it's only been like 2 weeks, stop being a pansy."

"Well, call us some extra-large pansies because we need you back in the game, bro!" Jamal said as he tried to fight back tears.

"Man, we need you, bro. We need you," Jason cried as he got up to hug O'Neil.

Sheena stepped aside as The Twins and O'Neil embraced and shed tears together.

"Man, we love you so much, bro. It's killing me to see you like this. I can't take it, bro."

"I know, cuzzo, I'm sorry. But it's okay." O'Neil attempted to soothe the Twins.

"Now cut it out, your tears and snots are gonna mess up my robe," he joked, trying to lighten the mood.

"Alright, let's let him sit down," Sheena said as she walked him to the couch and helped him sit down.

"I never thought I'd see the day that Chrissy would be a mute. What's up, blockhead?"

Chrissy sat in silence, lost for words, staring at O'Neil. She became teary-eyed when she saw how thin he had become in just two weeks.
"Awww, Chris, come here, girl," O'Neil said as he watched her grow more emotional.

Chrissy walked over to him and sat down beside him as he wrapped his arms around her, and she hugged his neck as she sobbed into his fluffy, oversized robe.

"I don't know what to say, I don't know how to help. I... I... I don't know what to do, Neil," she rattled off between cries and sniffles, clearly flustered.

"Awww, come on, my little blockhead, it's okay. I didn't mean to make you cry. Come on, stop crying. It's okay, I just need you to do what you've been doing for the past twenty-plus years. Show up, show out and be the annoying ass Chrissy that gets on my last damn nerve, okay?"

O'Neil kissed Chrissy on the top of her head.

"Okay, okay, I can do that," Chrissy sniffled as she tried to compose herself.

"Good. I love you my little brown butthole," O'Neil joked as he playfully slapped her upside her head.

 In return, Chrissy buried her tear-stained face and runny nose into his fluffy robe and rubbed her face in circles around his chest.

"And here I was thinking I needed a Kleenex," Chrissy said sarcastically as she sat upright, smirking.

"Damn this robe is absorbent."

"Ugh, you're annoying. Move nasty, you put your snot on me. Eww, go."

"And I love you too," Chrissy said with a smile.

She kissed him on the cheek, got up, and returned to her seat.

"Aight bro-bro, whatchu need to tell us?" Jamal asked as he subconsciously started shaking his head no, as if he could stop his fear and anxiety from increasing.

O'Neil looked at Sheena.

"Ready?"

"Hold on. Everybody, we need you to get the family on the phone. Hold on, Neil. I have to call your parents and Krystal. We'll let you know when we're ready," she said as she started pressing prompts on both her and O'Neil's iPhones.

"Aight, I got Pop-Pop on the line," Hakeem confirmed.

"Got uncle Mike," Chrissy added.

"Bro and cuzzo on the line." The Twins announced.

"Hi Mama Jodi, hi Pops! Give me a second. Hey Krystal, hold on. We're just getting everybody together," Sheena said as she spoke to both phones.
"Okay, everybody's all here. Neil wanted to speak to us all himself."

"We love you, baby, so much," his mother shouted.

Everyone turned their phone cameras on to O'Neil, waiting for him to speak.

"I love you too, Ma," he said somberly.

O'Neil took a deep breath and exhaled before continuing.

"It's been almost a year of treatment. Nothing's working. It's too aggressive. I need y'all to know I tried, I tried really hard because I didn't want to have to tell any of you any of this. I didn't want to disappoint any of you. But there's nothing else they can do. I don't want to try a clinical trial, I'm sick and I'm tired of being too sick and tired to enjoy my life."

"No, no, no, noooo. Son, what are you saying?" His mother cried out.

"What are you telling us, son?" She frantically pleaded as she tried to make sense of his words.

Sheena avoided eye contact with everyone in the living room and on the mobile devices out of fear of becoming emotional. She wanted to stay strong for O'Neil, so she held both phones up as he tried to explain his wishes to everyone. Sheena continued to look down at the floor. She could hear various people crying and denying what was happening. "Ma, I don't think I'll make it to Thanksgiving, I'm dying, Ma."

Once he spoke those words, a bomb of grief exploded in the room. Wailing and pleading could be heard even louder than before. Sheena could see the Twins pacing back and forth.

"Nah, nah, nah, come on, man. Nah, no way, nah. You're not saying this, cuz." Jamal argued.

"Come onnn, come on! You got this, bro. Come on, you got this. You're too strong, man. Come on! We Harris and Harris, we're blowing up, man. We're living our dream, bro! All because of you, man. Come on, no, you're not going nowhere. You got this." Jason cried.

Sheena continued to look down at the floor, trying to remain calm. She held onto both phones, trying to keep her hands from trembling.

"I'm sorry. I didn't mean to let everyone down. I'm just tired, I'm weak all the time, and nothing else can be done.

He pleaded, "I'm sorry, Ma, I'm sorry, Pops, I tried. I promise you, I tried so hard to beat this, but this cancer fight is over. I just want to focus on enjoying all my family and friends until my time is up. I need everyone to support me and my decision," he cried softly.

"Just be okay with my decision to finish this on my terms, please... please," he begged weakly.

"I'm just so tired."

Jodi continued to sob and was inconsolable as her husband held her tightly.

"Son, don't you ever apologize. You never have to be sorry. We love you; we support you, and you're the bravest man I know," he said as he became overcome with emotion.

"It's your life and your journey, and we will be there supporting you every step of the way. Alhamdulillah, all praise to Allah, you are a gift, son. Mashallah! If this is what you want and what Allah has willed, we must accept, no matter how devastated we are. I know you have made the right decision for you, son."

Kenny could barely finish his sentence as he tried to compose himself.

"Baby boy, we're on the next flight out. We will be there soon, son, anything for you, always."

O'Neil's voice grew weaker as his energy depleted with all the emotions.

"She-She, tell them the plan," he said with a strained whisper.

Sheena took a deep breath and tried to muster a comforting and joyous tone.

"Okay, everyone, Neil wants to celebrate Thanksgiving early! So, you know what that means. Family, friends, food, drinks, music, spades, and fun! So, early Thanksgiving at our house on

Saturday. Let everyone know that now is the time to visit. Neil has made it clear he wants this Thanksgiving to be epic, so we all have work to do to make this happen. Neil wants this to be an epic celebration! A happy, fun, love-filled celebration with everyone that can make it, okay? So, we will see everyone when you get here. Okay, we love you all," Sheena said as she and O'Neil waved goodbye.

15

CELEBRATION OF LIFE

"Hey, Love, come here. Gimme a hug. I'm so sorry, I know it's hard. You've been dealing with this day in and day out. I know it's hard. We all appreciate everything you've done and what you continue to do," Hakeem said as he wrapped his arms around Sheena.

"You're so fucking dope, you're the best thing we have in our lives. I just can't believe this shit is happening, he can't leave us, I can't lose my brother, I just can't. He's the glue. He holds us all together. He's been speaking life into us for years, and he's like a prophet. I swear, that man could see the future. There's so much shit he told us would happen and it did. But he never saw this? Sheena, he never saw this? My bro knew we would all be friends, he knew you would be the best thing in my life, he knew we would all do what we said we would do and be successful. He knew that we all needed each other, my boy can foresee shit before it even happened for as long as I can remember. But, he never saw this?" Hakeem questioned woefully as tears ran down his face.

"Babe, I know, I know. Right now, we can't ask why; we just need to be here for him. All he wants to do is celebrate life with everyone. So, we're going to do just that. He's accepted that he's transitioning; now is not the time for us to mourn, but it's time for us to love and celebrate. That's what I keep telling myself because it's definitely what he wants. I know it's hard, but one day at a time, we'll all get through it together."

Sheena tried to fight back her tears as she hugged Hakeem tighter and nuzzled into his chest.

"It's okay, Love. Like you said, we'll all get through this together."

The front doorbell rang as Hakeem and Sheena consoled each other in the kitchen.

"Who the heck is that at this time of night?" Sheena asked, perplexed.

"I'll get it!"

Chrissy called out from the living room as she rushed to the front door and peeked out the peephole before she sucked her teeth and opened the door.

FOR THE LOVE OF YOU

"Hey. Sheena's in the kitchen, Neil's asleep."

"Who's she talking to?" Hakeem asked Sheena as they both looked toward the kitchen entryway.

"Krystal!"

Sheena shrieked as she ran to hug her. Krystal dropped her luggage and handbag to the floor and fell into Sheena's arms, sobbing.

"I got here as fast as I could. Sheena, I'm sorry, I would have come sooner, but he kept saying he was okay and not to worry. I'm sorry, I would have been here if I knew. Why didn't he tell me? Whyyy?"

Krystal cried as she clung to Sheena.

"I know, Krystal, it's okay. You know, Neil, he didn't want to worry anybody or be a burden. He also didn't want you taking a bunch of time off from work, or feel obligated to fly back and forth. I don't want you to feel like I was keeping anything from you, but I was trying to respect his wishes. It's his story and his journey to share, not mine. It's been killing me; all of this feels so surreal. I've been trying to hold it together. I just don't understand why this is happening, him of all people."

Sheena wailed uncontrollably as Hakeem rushed over to console her and Krystal.
"It's aight, we're all here together now, and there will be more of us here later. We will make this time everything he's

asked for and more. We have to keep it together for him right now. The Twins said his parents and grandfather should be here in the morning, so we have to pull it together as best we can."

"I know." Sheena agreed as she wiped tears from her eyes and regained her resolute demeanor.

"Now is not the time to fall apart. Babe, can you bring Krystal's luggage to my room? Come on, Krystal, you can stay in my room with Neil while you're here. Are you ready to see him?"

Krystal took a deep breath and grabbed Sheena's hand.

"Yes," she uttered, her voice quivering, and her hands trembling.

Sheena squeezed her hand.

"It's okay, I'm glad you're here. I know he can't wait to see you." Sheena assured her as she led Krystal to her bedroom.

"Hey Twins," Krystal excitedly whispered as she walked into Sheena's bedroom and saw them both sitting and keeping O'Neil company.

"Yoooo! What up, sis?" Jamal greeted her as he got up and hugged her.
"Glad you're here," Jason said warmly as he got up and kissed her on the cheek.

"How's my superhero doing?" Krystal asked, looking at O'Neil, who was sleeping comfortably but appeared gaunt.

"He's sleeping off and on; he just dozed off not too long ago. We'll let you get some smoochie time in." Jamal said with a smirk, giving her another hug and walking towards the door.

"Wake up, sleeping beauty," Jason said, rubbing O'Neil's head.

"Your boo thang is here," he said before leaving the bedroom and following Jamal.

Krystal stood at the side of the bed, staring at O'Neil.

"Go ahead, climb in there and snuggle with your man, girl. Did you eat anything? There's Thai food. Do you want some?"

"Yes, I should try to eat something." Krystal agreed.

She climbed into the bed, spooned O'Neil, kissed him on the lips, and held his hand.

"I'll bring you both a plate, you can try to see if you can get him to eat a little."

"Wake up, handsome. Wake up." Krystal whispered in his ear as she wrapped her arms around him, rested her head on his shoulder, and kissed his neck.

"He's still sleeping? Girl, if you don't shake his ass awake already!" Sheena joked as she set the tray of food down on the bed.

"But he looks so comfortable."

"If we don't wake him up, he'll be complaining tomorrow, and you're not getting me in trouble with your little tyrant." Sheena snickered as she reached over and pulled the covers back from O'Neil.

"Wake up, kiddo," she said as she rubbed his sternum.

"Got a surprise for you, wake up."

O'Neil moaned as he slowly roused.

"You up?" Sheena asked as he began to move.

O'Neil slowly opened his eyes.

"Awwww man, Ciara was just about to show me her goodies."

"Whoopsie! Now, what would Krystal think about that, huh?"

"Woman, I wear the pants, she knows I get a pass for my true love, Ci-Ci."

"Oh! Is that right?" Krystal interrupted as she leaned over O'Neil so he could see her face.

"You came," O'Neil said with surprise as he looked at Krystal with love.

"I'm so glad you came!"

"Of course I came; you know I missed you," Krystal reassured O'Neil, repeatedly planting kisses on his lips as she cried softly.

"What's wrong? Why are you crying? Babe, what's wrong?" O'Neil asked, seemingly confused.

"I just missed you, that's all. I'm okay," she said, kissing him again and snuggling beside him.

"Okay, I don't want to interrupt the love fest, but you two need to eat something. Here, let me know if you need anything else," Sheena said as she placed the food tray on Krystal's lap.

"Everybody's staying over so we can finish making arrangements for his Thanksgiving celebration."

"You mean my epic celebration." O'Neil corrected.

"Yeah, this list of people keeps growing. We're going to have to do this at a function hall. Are you okay with that?" Sheena asked O'Neil.

"I don't care where it is, I just need everyone to make it happen."

"Say less, your majesty. Your wish is our command. Alright, I'll leave you two lovebirds alone."

Sheena returned to the living room, where Hakeem and the Twins were busy talking on their phones, and Chrissy was sitting alone in the dining room.

"Hey Chris, what's up?"

"Hey girl! I just texted my uncle about the hall. If we need it, we're all set. VFW Post on Morton Street. I just need to confirm with him once we decide on a date and time."

"Okay, we should do Saturday, 2 PM to 8 PM."

"Bet, I'll let my uncle know now so he can lock it in. I already talked to my cousin Nessa, she'll decorate for us, just let me know the color scheme."

"White and yellow, I already know that's what him and his mom will choose."

"Cool, I'll go with Nessa to pick out the decorations and center pieces. Go check on them fools in there, they're working on the guest list. We're definitely going to need some food catered. Once we have the numbers, we can figure out this food situation. So, go check on them douche nozzles and get back to me."

"Be nice, Chris," Sheena said as she rolled her eyes and entered the living room.

"Hey, how's it going in here?" Sheena asked as she sat beside Hakeem and put her head on his shoulder.

"We got this, Love. You already know everybody loves O, so they're definitely gonna come out and show love."

"Good, so you can let everyone know Saturday, VFW on Morton Street, 2 PM to 8 PM."

"Say less." The Twins responded.

"The number of people reaching out and showing love is wild, man. I hope he knows how much he's loved," Jason said.

"Because this will be epic, our bro is going to love this."

■

"Krystal, you're a lifesaver. Thanks for helping me cook breakfast. Time is slipping away, I just need everything to slow down, damn it!"

Sheena bawled as she slammed down the dish she was washing in the sink and began to weep.

"I can't, Krystal, I can't handle this. Please tell me this isn't happening today; this can't be his goodbye to people. Krystal, tell me this isn't happening."
Krystal walked towards Sheena.

"Come here. No, put that down. Come." Krystal instructed as she turned off the kitchen faucet and sat Sheena down.

"Look at me, look. Sweetie, this is happening. As painful and unimaginable as it all is, it's happening. We have to pull ourselves together. His parents are in there with him and the hospice nurse. We need to stay strong for them and Neil, just until after we make today happen, okay? After today, I promise you and I can hide and cry our little hearts out, but for now, we have to stay strong and make sure we pull this off and get it right."

Krystal hugged Sheena tightly.

"We're in this together, you can lean on me, okay? You're not alone. I love you, girlie."

"I love you, too. Whew! Sorry, I didn't think I would get this emotional this early in the day."

"Excuse me, Sheena. I just wanted to let you know I'm wrapping up now." Susie said as she walked into the kitchen.

"I was able to talk in detail with Neil's parents. It seems like pain management is going well. He has less of an appetite and is sleeping more now, all of which is to be expected. I understand today is a big day for Neil. Would you like a palliative care nurse to be available at the event?"

"No, but thank you. I think Krystal and I can handle it. If anything changes, I will reach out."

"Very well then. I also discussed with Neil's family some of the additional physical and mental changes they are beginning to see. I understand that Neil does not want to discuss any presumed timeframes, so I wanted to honor his wishes, but I also wanted to educate his family on what to expect as the transition nears."

"No, that's fine. We understand. Thank you so much, Susie. I appreciate all your help."

"Well, I'm glad I could be of some help. I'll be back tomorrow, but if you need anything before then, just contact our 24-hour line; a colleague can assist if it's after hours. Enjoy today's celebration, and I will see you all tomorrow."

"Thanks, Susie. Have a good day, I'll walk you out," Krystal offered as she stood up to escort Susie to the front door.

Sheena looked at the time. It was already approaching 11:30 AM, and there was still so much to do and finish. The cooking timer began to buzz, refocusing her attention as Krystal walked back into the kitchen.

"Alright, the turkey is done. I'll be able to pack up the food so The Twins can drop it off at the Post."

"Good. In about 20 more minutes, the macaroni and cheese will be ready, and everything else is all set," Krystal confirmed. "Chrissy said they're almost done with the decorations; I'm waiting for her to send pictures. She's gonna stay there and wait for the caterers to set up and for The Twins to drop off the rest of the food."

"Before I forget, Hakeem needs to give him a haircut so he can get showered," Krystal reminded Sheena.

"Oh, damn it! I totally forgot about that. Let me go tell him to do it now," Sheena said hurriedly as she rushed out of the kitchen.

■

Sheena rushed out of her bathroom and into her bedroom as she heard her cellphone ringing.

"Hey Chris, wassup? Getting dressed now. How's it looking over there? Well, I've been patiently waiting for the pictures!" Sheena responded, clearly annoyed as she rolled her eyes.

"No, I'm fine. Really, I am," Sheena said with a softer tone.

"I know you're making sure everything looks good. Really? Thank you. Okay, what time? Okay, we'll see you soon. Love you too."

Sheena sat down on her bed and quickly composed a group text message.

"Chrissy's uncle will pick us up in a Sprinter at 2 PM to drop and pick us up."

Sheena hit send and began to get dressed. Tears began to fall as she looked in the mirror and attempted to apply her makeup. She buried her face in her hands and whispered aloud.

"I can't. I can't do this. No, no, no, no, nooooo. I just can't. Please, God, please! You can't take him from us, not now. Please, please, please. Don't do it, not yet."

Sheena heard a knock at her bedroom door.

"Come in," she said, quickly drying her tears and composing herself.

"You look beautiful." Krystal complimented as she walked into the bedroom.

"Thanks, girl!" Sheena responded as she began blowing her nose, trying to look and sound upbeat.

"Awwww, Sweet Pea. I know, I just finished doing the same thing." Krystal said lovingly as she hugged Sheena from behind.

"Want me to put your face on?"

"Girl, yes. Glam me up." Sheena said playfully as she dried her eyes with a Kleenex and blew her nose again.

"Let's go with a light and subtle glam today. If it gets too emotional, we don't want you walking around looking like your face is running away from you."

Sheena chuckled.

"Good point."

"Alright, I'm thinking a subtle and demure cat eye, a light rosy cheek, and a pink glossy lip. What do you think?" Krystal asked as she began to rummage through Sheena's makeup supplies, putting aside what she needed.

"Work your magic." Sheena agreed as she closed her eyes and tilted her head up.

"How are you doing today?"

Krystal let out a forlorn sigh.

"At this point, I'm just taking it one hour at a time. I can't think too much of what's ahead. If I get through the hour emotionally intact, it's a blessing, and I'll deal with it in the next hour. So my motto right now is, one hour at a time, girl. So... that's how I'm doing. Alright, almost done."

Krystal opened the blush palette and blotted the angled brush before lightly dusting Sheena's cheekbones.

"Done, what do you think? Like it?"

"You nailed it!" Sheena said, smiling, and expressing her approval as she untied her headscarf and let her straightened hair fall to her shoulders.

"Here, gimme," Krystal instructed as she took the comb from Sheena and proceeded to part her hair in the middle and tuck both sides of her hair behind her ears.

"Perfect!" Krystal praised as she stepped back to get a better look.

"Stand up."

Sheena stood up, put her hands on her hips, and slowly twirled around. She ran her fingers through the right side of her temple and pushed the hair behind her ear again.

"Ohhhh, you did that!" Krystal gushed as she snapped her fingers three times.

"Yassss honey. Yasss! This mustard yellow scrunched midi dress is giving me life. Body is snatched to the Gods, okay sis!"

Sheena playfully batted her eyes.

"What? This old thing?" She asked theatrically as she bent over and started twerking.

"Girl! You're a hot mess." Krystal said while laughing.

"Your inner Chrissy is showing."
"Well, goddamn! Why didn't we get this party invite?"
Hakeem teased as he began to pump his hips back and forth

as he walked behind Sheena, grabbing her hips.

O'Neil smiled softly as he slowly walked over to Krystal and gave her a soft peck on the cheek before singing.

"Girl, you look good, back that ass up. I'm big daddy so back that ass up."

Krystal danced around O'Neil flirtatiously.

"Aww, bro, look at all this black love," Jamal commented to Jason as they entered Sheena's bedroom.

Sheena, Hakeem, Krystal, and O'Neil playfully danced and laughed.

Jason was holding up his cellphone and recording.

"Ya'll so damn cute, I can punch all of ya."

"Don't hate the playa, young blood, hate the game." O'Neil wisecracked as Krystal hugged and kissed him passionately.

"Well damn, get a room sis," Jamal yelled as he pretended to be disgusted.

"Aight, Lovebirds, I gotta get a pic of this. I ain't even gonna front, ya'll look good. Get closer." Jason instructed as he raised his cellphone again.
Sheena, Hakeem, Krystal, and O'Neil leaned in close and posed.

"Alright, new pose," Jason instructed.

Sheena and Krystal stood on each side of O'Neil, wrapping their arms around his waist, while Hakeem stood behind them with his arms around all three.

"This is the one right here!" Jason announced excitedly.

"Aight, show the man of the hour some love, ladies."

Sheena and Krystal laid their heads on each of O'Neil's shoulders, hugging him tighter. They all beamed with pure joy and love.

"Love it, love it," Jason said, taking photos from different angles.

"These are dope. Let me air drop them to you now," he said as he began sending the images to everyone's phones.

"My squad, ready for a legendary day?" O'Neil asked as he kissed the back of Krystal's hand.

"Come on, bro! You already know." Hakeem responded assuredly.

"We're gonna rock out," Jamal added.

"With our cocks out." Jason finished.

"On dawgs!" The Twins and Hakeem yelled out in unison before dapping each other up with excitement.

"We got you, bro, we got you!" Hakeem said as he began to choke up.

He gave O'Neil a long, loving embrace, and the rest of the group joined in, making it a group hug.

"Neil, we love you. I love you so much." Sheena said as she clung to Hakeem and Krystal.

"I love you, baby. I hope you know how much." Krystal whispered as she kissed his lips.

"You're my person," she whispered, holding back tears.

"I love you. I love all of you. You all make life worth fighting for. Every day is a fight against this monster. Every fucking day." O'Neil declared as his voice trailed off.

"Alright, enough of this. No pity party today. Let's get ready to party and eat good! Let's roll, squad."

16

LEGACY

The sprinter van pulled up to the VFW Post, and Chrissy's uncle Pete slowly approached the front of the venue.

"Okay, we're here. Let me set up and get you all inside." Pete announced as he put the van in park and opened his door.

"Baby girl, I just pulled up. Okay." Pete said into his cellphone as he walked over to the van doors and slid them open.

Soon after, Chrissy walked out of the venue with Shizz following behind her as he carried a large cardboard tube.

"Neil, look! You see who that is?" Sheena asked excitedly.

"Ohhhhh, that's what I'm talking about!" Hakeem responded with equal excitement.

"Bro! Shizz made it. Damn man, that's respect right there. Ya'll know him and his girl moved to Atlanta not too long ago."

When Shizz and Chrissy reached the sprinter's open door, Shizz placed the large cardboard tube on the ground, opened the top, and flipped it around. A rolled-up red carpet slipped out of the tube. Shizz then took the rolled-up red carpet runner, placed it on the ground, kicked it open, and began unrolling it from the sprinter door to the venue entrance.

"Alright, beautiful family. It looks good in there. Enjoy." Uncle Pete said with a smile as he began helping everyone exit the sprinter.

"Not the red-carpet treatment. Oh yeah! I knew my squad wouldn't disappoint." O'Neil praised Hakeem and Jamal as they helped him exit the sprinter.

"Aww, man! What's up, my dude?" Shizz greeted O'Neil with respect and appreciation.

"I hope you know I would have never missed this. I don't care how many miles I had to travel." Shizz said as he hugged O'Neil.

"Thank you, thank you so much. You and Gizmo were always real ones. Much respect, always," O'Neil responded as he dapped up Shizz and leaned in for another hug.
"Yoooooo! What up, Shizz?" The Twins said as they each gave him their own personalized handshake and hug.

"Damn, it's good to see all of y'all. Mr. and Mrs. Harris, my mother sends her love. She wanted to make it out here, but it just didn't work out. But she definitely sends her love and is keeping you all lifted in prayer, just like you all did for us with Giz."

Shizz leaned in and kissed Jodi on her cheek, followed by a hug, then wiped a tear from his eye.

"We appreciate you being here," Kenny muttered, trying to hide his tears.

"This means a lot to us, more than you'll ever know," Jodi added as she held on tightly to her husband's hand.

"Okay fam! We have a whole function hall filled with people here to celebrate and a ton of food. Let's get our asses in there because I need a shot!" Chrissy interjected.

"Same ole Chrissy, I see." Shizz laughed.

"Aight, Chris, you got that. Let's get in there." Hakeem agreed.

The Twins stood on each side of O'Neil, helping him walk the red carpet toward the entrance. Everyone followed behind slowly, as O'Neil plodded with dwindling strength, with Jamal and Jason supporting him.
As Chrissy opened the door to the function room, the familiar aroma of Thanksgiving dinner permeated everyone's nose.

"Mmmm, that smells so good," O'Neil murmured, his eyes closed as he smiled while leaning on Jamal.

As they stepped further into the room, the sound of thunderous applause and cheers reverberated throughout.

"Neil, welcome to your celebration!" Chrissy shouted as she held her hand out, ushering O'Neil into the room.

"Look! Open your eyes!" she shrieked, as everyone in attendance clapped and cheered.

"Oh, my word! Look at this, I'm speechless, absolutely speechless." Jodi cried as they looked at the beautifully decorated room filled with many familiar and loving faces.

"You know me and my family know how to put together a good time. Don't worry, we got this. Follow me, we're all going to sit at the center tables up front." Chrissy instructed as she led them all to their tables.

"We love you, Neil!"

"Looking swaggy, my G!"

"God bless you, Neil!"

Cheers and words of encouragement rang from all sides of the room as they made their way to their tables.

"Chrissy, this is beautiful. I can't believe you got all this done. This is perfect." Sheena gushed as she admired the white and yellow linen tablecloths, chair covers, and flower arrangements.

Each table boasted a glass vase with white and yellow roses, white daisies, yellow carnations, white lilies, yellow alstroemeria, and green huckleberry, along with a gold-framed photo of O'Neil, ranging from baby photos, yearbook photos, photos with family and friends, and business photos. Each table represented a pivotal time in his life.

"Do you see this? I can't believe they pulled all this off." Sheena commented to Krystal as her eyes filled with tears.

"I didn't know what to expect. But this right here, this definitely exceeded my expectations! Thank you, Chrissy." Krystal leaned in to hug Chrissy as she continued expressing her sincere gratitude.

"It was the least I could do. I'm happy you all like it. Okay, enough of this mushy shit!" Chrissy joked as she slowly released from Krystal's embrace.

"The food has already been blessed, and plates are coming out to all the tables. Have a seat, get comfortable, and we'll be served shortly. Neil, big bro! I need you in this center seat right here, relaxing, eating, and enjoying what's coming. Some people have a few things they want to say to you. Ready? Chrissy asked with a grin.

"You ready for your celebration, bro?"

"Sis, ready," O'Neil said as he slumped into his chair.

"You okay?" Krystal asked with concern as she noticed O'Neil had become increasingly feeble than earlier.

"Babe, I'm okay. Just hungry."

"I gotcha. The food is coming now," Chrissy interjected as the venue staff served the food to the main table.

"Okay, everyone, sit down, eat, and enjoy. Now let me go play event host," she said as she was handed two full shot glasses, as the food was served.

"Good looking out."

Chrissy swiftly downed both shots one after the other.

"Aight, let me get this started," she asserted before walking to the podium.

"Good afternoon, beautiful people. Thank you all for taking the time out of your day to help celebrate our amazing friend, brother, son, and man, Neil. I hope you all are enjoying your meal and each other. I'm your host for the night. Feel free to leave me a tip or pay me in premium tequila shots if you're enjoying yourselves."
"Say less, beautiful. All your shots are on me tonight!" A male voice screamed out from the crowd, and a few chuckles could be heard around the room.

"Ohh, I like your style, Big Sexy," Chrissy responded seductively.

"What the hell is she doing?" Hakeem leaned over and

whispered to Sheena.

"This fucking girl never fails to be an asshole," he muttered under his breath.

"Chris, move it along!" Hakeem yelled out.

"Focus!"

Chrissy turned to Hakeem, rolled her eyes, and stuck her tongue out before turning her attention back to the guests.

"Alright, peeps. Many of you want to share a story, remembrance, reminisce, or have words of encouragement, so let's get to it."

Chrissy looked down at the piece of notebook paper in her hand.

"Okay, first up is Cousin KJ, where you at? Come on up."

"Karon! Aight cuzzo. I see you!" Jamal yelled out as Karon walked up to the podium, hugged Chrissy, and took the microphone.

"I love y'all. I love you, baby boy." Karon commented as he looked over in O'Neil's direction.

"I love you too," O'Neil mouthed as he held his fist up in the air before gently beating on his chest two times.

"Aight y'all, for those that don't know. I'm Karon, my people call me KJ, and Neil is my little cousin. And, I know what y'all are thinking, my big ole' ass was his mentor, right? I was teaching my knucklehead cousins over there how to be solid, right?" Karon asked as he pointed over toward O'Neil and The Twins.

"Bullshit! Those three little funny-looking bastards over there taught me my greatest lesson. Sometimes you just need to shut the fuck up and listen. Listen and learn. Neil, I never told you this, but I always looked up to you, baby cousin. You've always been that light, that bright light that always exuded character, love, compassion, morals, ethics, and discipline. You've been a man before you even knew it, but everyone in the family knew. You pour into everybody and everything that you love. I have so much respect for the life you live and the life you've made. If I could just return a small fraction of the joy and love you've given me and this room of family and friends, I would do it in a heartbeat. And I just want to let you know, you're not walking this journey alone, baby cousin. When you're tired, we got you." Karon assured O'Neil as he pointed around the room.

"We got you. When you feeling down. We got you. When you're feeling down, we're gonna lift you up. When you feel like your light is dim, we're gonna be your high beams lighting your way. We gonna be that light for you, like you always been for us, cause baby cousin, you ain't alone. We are in this together. You've been my hero since we've been blessed with you."

Karon took a deep breath to hold back his emotions as he tried to finish his sentence. "And I'm never gonna let you go! You hear me? I ain't ever gonna let you go, I can't. I can't!" Karon cried out as his chest heaved up and down as he tried to compose himself.

A voice screamed out from the crowd. "It's okay, KJ. It's okay, let it out."

Chrissy rubbed his back, hugged him, and took the microphone.

"Thank you, KJ, that was beautiful. Alright, we have so many people wanting to spread love. Next up, and this one shocked the shit outta me. Ladies and gentlemen. . . I honestly can't believe this. Come on, Mrs. Fournier. Can you believe our fourth-grade French teacher is here? Come on up, Mrs. Fournier."

"Yooo! Mrs. F?"

The Twins and Hakeem shouted as the three of them stood up and began to applaud gleefully. Sheena covered her mouth in shock as she watched Mrs. Fournier slowly make her way to the podium and started to wave in their direction.

"Oh, my God. Hi, Mrs. F!" Sheena yelled.

"I can't believe she's here!" She said, surprised, looking at O'Neil, who was sitting there beaming with gratitude.

"Good afternoon, everyone. I had the pleasure of teaching O'Neil, Sheena, Jason, Jamal, Hakeem, and Chrissy in fourth and fifth grade. I know many are probably wondering how or why I'm here. Well, let me tell you. As a teacher in the Boston public school system for almost forty years, I've taught countless students and, out of all those students, this group," Mrs. Fournier said as she pointed to O'Neil's table.

"This group of kids I always knew were special. The love, dedication, and care they showed for each other as they began to forge their friendships was magnificent. They held each other accountable, kept each other in line, and most importantly, loved each other. A true testament to present day as I stand here looking at my former students, who are my greatest dream as a teacher."

"Now, bear with me because I want to share a story that I'm sure no one else knows. It was the fall of '99, and my husband and I were leaving his neurology appointment at Mass General. We just got the news that my husband was diagnosed with amyotrophic lateral sclerosis, commonly known as ALS. Being the gentleman he is, O'Neil stopped me once he recognized me. He said hello and wanted to thank me for being one of his favorite teachers. My husband instantly took to O'Neil, commenting on how courteous, intelligent, and personable he was. And once O'Neil shared that he would attend M.I.T. and how much he enjoyed renovating and building with his grandfather and uncles, my husband quickly found a friend." Mrs. Fournier said with a quick smile.

"From that day forth, O'Neil called every week to check on my husband and came to my house to finish a project my husband started before the muscle weakness set in, or complete a project my husband had hoped to do. During this time, O'Neil became the son that my husband and I never could have. As the weeks turned to months, months turned into years, my husband grew weaker as the disease progressed, taking his speech and total mobility. During this time, O'Neil showed up without fail, ensuring the house was conducive to making our lives manageable. He installed ramps, remodeled the bathroom, built a deck, completed the laundry room, and most importantly, he became our family. I could never thank him enough for the joy he brought into our lives at such a difficult time. He helped make my husband so happy and fulfilled, and for that, O'Neil, this little old teacher, and her adoring old husband, may he rest in eternal peace. We thank you, you were, and you are the light that your cousin spoke of earlier. You gave my husband that spark and care that he needed. I truly believe you were the reason that we got to have him around that third year. May you be forever blessed in this lifetime and beyond. The biggest lesson you taught me, and I need you to know this, is don't let the pursuit of tomorrow diminish the joy of today. Live! Live in your moments and don't ever forget to be kind."

"Merci, merci mon cher ami. Thank you, my dear friend. May love and light continue to guide you in your purpose. I'm eternally grateful for you." Mrs. Fournier held her hand over her heart.

"I sincerely hope you know that," she whispered, her voice

trailing off as she handed the microphone back to Chrissy.

People walked up to the podium one by one to share a humorous, silly, sweet, sentimental, poignant, and soul-stirring story. Laughter, tears, and declarations of love, respect, and admiration for O'Neil were expressed by each attendee who took hold of the microphone and spoke their truth.

"Aww man, I wasn't expecting so many people to be able to speak this beautifully about my annoying ass friend!"

Chrissy attempted to laugh through her tears while slurring her words as she downed another shot.

"Neil, you know I love you. You know how much you mean to me. I . . . I just can't right now."

Chrissy cried as she swayed back and forth. Sheena quickly stood up and walked towards Chrissy, who was clearly intoxicated.

"No worries, sis, I got you," Sheena whispered as she took the microphone from Chrissy.
"Go take my seat. You did a great job. I got it from here. I got it from here, go ahead, relax."

As Chrissy stumbled towards the table to sit next to O'Neil, Sheena took a deep breath before continuing.

"Good evening, I'm so happy that all of you were able to come out and show support for Neil and his family. He kept saying he wanted today to be epic, and this has certainly turned out to be more than what we imagined. So, thank you all. I'll try not to ramble, but for those that don't know, I'm Sheena and Neil, and I have been friends since we were kids, fourth grade to be exact. He's been my friend, my family, my protector, my confidant, my cheerleader, my strength, my rock, my peace, my will, my life. He's my life, you hear me?" Sheena asked as tears began falling down her face, and her voice quivered.

"This man right here is the only person in the world that sees me, truly sees me. I couldn't fathom what life would have been without him all these years. What you and your family have done for me, I could never put into words how grateful, thankful, and appreciative I am of all of you. Neil, you know my thoughts, my fears, and my pain. You are the reason I can stand here today as I am, and thank you for being that angel here on earth that I needed. You are my hope, my love, and my inspiration. It's because of you I am, and I can. I love you now, I loved you then, and I'll love you all of our tomorrows."

Sheena sobbed as she blew O'Neil a kiss. She watched him break down in tears, and his mother and father hugged him while they all cried together. Krystal walked towards Sheena and hugged her.

"That was beautiful, I got this now," she reassured Sheena as she held her hand and took the microphone.

"Hello everyone, I'm Krystal, and I'm going to try really hard to keep it together. Babe, you know how I feel about you. And you have given me meticulous instructions on what you want me to execute today. And I'm here to make it happen. With that being said, I need Mr. and Mrs. Harris to make their way over here. Twins, can you help Neil come up here, too?"

Krystal and Sheena grabbed three chairs and placed them on the parquet floor. The Twins slowly walked O'Neil to his seat, and his parents positioned themselves behind him, each with a hand on his shoulder.

"Neil wrote something he wanted me to read today."

Krystal slowly unfolded the handwritten paper that O'Neil had given her the night prior and began reading it.

"To my incredible mom and dad, first, I want to thank you. Your love, kindness, and faith helped me become the man I am today. You taught me that I could conquer anything as long as I worked hard, remained humble, and gave anything I cared about my complete dedication. You two are the blueprint to my wonderful life. I couldn't ask for anything more. You taught me love without conditions, to give without the expectation of reciprocation, to be honest to a fault, to be loyal to those that have genuine intentions, protect the ones you love and those who cannot protect themselves, stand on your beliefs even if you have to stand alone and to operate from love and to live graciously. My love for the two of you has no end. I'm thankful to Allah for giving me two loving parents that showed me so much love, understanding, patience, and wisdom. I pray that you are proud of me and that you understand my decision. My prayer for you all, in the name of Allah, the Beneficent, I lift everyone I love up who needs healing. I pray you surround my loved ones with your love and grace, bringing healing, understanding, and comfort to their minds and spirits when I am no longer here to comfort them. May peace be upon you all, Alhamdulillah."

Sobbing could be heard throughout the room as Mrs. Harris clung to O'Neil, hugging him tight. Mr. Harris cried softly while holding O'Neil's hand. O'Neil whispered into his mother's ear before waving Krystal over. Krystal leaned down and kissed him on the cheek as he took the microphone, and Krystal began to comfort Mrs. Harris.

With a strained voice, O'Neil began to speak.

"My granddad once told me, honor thy mother and father for thy days on this earth will be longer. And today, listening to you all, because of my mom and pops, all the love and lessons made me who I am. My physical days on earth may not be longer, but I will live on through each and every one of you. I love you all. No more tears, let's celebrate life, love, family, and friendship."

O'Neil handed the microphone back to Krystal.

"Okay! My man has spoken; no more tears. It's time to continue with the celebration. So, the next task on my honey-do list is dedicated to his Pops, Mr. Harris. Not too long ago, Neil and I were having a conversation about random things we haven't done yet. As we were talking, Neil says, Babe, my Pops and I always like to play around and dance. But you know what, I've never actually danced with my father. So, with that being said, Chrissy, queue the music!"

As the instrumentals began to play, Mr. Harris helped O'Neil stand and guided him onto the parque dance floor, holding him tight. Krystal then began to sing the lyrics to "Dance with My Father" with her flawless voice.

She belted out a heartfelt plea for another chance to spend more time with an adoring dad, just one more time, one more chance, one final act of love.

Mr. Harris held his son tightly as they swayed back and forth to Krystal's perfect vocal range, pitch, and resonance as she sang from her soul.

Sheena held Mrs. Harris' hand as she watched her husband and son dance affectionately while trying to maintain her composure.

Once the song ended, Mr. Harris helped O'Neil back to his seat as he wiped his eyes and kissed him.

Sniffling and sobs could be heard around the room as people began to rise and give a standing ovation.

"Whew, I don't know how I got through that one," Krystal said, relieved as she sighed and wiped her brow.

"So, the last on my honey-do list is for his mom, Mrs. Harris. Neil said that for as long as he could remember, his mother would make sure this song was played at every party, family gathering, cookout, and any other celebration. They would dance and laugh and sing. For Neil, this song is happiness and will always remind him of his mother's joy and love. I'm ready, Chrissy, go ahead."

As soon as the instrumentals began to play, Mrs. Harris giggled.

"Time to cut a rug, baby!" Mrs. Harris yelled out as she took O'Neil's hand and helped him out of his seat.

Krystal began to sing as she snapped her fingers and tapped her foot to the beat of the Isley Brothers singing "For the Love of You."

"Come on everybody, get your butts out your seats, this is a party!" Mrs. Harris yelled out with a smile as she held O'Neil as they moved side to side.

People began to rise from their seats and two-step with each other or alone, laughing and singing until their crying eyes were replaced with joy and smiles.
Sheena pulled Hakeem onto the dance floor next to O'Neil and his parents, as they held onto him as they danced and laughed together.

Sheena caught O'Neil's gaze as he beamed with contentment and mouthed to her, "Thank you. I love you," with the biggest smile he could muster.

17

I'M READY

"Doc, he was so happy that day, but two days later, we lost him. He passed away at home, in my bedroom, surrounded by all of us, just like he asked. I know in his last days he was at peace and was showered in love, but..." Sheena stammered as she wept.

"When he left, so much of me went with him. Imagine half of you ceasing to exist, that's how I felt."

"It sounds like he lived a wonderful life, and I'm absolutely gobsmacked at such a beautiful tribute all of you pulled together. A living memorial, how splendid! How utterly marvelous it was that everyone was able to get a chance to share lasting words or stories directly to him. The ability to say final goodbyes should never be underestimated; it's a gift not usually bestowed upon us. I know it didn't lessen the pain of your immeasurable loss, but think of all the things you both were able to do and express as you both navigated that journey together, Deary."

Sheena folded her arms across her distended belly and crossed her legs as a faint smile formed.

"I know you're right. I am grateful for that."

"Bereavement is a process. You were able to recognize you needed support navigating your grief journey, and you're now at the point where you can choose to celebrate and reminisce on the memories. However, I encourage you to find support in those closest to you as you continue to work through your process. Dear, having a baby is such a delicate and amazing time. I want to ask if you have given more thought to opening the lines of communication with your mother one day?"

Sheena sighed as she looked up at the ceiling, taking a long pause as she massaged her tight belly.

"I'm considering it, I am. Ummm, I at least want the baby to know who my mother is and let Evelyn hear it from me that I'm having a baby."

Sheena let out another sigh.

"Yeah, I'm ready to talk to her, I can do it."

Sheena looked at Dr. Angel with gratitude and self-assurance as she smiled.

"Yes, I'll speak to her and let her know. I'm not reaching out with any expectations, but I'm willing to take the step to make contact."

Dr. Angel smiled slightly as she tapped her pen on the tip of her nose.

"Sheena, I want to remind you that you don't have to reach out now if you're not ready. You can continue to think about it if you're not certain. I want you to proceed at your own pace, and it's okay if it takes longer or you never get there. I don't want you to feel pressure to reach out if you're not ready or unsure of your readiness."

"I know, I won't reach out unless I'm sure, Doc. Ugh!" Sheena groaned as she massaged her belly.

"My goodness, she is giving me a hard time today," she muttered as she sat up.

"My poor bladder is being pressed on like a panini," she whined as she got up and waddled towards the bathroom.

"One sec, Doc."

"Take your time, Deary. I think we've accomplished everything we needed to." Dr. Angel concluded as she got up and began closing and taping a medium-sized cardboard box while she waited for Sheena to return.

Sheena was breathing heavily upon entering the room.

"Oh dear, are you okay?"

Groaning loudly, Sheena continued to waddle back to her seat.

"I'm fine. This baby is just rearranging and pressing on every single organ. Whew, Doc, I can't wait. No matter how many pregnant women I've treated, I was not prepared for all these pregnancy symptoms. Goodness gracious!" She exclaimed as she rubbed her stomach.

"Don't fret, Deary, you're at the finish line." Dr. Angel reassured as she walked towards Sheena and stuck her hands out.

"May I?"

"Of course."

"Ahhh, yes. I can feel the tightness. Strong baby! I can't wait to see the face of this little cheeky cherub once she arrives." Dr. Angel chuckled as she rubbed Sheena's stomach. "Your mumzie loves you, take good care of each other."

Dr. Angel leaned down and whispered to Sheena's stomach, "You have a magnificent mum."

"I appreciate that and everything that you've helped me with. I promise, I'll use the tools and coping skills I have. This little nugget is depending on me, so I'll make sure I get this right as long as I'm someone's mother. I'll always protect my baby by any means. She'll never have to worry about someone hurting her, taking advantage of her, or making her feel like a burden as long as I'm breathing. I promise to give her a beautiful life, surrounded by loving people, Doc."

"Splendid! I'm certain you will. I have no doubts about that. Your work here is complete, and you are on to the next phase of your life as a mum. You reach out if you need me, and be sure to send me pictures of this sweet little babe once she's here. You also have the names and numbers of my colleagues here in Boston if you ever need to speak to someone in person."

"Yes, thank you so much."

Sheena leaned in for a hug.

"You've been such a lifesaver. I'm sad to see you go, but I'm happy you can be with your family and enjoy being a Glam-ma."

Dr. Angel let out a belly laugh.

"Glam-ma, oh Deary, I can't wait to share this with my daughters. They will certainly poke mullocks at this for certain! Okay, Dear, I know we went over the time today," she said as she rubbed Sheena's back before releasing her hug.

"Go on now, get back to your day. I know you have important things to do."

■

As Sheena drove away from Beale Street for the last time, she decided to take the long way home by driving down Quincy Shore Drive and stopping at Wollaston Beach. As she pulled into a parking spot, she was flooded with fond memories of coming to this exact spot with O'Neil to ride bikes, take a long walk, buy fried clam baskets, and watch the sunset.

Sheena slowly exited the car, holding onto the steering wheel for support. Once out of the car, she stretched and gently massaged a small part of her back before waddling towards a vacant bench and plopping herself down.

As she looked out to the beach and admired the beautiful skyline, she reached into her purse and pulled out O'Neil's old iPod Nano. She stuck one earbud into her left ear and hit play. Her mind wandered as she recalled the time O'Neil gave her the iPod.

It was the day after his celebration of life party. He grew increasingly weaker and more unresponsive. Sheena smiled as she climbed into her bed, holding O'Neil's hand as he slept. She leaned over and kissed his forehead, whispering in his ear. O'Neil slowly roused and gave a slight smile as he struggled to talk, his voice a strained whisper as he pointed to the iPod next to him.

"For you, when you miss me, just listen."

As she reflected on that moment, Lean on Me by Bill Withers began to play. Sheena's eyes became misty as she chuckled and said aloud, "You always know what I need to hear, huh?"

Sheena closed her eyes and hummed to the music as she got lost in the lyrics. Each song brought back a significant memory of their lives together. Before she was interrupted by her cellphone vibrating, she stopped the music, removed the earbud from her ear, and answered the call.

"Hey Keem. Hello? Keem."

Sheena could hear muffled noises in the background.

"Hello? Keem!"

"Nah, hold up. Lift your side up. It's not level. Now run that wire through." Hakeem was instructing someone in the background.

"Keem, hello."

"Aight, the left should pop right in there. Boy, I told you I'm the TV mount king!"

"This damn boy butt dialed me again," Sheena mumbled. "Keem! Keem!" Sheena yelled into the phone again.

"It looks good, bro. Told you it would fit," Hakeem declared as Sheena tried to get his attention again before hanging up the phone.

"Alright, it's time to get home, little nugget," Sheena said as she returned her belongings to her purse and walked to her car.

Sheena pulled up to her house and grabbed her bags.

"Home sweet home," she muttered as she climbed the front stairs.

Once in her apartment, she walked to her living room, sat down, and kicked off her shoes. She could feel her stomach tightening as she rubbed the sides of her belly.

"What are you doing in there, huh?"

Sheena turned on the television and flipped through the channels before stopping on the 1976 classic movie Sparkle. Instantly, nostalgia flooded her senses, transporting her back to when she first watched this movie.

It was the summer of '93, and she was hanging out with O'Neil at his grandparents' house while his parents cooked on the grill and played old school music. The house was filled with so much love, laughter, family, and friends coming in and out to stop by to eat, drink, and laugh. Sheena was in awe at how much love and family could be in one place simultaneously. Once the night came and everyone left, it was just O'Neil, his parents, and his grandfather left.

■

"Who wants to watch a movie?" Jodi yelled out from the kitchen.

"Ma, what you wanna watch?" O'Neil yelled back.

"Put on something good, baby. None of that shoot 'em up, bang, bang nonsense you kids watch."

"I know what you want to watch," he remarked as he opened the cabinet on the entertainment stand and perused the VHS tapes neatly lined up in a row on all three shelves.

"Got it," he said triumphantly as he popped the tape in the VCR and hit rewind.

Jodi walked into the living room with a bowl of freshly popped Jiffy popcorn and sat in the middle of the sofa as O'Neil pressed play.

"Baby boy, what's the movie of the night?" Jodi asked as she waved her hand, signaling for Sheena and O'Neil to sit beside her.

"Come on, my beautiful babies," she said sweetly as Sheena and O'Neil snuggled on each side of her as Sparkle began to play on his grandfather's floor model television.
"Now, this is a real movie!" Jodi announced with a smile as she nudged Sheena with the bowl of popcorn.

"Here, sweetie."

Jodi settled into the sofa and wrapped her arms around Sheena and O'Neil.

"This is my favorite movie," she added, kissing them both on the tops of their heads.

Jodi lovingly held them both close as they watched the movie. Jodi sang along to her favorite songs, playfully pinching their sides and encouraging them to try to sing along.

Sheena felt grateful for each Harris family member, who treated her like family as she sat there being loved on by Jodi. She wrapped her arms around Jodi, who smiled at the television and sang her beautiful heart out along with the cast, Sparkle, Sister, and Delores as they pranced around the stage singing Aretha Franklin's song, "Giving Him Something He Can Feel."

"Come on, dance with me, my babies!"

Jodi stood up, grabbed Sheena and O'Neil's hands, and pulled them both close to her. She continued to sing, and they all danced around the living room until the song ended. Then, they all fell backward onto the sofa, as Jodi giggled.

Sheena looked up at Jodi with admiration.

"Mama Jodi, I wish you were my mother. I love you."

"Aww, sweetheart. You're my baby, too. You're family, you hear me? We are your family; don't forget that. You are my chosen daughter," Jodi replied, enthused, holding Sheena's hand through the rest of the movie while O'Neil hugged her arm.

"She-She, you know what's mine is yours. I got your big headed back." O'Neil joked as he tossed a handful of popcorn at her.

■

"That damn boy always had something smart to say," Sheena chuckled as she sat there reminiscing as the movie credits began to play.

"Okay, little one. It's time to put the finishing touches on your room," she grunted, holding her lower back as she got up from the couch and walked towards the baby's room.

Once inside, she admired all the work that Hakeem and The Twins did to make the baby room perfect. Jodi also gave her O'Neil's old baby crib, which was in pristine condition and made of solid oak wood that Hakeem re-stained and lacquered.

Sheena walked over to the closet and pulled out some shopping bags as she began to put the finishing touches on the room. She unzipped the bedding bag and began to cover the crib mattress with pastel yellow fitted sheets and a yellow and white comforter. She smiled as she pulled out the pastel yellow, grey, and white butterfly mobile soother as she carefully attached it to the crib, while slowly tracing her hands over the soft felt pastel-colored butterflies before turning on the switch as the mobile began to turn and softly play the Rock-A-By-Baby lullaby. She listened to the mobile continue to play lullabies as she unpacked the rest of the bags and boxes, neatly folding onesies, rompers, pajamas, sleep gowns, and socks before putting them in the dresser drawers. She unboxed the diapers and stacked them neatly on the shelving with all the baby products as she hummed to Twinkle, Twinkle Little Star.

Once everything was tidy and complete, Sheena looked around the room again, studying every detail.

"Wait, something is missing," she muttered, massaging her lower back.

"Aha, the butterflies," she remembered as she waddled to the living room to retrieve her bag.

Upon her return, she pulled out the butterfly stickers she purchased from Family Dollar to affix to the wall by the crib.

"Perfect! All done."

She was content as she sat in the nursery swivel glider, as lullabies continued to play, and she began to fall asleep when her cellphone rang and interrupted her nap.

"Hey Keem," she said sleepily.

"Hello?"

She could hear Hakeem yelling.

"Jay, don't forget my strawberry milkshake and don't be eating my fries neither! Ya big-headed little thief. Mal, watch this fool come back to this truck with half-eaten boxes of fries for us while his is full to the brim."

"Bro, you know you can't trust his greedy ass around no damn food." Jamal joked.

"Keem, hellooo. Keem?" Sheena screamed into the phone.

"Man, look at this! Look, look at him. I know his trifling ass is munching on my damn fries."

"Keem!" Sheena screamed again in the phone as she could hear the car door open and close.

"If you touched my fries, it's lights out for you, punk!"

Sheena sucked her teeth and disconnected the call.

"Why does this fool keep butt dialing me," she muttered to herself before calling Hakeem back.

"Hello?"

"Keem!"

"Hey, Love, what's up?"

"Dude, you keep butt dialing me. What's up with your phone?"

"Awww man, I'm sorry, Love. Working with these damn knuckleheads, I dropped my phone and Tweddle Dee and Tweddle Dumb rolled over my phone with a cart. The screen is smashed to smithereens, my bad, sweetheart. I'll get it fixed tomorrow."

"She-She, where you been all my life, I miss you girl!"

"I miss you too, Mal, but I just saw you the other day, you nut!" Sheena playfully yelled into the phone.

"Stop blowing your hot ass breath in my face, damn! Did you ask for extra onions or something? Love, let me call you back. These fools are driving me nuts. You feel okay, though?" Hakeem asked with a more serious tone.

"Yeah, I'm good. I just finished putting her clothes away. But I'm not going to lie, I'm so uncomfortable. I can't wait to get this pregnancy over with. I need my body back."

"Well, take it easy and relax. I'll be there later tonight; we have one more project to finish. Let me know if you need anything, okay?"

"Okay, I will. See you when you get here."

"See you later, I love you."

"Love you too, see you soon."

Sheena settled back into the glider when she noticed the lullaby stopped playing.

"It's too quiet in here," she mumbled as she reached back into her bag, pulled out O'Neil's iPod, leaned over, and slid it into the iHome docking station before pressing play.

She began to slowly rock back and forth in the glider as she rubbed her stomach.

"What do you think, Munchkin, should I call Evelyn today? Hmmm. Ouch! Was that a yes?"

Sheena chuckled as she held the side of her stomach and rubbed the tiny foot protruding from the side of her belly.

"Okay, message received."

She huffed as she got up, tottered to the bathroom, and returned to the baby's room, dressed in an oversized T-shirt and terrycloth bathrobe. Sheena let out a long sigh.

"Okay, here goes nothing," she whispered as she began scrolling through her contact list on her cellphone until she reached the entry for Evelyn Williams.

"Hopefully, this old battle ax has grown a heart in her old age," she mumbled as she hit the call button.

18

FREE

Sheena put her feet on the footrest and leaned back in the glider. The phone rang three times.

"Hello?"

When Sheena heard her mother's voice after all these years, she immediately felt a tinge of apprehension. A lump in her throat quickly formed, and she couldn't speak.

"Hello!" Evelyn roared into the phone, noticeably agitated.

Sheena felt her body flinch then stiffen as she began to stammer.
"Hi... hello, Evelyn?"

"This is Evelyn, who's this?"

"Hi, it's me. Sheena," she responded meekly as she fumbled for words.

"Sheena? Sheena!" Evelyn asked with confusion and then surprise.

"I can't believe it."

Sheena chuckled nervously.

"Yes, it's me. How have you been?"

"Same shit, different day but, I'm good. I can't complain. I can't believe it's you."

Still stammering, Sheena continued.

"I... I know it's been a while, but I wanted to talk. I wanted to talk to you," she managed to get out with a little more conviction in her voice.

"Talk to me? Whatchu' need to talk to me about? I know one thing; you better not be calling to ask me for money." Evelyn asserted with a stony reply.

Sheena rolled her eyes and sucked her teeth.

"Good ole Evelyn, still colder than a witch's titty. Listen, let me make this clear before I go any further," she demanded with a steely and austere tone.

"Ha! Go ahead, chile. Make this clear to me." Evelyn said snidely as she huffed into the phone.

"Like I said, I wanted to talk to you—emphasis on talk. I'm not calling to ask you for anything. Got it? Furthermore, I don't need money, and if I did, I certainly wouldn't call you, of all people, for anything.

Evelyn snickered, "I guess you told me. Feel better now, lil girl?"

Sheena ignored her passive-aggressive taunts and continued.

"I have my MSN, I work hard, and I'm doing well. Neil and I bought a house a few years ago, so no, you don't have anything I need to ask you for."

"I heard about Neil. Sorry to hear about what happened. I know you two were close for all those years," she said with a softer and somber tone.

"Thank you. Neil and his entire family have always been a saving grace, and my family."

Sheena's voice began to tremble.

"But that's not what I called to talk about. I called because I wanted you to hear it from me. I'm pregnant. I'm having a baby, and I just wanted to let you know that you'll be a grandmother, real soon."

"A baby? Baby! Whew, child. You ready for all that mess?"

"Contrary to your twisted beliefs, some people actually want children and love children."

"I mean, I'm just saying. Sounds like you got the perfect setup now. You finished your education; you got all those degrees, which means you're the head chick in charge. Got a house, got money. You can come and go as you please and do whatever you want at the drop of a hat. You ready to be tied down to a screaming, snotty-nosed baby, with no help?"

"I have help, I'm not alone! Just because my father left you and you left me, that doesn't mean I'm alone. My baby and I have her dad, uncles, aunt, and grandparents. I haven't been alone since you forced me out of your house that day. Make no mistake, I absolutely have help. And this baby is already loved, and she's going to be here real soon."

"Forced? I never put you out. You chose to leave."

"Yeah! Because you made a choice, and it wasn't to be a mother and protect or love me, I had to leave," Sheena yelled.

"Look, I didn't call today to rehash the past. I just wanted to let you know that I was having a baby, which means you'll technically be a grandmother. My door is open if and when you ever want to meet her once she gets here."

"That's fine. I'm not trying to revisit that nonsense either, cause I know I took care of you. I'm not the one that decided to walk away and not raise you like your no good for nothing piece of shit daddy. I had to figure shit out on my own, with no help. I had to work all these hours to keep a roof over your head, food on the table, and clothes on your back. You never wanted for nothing. I did my job, clearly. Look at you now. It doesn't look like you had it so horrible. Now, does it?"

Sheena let out an incredulous laugh.

"Unbelievable! Un-fucking-believable. You can't be serious. I wanted a mother! More specifically I wanted a mother that actually fucking loved me. Do you not understand that?"

"I took care of you, I fed you, I clothed you, I housed you! Who does all that if they have hate in their heart for something they birthed?"

"Is that really a question, Evelyn? Are you okay? Because this is insane to me. Outside of providing financially, what other motherly duties did you ever fulfill? You ever spend quality time with me? Talk to me without barking demands at me like I was your maid? You ever tell me you loved me? Hell, did you ever treat me like you cared about me? You ever come to any parent-teacher conferences? You ever ask about my hopes, dreams, or what scared me? Did you ever want to even know me? You treated me like I was a stranger, a nuisance, like I was expendable. Correction, I was expendable to you!"

331

"Sheena, I worked my ass off twelve and sixteen-hour shifts to provide. I was tired. Do you think I had it in me to give even more of myself to you? I barely had the capacity for my damn self. You had what you needed, and you're upset about not getting what you wanted? Spoiled, spoiled rotten, and ungrateful is what that is. I made sure when I couldn't be there for you, you were with people that loved you, like Mrs. Mattie and the Harris family. So, sue me! Sue me and hate me for doing what I could do, alone with no help from that bastard that knocked me up and promised me the world. You're not the only one that feels cheated; I got cheated out of my life, you understand? Talk about expendable, you and your daddy left and never looked back. So, I guess we're all even now."

Sheena began to feel her stomach tighten. She let out a faint grunt as she tensed up with aggravation, then mumbled under her breath.

"Accept the shit you can't change; you won't steal my joy. You don't control my happiness."

Sheena paused, took a deep breath, and continued. "Look, I don't want to argue about the past. Can we just start here, at this moment? My intention for reaching out was to reconnect and give you the option to meet your granddaughter, if you like. No pressure, but I wanted to give you the option. I would love for my daughter to know who her family is, biological and chosen. And that includes you. Maybe you couldn't be the mother I needed, but that doesn't mean you can't be the grandmother my daughter could love. I'm open to giving you that opportunity, if you want it. Again, no pressure."

"Well, if you're so dead set on having this baby and think you're making the right decision, I guess I can," Evelyn responded nonchalantly.

"I just hope you're prepared in case things don't work out how you plan. If that man runs off, I can help babysit sometimes, but that's it."

Sheena let out an irritated huff.

"That's fine, Evelyn, trust me, you don't have to worry about me asking you for anything, okay?"

"You say that now. But I get it, you're grown now. You know everything." Evelyn said sarcastically.

"Unh, uh. Nope! Sheena, hold on. Fool, what the hell you think you're doing? Get that shit out my house. Does my living room look like a goddamn junkyard to you?"

Sheena could hear a male voice in the background, but couldn't determine what was being said.

"Get it out! Don't step another foot in here, turn around and bring that shit back to your raggedy ass truck."

"Woman, cut all that hollering out! All you do is complain. Now, you done told me to go make some money, and now you wanna holler about me making some money. I can't win with your old bipolar ass!"

"If you don't like it, get out."

Soon after, Sheena heard a thud.

"Owww! That hurt, why you so goddamn mean, woman? You wicked, throw another shoe at me and see if I don't put my fancy feet up yo' ass."

"Motherfucker!"

Thud.

"Ahh, goddamn bitch, you got me right between the eyes. Baby, why you gotta be so mean? I was just playing. Now, since you making me haul this on up outta here, I'mma need $150 for lost wages, noooow. Whoa, whoa. Hold up now, why you got that in ya hand?"

"I'm sick of your shit! Donnie, get your stupid ass out my face before I slice you up and put your useless, dusty ass in them trash bags and dump you on your ugly ass mother's doorstep."

Sheena jolted out of her seat like a thunderbolt and began pacing around the room once she realized who was speaking on the other end of the phone. A flurry of rage overcame her, and she became hot with outrage. Angry tears began to fill her eyes as she began to replay the last night she was stuck alone in the same house with him.

"I can't believe this! Are you fucking kidding me? Are you fucking stupid? He's a fucking pedophile, a fucking pedophile! How dare you?"

Sheena rattled off in a flurry of rage as she continued to pace back and forth.

"You will never, ever see my daughter, you hear me? Never! I will always protect my baby from people like you two. No one will ever hurt her, you won't ever get to show her how vile, uncaring, selfish, heartless, distant and no morality you have! No one will ever hurt her; no man will ever take advantage of her. Not her mind, not her body, not her innocence! I will protect her at all costs; I will protect her until my last breath. I will do everything in my power to make up for what you didn't do for me. I hope and pray that you both have the fucking lives that you both fucking deserve!"

Unable to interject, Evelyn was forced to listen to Sheena's contempt for her and Donnie as she fired off words of fury and vitriol between sobs. Once Sheena paused to take a breath, Evelyn took the opportunity to respond.

"I didn't call you! Did you forget, you contacted me? It's not your damn business what I do with my life and who's in my house. Who the hell do you think you are? I don't owe you shit, little girl!"
"You don't deserve to be here. You should be the one six feet under, not Neil! You fucking worthless piece of shit."

Sheena immediately disconnected the call and began to sob uncontrollably as she stumbled back to the glider and fell into the chair as she held her stomach.

"I can't believe this. Why did I call her? I should've known better, I should've known," she cried as she felt a sharp pain on her right side.

"Ahhh! Whew, calm down, Sheena, calm down," she said to herself as she took slow, deep breaths.

"Relax. That woman cannot steal my joy. Her actions do not reflect me, nor do they define me. Accept the things I cannot change, surround myself with those who love me, and invest in those who truly care for me."

Sheena repeated this three times like a mantra as her breathing steadied. Her anxiety lessened enough for her to attempt a phone call.

"Pick up, pick up, pick up," she whispered as the phone rang five times before the voicemail answered.

She immediately attempted to make the call again.

"Keem. Pick up. Pick up, damn it!" Sheena murmured as she sucked her teeth and hit the call button on another contact.

"What the heck, Chrissy!" Sheena yelled in frustration as she slammed her phone down on her lap after Chrissy's voicemail picked up.

Sheena leaned back in the chair, put her feet up on the footrest with her left hand on her forehead, and rubbed her stomach with her right hand before exhaling deeply.

"Where the hell is everybody at? I wish you were here, Neil; I swear to God I do. I just want to talk to you and hear your voice again. I need to talk to you."

Sheena closed her eyes as she listened to the music in the background. As she spoke aloud, she thought fondly of her memories of O'Neil.

"What would you say to me right now if you were here, huh?"

As the next song on the iPod played, Sheena began to smile.

"I hear you; I hear you loud and clear," she chuckled as she began to sing along with Michael Jackson's You Are Not Alone.

As Sheena began to feel more relaxed, she was interrupted by a text alert. She picked up her phone and read the message.

Chrissy:	My bad sis. Busy. Can't talk. U ok?
Sheena:	OK. Talk to you when you get here.
Chrissy:	U sure U ok?
Sheena:	I'm good. See you later.
Chrissy:	K! Luv U.

Sheena: Love you too

Shortly after, Sheena's phone began to ring.

"Hello."

"You got your charger?"

Sheena could hear Hakeem in the background.

"Plug this in."

"Hellooooo! Keem."

"Mind ya damn business, just plug it in. Nosey ass!"

Sheena sucked her teeth.

"Not this again," she mumbled.

"Keem!"

Sheena waited for Hakeem to realize he butt dialed her again as she waited to hear one of The Twins return a snarky reply.

"So, when are you going to tell her?"

"Nah, don't start this again. Come on, man."

"Whatchu' mean? We gotta tell, this baby is coming soon. You wanna wait till both these kids are here looking alike?"

Sheena quickly hit the mute button and gasped.

"Chrissy? What the. . ."

"Let me handle it! Let me handle it my way. Chill the fuck out!" Hakeem snapped.

"Who do you think you're talking to? We've been handling it your way for over fifteen years. Grow some fucking balls and stop acting like a pussy!"

"Ayo, Chris, watch your damn mouth. I'm not playing with you, for real."

Sheena clutched her chest, beginning to hyperventilate. She continued to listen, hanging on to each word as it was spoken.

"Boy, please! I ain't scared of you. Take off your fucking panties, stop being a bitch and tell Sheena about us, about this baby I'm carrying. About your baby, I'm carrying."

Sheena let out a piercing shriek as she doubled over in pain at the intense cramp she felt in her stomach.

"Aargh! This can't be true, please. This can't be real," she cried out.

"Chrissy don't make me pull this fucking car over. I'm not gonna tell you again, watch it."

"Pull the damn car over, bitch! I'm sick of this shit. You need to be real with Sheena, yourself, and everybody. If you don't do it, I will. And I'm dead ass serious, play with me if you want to."

Sheena could hear the tires screech, and the music playing in the car abruptly stopped. Muffled movements could also be heard.

"What I say? What I say, Chrissy? Can't talk shit now, huh?"

Sheena could hear what she thought was choking before hearing huffing and panting.

"I'm the bitch that needs to be real, huh? What about you? Sheena's supposed to be your best friend and your sister, right? How the fuck we even get here Chrissy? Huh? You've been plotting for years, the only thing real about you is, you're real grimy!"

"Mmmm, do that shit again. You know I like it rough, daddy. I mean, baby daddy," Chrissy said seductively.

"Gimme, let me see it. You know you love it when I make you mad. You already told me that hate fuck hits different. And we know you're not trying to give this up."

"Quit fucking playing with me, I'm serious! This shit ain't funny. I'm not telling Sheena nothing until I see some goddamn DNA results. Everybody knows you're like a goddamn bank. You accept everybody's deposit. Told you not to go through with this shit, but you always trying to run game on somebody. Doesn't your so-called boyfriend think it's his baby? Yeah, you think I don't know about that, huh? Fuck outta here with this bull."

"Oh! So now I'm a grimy little hoe? Like you're too good for me? Is that what you're saying? Speak up, you had all that heart two seconds ago, right?"

"I said what I said. Everybody knows you're like the community playground. Everybody in the neighborhood comes to slide and ride you."

"I know you ain't talking cause you been coming to this playground since middle school so, cut the shit. Again, be real with yourself. You love this shit, and you love me. Just admit it, you ain't the settling down type. I understand, you want both of us, admit it, Boo."

"Come on, stop! I don't feel like doing this shit with you right now. Get your hands off me. For real, stop!" Hakeem demanded with irritation in his voice.

"You want me to stop? Because it doesn't feel like you want me to stop anything. Mmmm, come here."

"I can't believe I let you get me into this shit. Fuuck!" Hakeem yelled as he beat on the steering wheel.

"You fuck everything up; you know that shit!"

"Boy, don't play victim now. I had you first; you're the one who wanted to pretend you didn't know me when you first met Sheena. We could have gotten this out of the way a long time ago. And let's not forget you never once stopped messing with me. You did that! I didn't have to chase you, trick you, or seduce you. You keep coming back because you love it here. Admit it. I always tell you a drunk man's words are a sober man's thoughts, right? How many fucking nights you crawl into my bed telling me how much you love me, I'm the only person that understands you. Remember, you're the one who said you wanted to live the life of a nomad, but no one would understand. But I understand, and what did I say? Fuck what everyone else thinks, if you don't want to be tied down to one person and want to wander, live your life. But no, you want to live the life you think your family and friends would respect more. And now, here we are. Time is up, Keem; it is time to be real finally. What do you want? Whatever you choose, we have to tell Sheena before this baby gets here."

"Fuck, I just need more time. She can't handle this shit right now. I can't do this to her, not now. She can't handle this, not this Chrissy. You know that this ain't right," he said despondently.

"Real talk, Hakeem, it's never been right. But we both chose to do it anyways. And once both these babies are here, it's a wrap on this secret. And you know I'm right."

Sheena had heard enough; she was inconsolable and yelling in disbelief.

"Why? Why? Why would they do this to me?" She managed to cry out between her sobbing.
"I can't, I can't. What did I ever do to deserve this?"

Sheena could feel herself growing nauseous as she got up and raced towards the waste basket to vomit. As she lifted herself up and wiped her mouth with her hand, she waddled back to the glider, picked up her cellphone, and unmuted herself.

"Was I a fucking game to you two? All these fucking years. Chrissy, how could you do this? I treated you like a sister. How could you do this shit to me, of all people. Me? Me!"

Sheena continued to scream and wail into the phone as tears flowed from her eyes and salty snot trickled down her nose onto her top lip.

"I know you two hear me, fucking answer me. Say something, now!"

"Oh shit! What the fuck," Chrissy could be heard sounding shocked.

"Chrissy, you evil bitch. You set me up!"

"I didn't, Keem, I swear!"

"Hakeem you stupid fuck. Your raggedy ass phone has been dialing me all day. Did you forget that you dip shit?"

"Fuuckk, fuck, fuck!" Hakeem yelled as he beat the steering wheel again.

"Sheena, baby, I'm sorry. I didn't mean for you to find out this way, Love. I promise you; I love you, I'm sorry." Hakeem pleaded as he burst into tears.

"I didn't mean for this to happen, I promise you. You have to believe me."

"I don't have to believe shit. I heard everything. Over fifteen years! All this time, Hakeem? We're all supposed to be family. You both are supposed to be the closest people to me now. Why? I don't understand. Why? Why do you all hurt me? How did I not see this shit, how could I be so fucking stupid. Hoooow?"

Sheena screamed as she doubled over in pain, her stomach tightening, and she began to breathe heavily.

"Sheena, baby, are you okay? Talk to me, what's wrong?"

"Sis, we're on our way. We can talk this out. I'm sorry, don't be mad at me." Chrissy attempted to bargain.

"No! Stay away, stay away from me. I don't ever want to see you two again. No one, no one gets to hurt me ever again. No one will ever get the chance to hurt my baby girl either. I'll never be a victim to any of you evil ass motherfuckers again. Not you, not Hakeem, not Evelyn, not Donnie, nobody! No one hurts me, no one will hurt my baby. Mark my fucking words, I win. You hear me, I fucking win. I win because I'm free, I'm free! Thank you, thank you, Evelyn, thank you; Hakeem, and thank you, Chrissy, my sister. Ha! My sister? Thank you all for exposing your truth. I'm now free. I'm fucking free!"

Sheena continued to scream, exhibiting fast and pressured speech, before disconnecting the call.

Sheena let out a scream at the top of her lungs as she doubled over.

"Whyyy, Neil whyyyy? I can't do this. How could they all be so despicable and vicious? All this time, all this time, it was all a fraud. My life with them was all deception. Everything is a sham, fake, phony. Neil, you were the only thing real in my life. I can't do this without you. This hurts too much. What do I tell my baby girl? She doesn't deserve this. Nooo, nooo! Why?"

Sheena felt an intense tightening in her stomach and back as she tried to straighten herself up and walk towards the chair. A warm, moist mucus plug landed on her foot, followed by warm liquid dripping down the inside of her legs.

"Argh! Owwww!"

Once she realized she was in active labor, Sheena immediately shifted her focus. She had to act quickly because she already felt the baby crowning. She waddled to the closet to retrieve her medical bag, the first aid kit, baby blankets, and her bag of newborn essential supplies. She laid the blanket on the floor before slowly sitting on top of it in front of the floor-length mirror and leaning back, preparing for another contraction.

"Okay, baby, it's just me and you, we can do this. Ahhhh!"

Sheena grunted, pushed, and breathed as she watched her reflection in the mirror. Admiring the full head of hair peeping out, she continued her slow and steady breathing, preparing for her next contraction.

"Neil, I need you to help me through this. Please let me know if everything will be okay," she prayed, cried, and pleaded.

"Aargh!"

She cried out as another contraction took over and she got the urge to push.

"Oh my God, I see you, baby. I see you," she cried joyfully as she watched her reflection in the mirror, where the baby's head and face were visible.

"One more big push. Come on, we can do it. We can do it. Come on, baby."

Sheena felt another jarring contraction as she bore down and pushed with all her strength.
"Ahhhh!"

She pushed and grunted and pushed.

"Neil, please make sure my baby is okay."

She prayed aloud before feeling relieved when she opened her eyes and saw her baby girl lying between her legs on the blanket. Sheena immediately leaned over, gently picked her up, held her close, and cleaned her mouth and nose with suction. She noticed no cries and quickly turned the baby over and swatted her backside twice. The baby let out a screeching cry, and Sheena exhaled a sigh of relief. Sheena hurriedly turned the baby back over, admiring her.

"Look at you! Sweetie, you're so beautiful," she cried as she kissed both hands and feet.

"Look at this head of hair, you're a little angel. Look at you. I'll never let anyone hurt you, and you'll always be safe with Neil and me. I can't believe your mines. Oh, my goodness, you're so precious. I could never let anyone hurt you, I promise."

Sheena cradled and admired her beautiful baby girl, promising everlasting love and protection from the world's ills.

"I'm not her, I'm not like Evelyn. I promise. The cycle stops here. You'll never have to worry about this nonsense. I promise, baby. You're my best friend, you're my soulmate, you're my world. You, you. It's only you."

Sheena cried as she kissed her baby's sweet face over and over, then cradled her close to her breasts as she rocked back and forth before her phone rang, interrupting her thoughts. Sheena quickly answered without looking at the caller ID.

"H...hello?"

"Sheena, are you okay? I'm on my way right now. Why do you sound like that?" Hakeem asked in a hurried tone.

"No! Don't come here. Don't ever come here," Sheena bellowed into the phone, which caused the baby to cry again.

"What the fuck. . . Sheena, is that a baby crying? What the fuck! Sheena, is that the baby?" Hakeem asked, stunned.

"I'm rushing to you now! I'll be there in..."

"I fucking hate you! All of this was a lie. Stay away from us. Don't ever come here again!" Sheena yelled before disconnecting the call.

"I don't understand. Why? Why would they do this? All this time, it's always been a lie." Sheena said to herself.

She began wiping her tears with the back of her hand, and then she felt her bracelet graze her nose, which caught her attention.

"You fucking lying ass homewrecker! I always defended you! I always saw the good in you, even when people tried to tell me not to. Fuck you, fuck you"! She screamed erratically as she looked down at the friendship bracelet she and Chrissy had purchased at the Corner Mall all those years ago.

"All this time, all these years of lies. You're even walking around with his baby, flaunting your fucking pregnancy in my face while I'm letting you stay in my fucking house. How could you?"

Sheena screamed as she tried to rip the bracelet off her wrist.

"Get off me, I want this off, now!"

Sheena slowly stood up while gently holding the baby before tenderly laying her down in her crib, swaddled in her blanket, soiled in amniotic fluid and traces of blood. She gazed down at her baby as her sneer turned into a loving smile.

"You're so beautiful. Neil, look. Say hi to your niece." Sheena chuckled as she continued to gaze down at her sleeping baby.

Her mood quickly shifted.

"I don't know, I don't know what to do. Just tell me, please. I can't do this; I won't let anyone hurt her. No, I won't," Sheena blurted out to herself, then mumbled incoherently.

"Tell me! Tell me what to do! Tell me how to protect her, please... please!" She pleaded as she clasped her hands together, praying for her pain to end as the music from

O'Neil's iPod continued to play in the background.

Sheena gasped as she covered her mouth in shock.

"I knew it; I knew you would have the answer. You always look out for me; now you get to look out for both of us," she said, leaning down to kiss the baby on the forehead.

She began to sing along to the song playing in the background, picking up the soiled blankets and tossing them in the laundry basket. Then, she grabbed some towels and dried the baby before re-swaddling her in a clean blanket as the music played and she began to sing the chorus to Wind Beneath My Wings.

Sheena was dancing around the room and singing aloud as she picked up the Rollo May quote Dr. Angel had given her earlier in the day. She unfurled it and admired the elegant calligraphy as she read it for the umpteenth time.

"The purpose of psychotherapy is to set people free."

She grabbed the scissors from the first aid kit and cut the quote with two snips before affixing it to the wall over the chair. She continued singing and swaying to the music, loudly yelling the lyrics repeatedly as if she were in a trance.

Sheena stepped back to observe her work.

"That's perfect! Neil, it's perfect, right?" She asked aloud as she read it to herself.

"The purpose is to set people free."

She smiled to herself before walking back to the crib.

"Hey, little nugget, do you want to eat?" She asked sweetly as she picked the baby up and walked back to the glider to sit.

Slowly, she removed her left arm from her bathrobe and lifted her T-shirt before gently grazing her nipple over the baby's lips to rouse her awake. The baby latched on quickly and immediately started nursing.

"Somebody's hungry, slow down, sweetie." Sheena chuckled as she rubbed the baby's full head of thick curly hair.

"You are absolutely perfect, my very own angel. You're mine, always and forever. I'll never let anyone hurt you. I promise, you'll never feel this kind of pain," she reassured her baby as she kissed her cheeks.

"All done? Okay, sweetie," she said as she gently held the baby to her shoulder and lightly patted her back until she heard a soft burping noise.

She continued to gingerly rock back and forth, humming to the music as she rubbed the baby's back. Sheena's attention was interrupted by the childhood friendship bracelet engraved with the word "Friends."

She became incensed all over again.

"Set people free. There's purpose in freedom," she mumbled as she laid the baby down on her lap and tried to yank the bracelet off again.

Sheena then leaned over, opened the first aid box, grabbed the X-ACTO knife, unwrapped the baby blanket, and carefully cut the umbilical cord above the clamp she had placed earlier. She meticulously swaddled the baby again as she continued to enjoy the music in the background.

She was startled when she heard banging on her front door. The chain lock prevented it from fully opening.

"Sheena! Sheena! Open the door, Love. Come on, please open up." Hakeem yelled as he continued to attempt to push the door in.

"You still got Neil's key on you? We can get in through his place and use the back staircase." Sheena overheard Chrissy suggest.

Sheena smiled as the next song began to play. She got up, cradled the baby, and turned the volume up on the iHome. Slowly dancing with her daughter, she sat back down in the glider and rested the baby on her lap. Sheena slowly rocked back and forth as she sang.

"Set people free," she said as she grabbed the X-ACTO knife and looked down at the bracelet she was ready to rid herself of.

"Arghhh. . . .arghhh" Sheena moaned as she held the bracelet in her hand.

"See, baby, free. No more pain and no pain for you, ever. Right, Neil?" She asked as she picked up the umbilical cord, wrapped it around twice, and held it firmly in her hands.

She continued to rock slowly back and forth, singing gently, and her eyes grew heavy; the urge to sleep overpowered her. As the feeling of peace began to engulf her, Sheena heard a blood-curdling scream.

"Ahhhh! Oh my God! Keeeem! Keeeeem!" Chrissy yelled as she slumped to the floor in the nursery's doorway.

Hakeem charged past Chrissy.

"Sheena! What the fuck did you do? What did you do?" Hakeem screamed as hot tears filled his eyes.

Sheena managed to open her eyes for a brief second before softly whispering. "Free," before slumping over.

"Nooooo! Noooo! What did you do?" Hakeem wailed as he grabbed the baby from Sheena's lap.

He looked down and saw the baby was slightly discolored with a bluish hue, and quickly uncovered the baby and noticed the umbilical cord wrapped tightly around her neck.

"No, Sheena! Whyyyy, whyyyyy? Love, why did you do it? Why? What the fuck Sheena. Why the fuck did you do it?"

Hakeem screamed at the top of his lungs as he observed all the blood pooling on both sides of the chair and floor before lifting the sleeves of Sheena's robe and noticing both her wrists had substantial lacerations to her radial arteries.

"I could've fixed this, Love. I could've fixed this shit! You didn't have to do this. I fucked up, I know I fucked up. But why this? Why?" He pleaded as he cradled his daughter close to his chest as he paced back and forth.

Chrissy continued to bawl while writhing around on the floor, screaming and wailing uncontrollably.

"Sheena, please," she pleaded as she crawled towards Sheena's slumped body.

"I'm sorry, Sheena, I'm so sorry. Please be okay. I'm sorry, sis! You can't leave me like this. I need you. I'm sorry. I'm fucking sorry. I don't know why I'm like this, I really don't. Sheena! Say something to me! Wake up, wake up. Please! Sheena! Aaargh! Sheena!" Chrissy yelled as she pulled on the collar of Sheena's robe while trying to shake her awake.

"Stop playing, get up. Get up and get your baby, Sheena. Please, get up." Chrissy continued to scream.
"They're gone, they're both fucking gone!" Hakeem yelled as he held his daughter while watching Sheena's breathing stop

entirely as the song "For the Love of You" ended.

"Chrissy, we did this. This blood's on our hands, Chrissy. Look at my fucking baby. Look!" Hakeem yelled while forcing Chrissy to make eye contact with his daughter.

"All this, all this is our fault, Chrissy!"

"Nooooo, noooo. Stop. Please. Stop," Chrissy begged as she tried to look away.

"Bitch, I said look!" Hakeem roared as he yanked Chrissy up by her hair. "Look at my family! They're fucking gone! They're gone!" He screamed as he collapsed onto the floor in uncontrollable agony, as Chrissy screamed with dread.

As they both slumped on the nursery floor, looking at both of the bodies, still in shock, the song "For the Love of You" continued to play on repeat.

"Sheena, why? Whyyyy? Why would you do this? I could've fixed this! I'm sorry, I'm sorry."

Chrissy yelled and sobbed as she balled up her fists and hit herself on the head over and over again as she pleaded to Sheena's lifeless body.

"I can't take it anymore, I just can't. Stop the music, please. I can't take that fucking song anymore," she wailed.

The End

Acknowledgments

I want to thank all my family and friends who help make life interesting. And a special shout-out to my beautiful sister, Tia, for going on this writing journey with me

www.ingramcontent.com/pod-product-compliance
Lightning Source LLC
Chambersburg PA
CBHW060351260626
47160CB00006B/2277